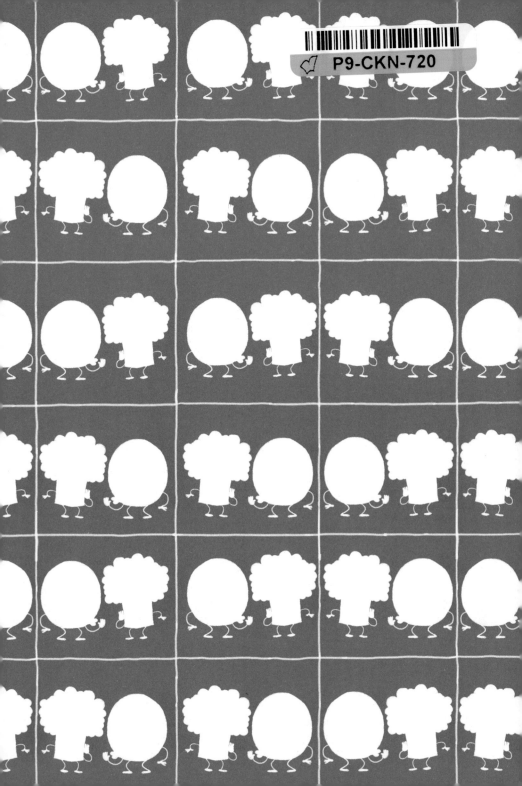

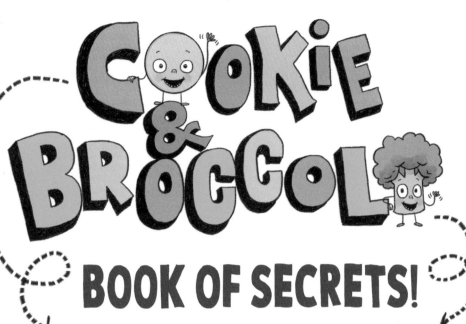

Cookie & Broccoli

BOOK OF SECRETS!

Whisper... Whisper whisper...
WOW! What an AMAZING secret!
Speak up! I can't hear you!

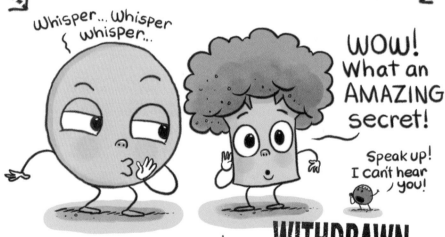

Bob McMahon

Dial Books for Young Readers

If you LOVE secrets you'll LOVE this book!

To Carol and the members of The Illustrators Table who made these books possible

DIAL BOOKS FOR YOUNG READERS

An imprint of Penguin Random House LLC, New York

First published in the United States of America by Dial Books for Young Readers,
an imprint of Penguin Random House LLC, 2022

Copyright © 2022 by Bob McMahon

Visit us online at penguinrandomhouse.com.

Library of Congress Cataloging-in-Publication Data is available.

Manufactured in China

ISBN 9780593529973 (hc)   10 9 8 7 6 5 4 3 2 1
ISBN 9780593529966 (pbk)   10 9 8 7 6 5 4 3 2 1

TOPL

Design by Jennifer Kelly

Text hand lettered by the author

This artwork was created digitally using Corel Painter and by eating lots of donuts.

CONTENTS

Chapter 1:
Broccoli's Big Secret!
1

Chapter 2:
The Secret Cure for Boredom!
33

Chapter 3:
Secrets of the Scary Forest!
71

Can You Solve the Secret Message?
84

Epilogue
87

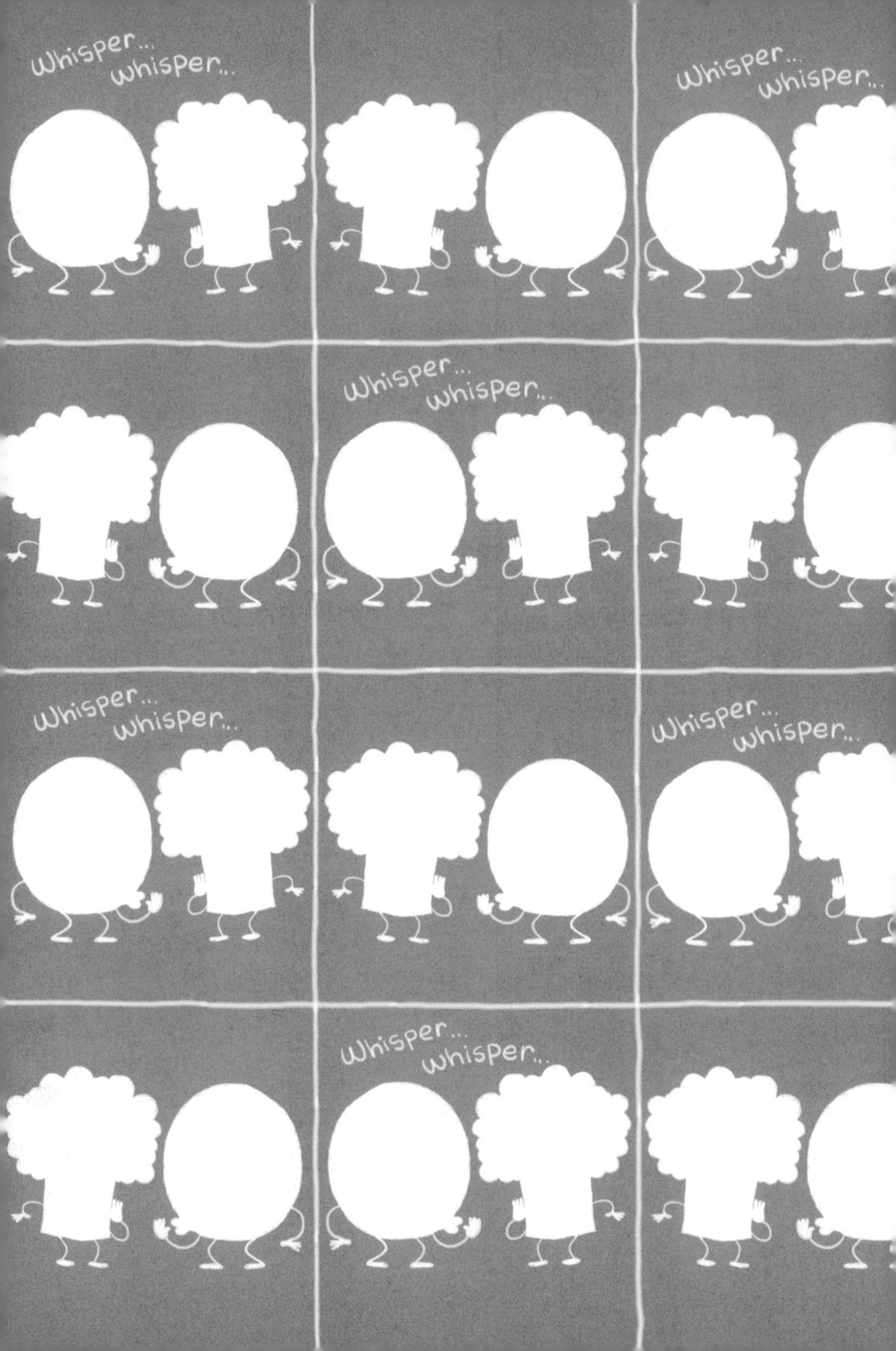
Whisper... whisper...
Whisper... whisper...
Whisper... whisper...
Whisper... whisper...
Whisper... whisper...
Whisper... whisper...

Chapter 1

BROCCOLI'S BIG SECRET!

I have a HUGE secret and I'm afraid someone may find out!

You can tell me, can't you?

TELL US! We won't tell anyone!!

Me too!

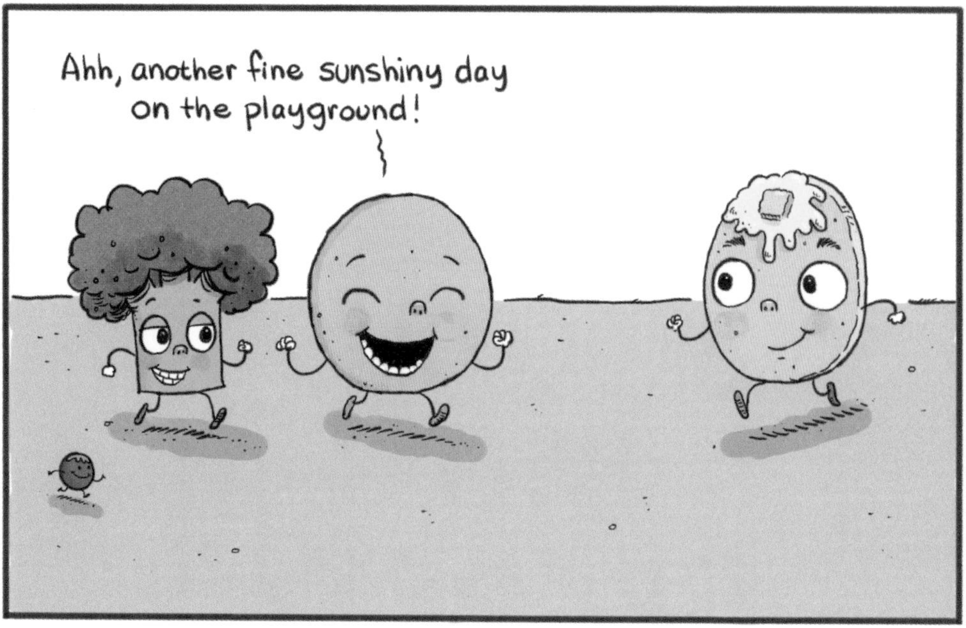
Ahh, another fine sunshiny day on the playground!

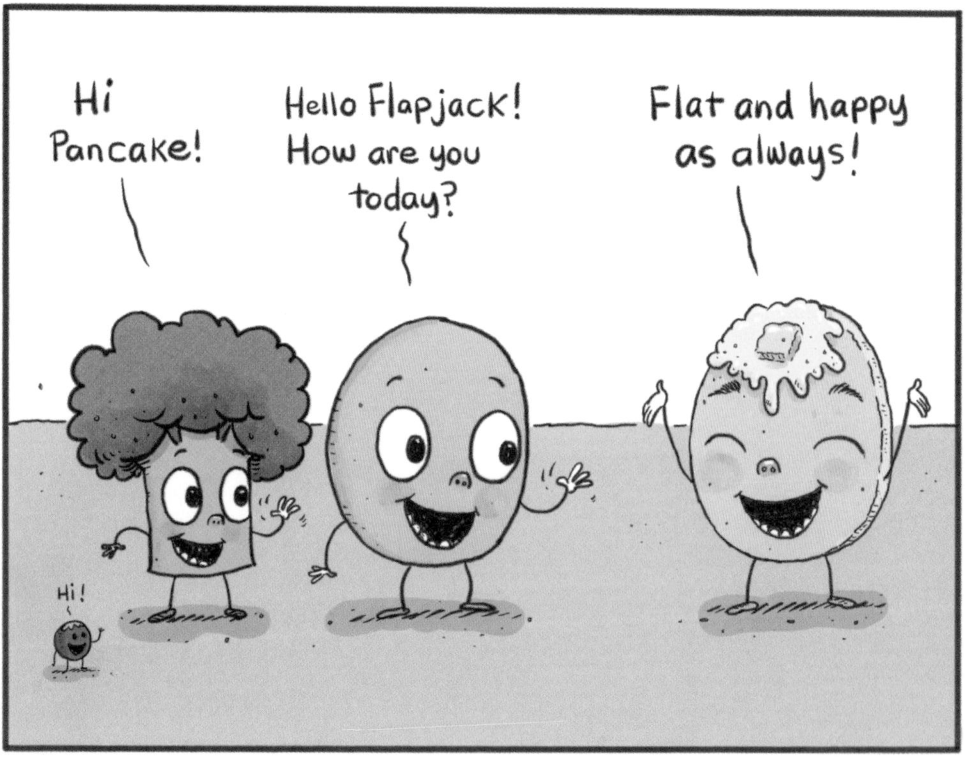
Hi Pancake!
Hello Flapjack! How are you today?
Flat and happy as always!
Hi!

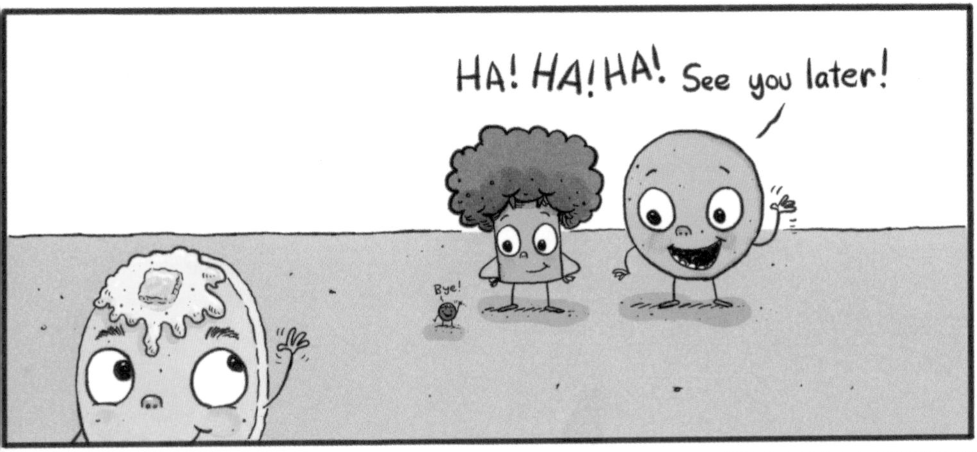
HA! HA! HA! See you later!
Bye!

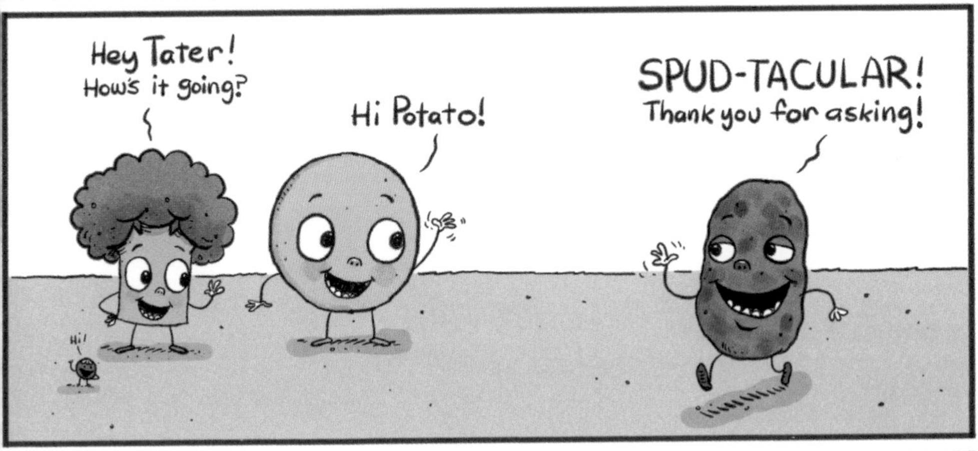
Hey Tater! How's it going?
Hi Potato!
SPUD-TACULAR! Thank you for asking!
Hi!

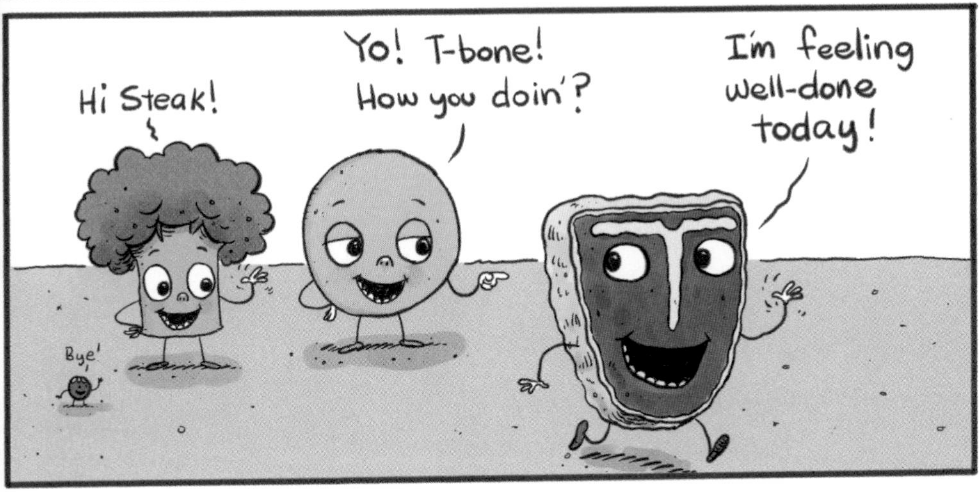
Hi Steak!
Yo! T-bone! How you doin'?
I'm feeling well-done today!
Bye!

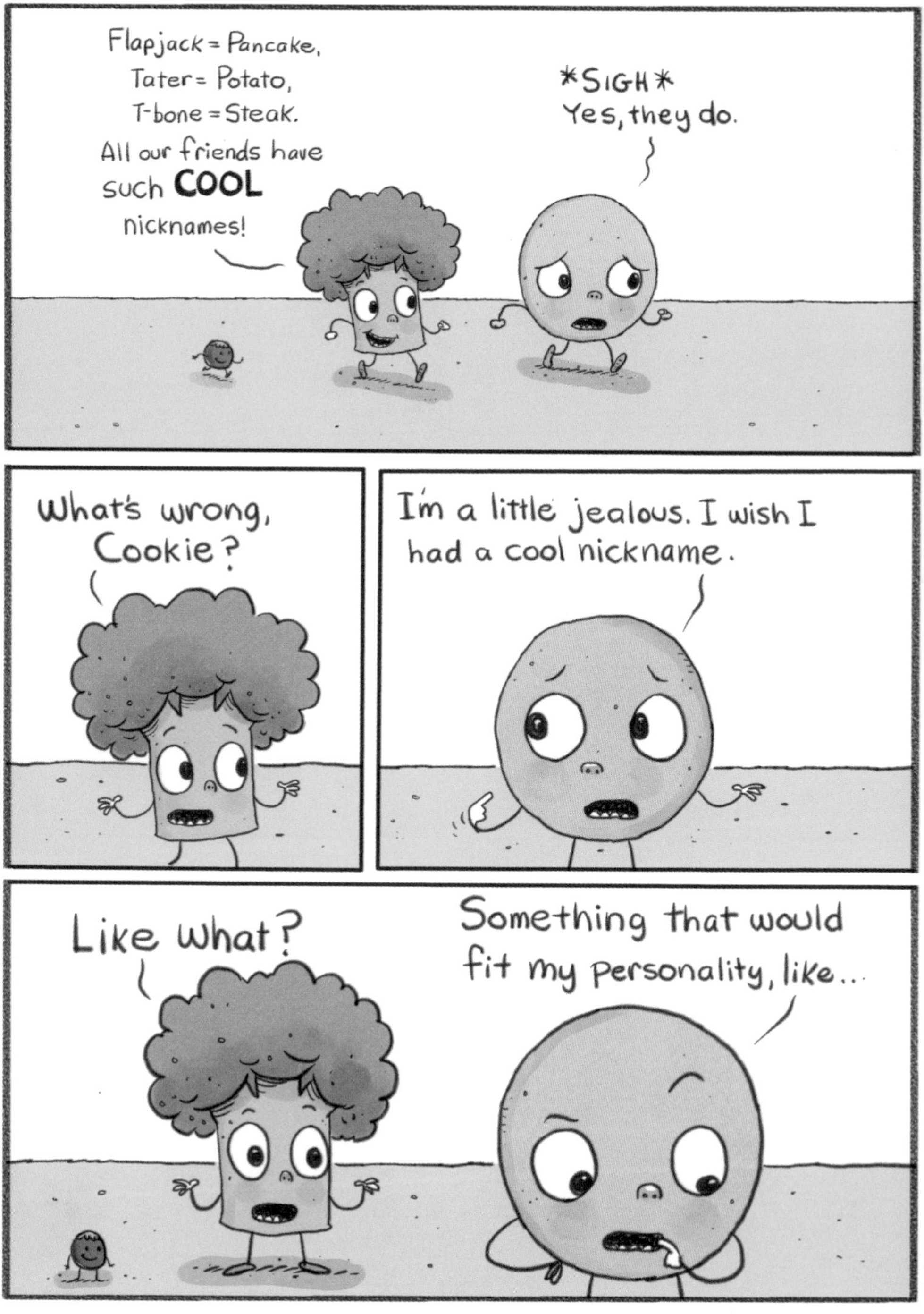
Flapjack = Pancake,
Tater = Potato,
T-bone = Steak.
All our friends have such **COOL** nicknames!
SIGH
Yes, they do.
What's wrong, Cookie?
I'm a little jealous. I wish I had a cool nickname.
Like what?
Something that would fit my personality, like...

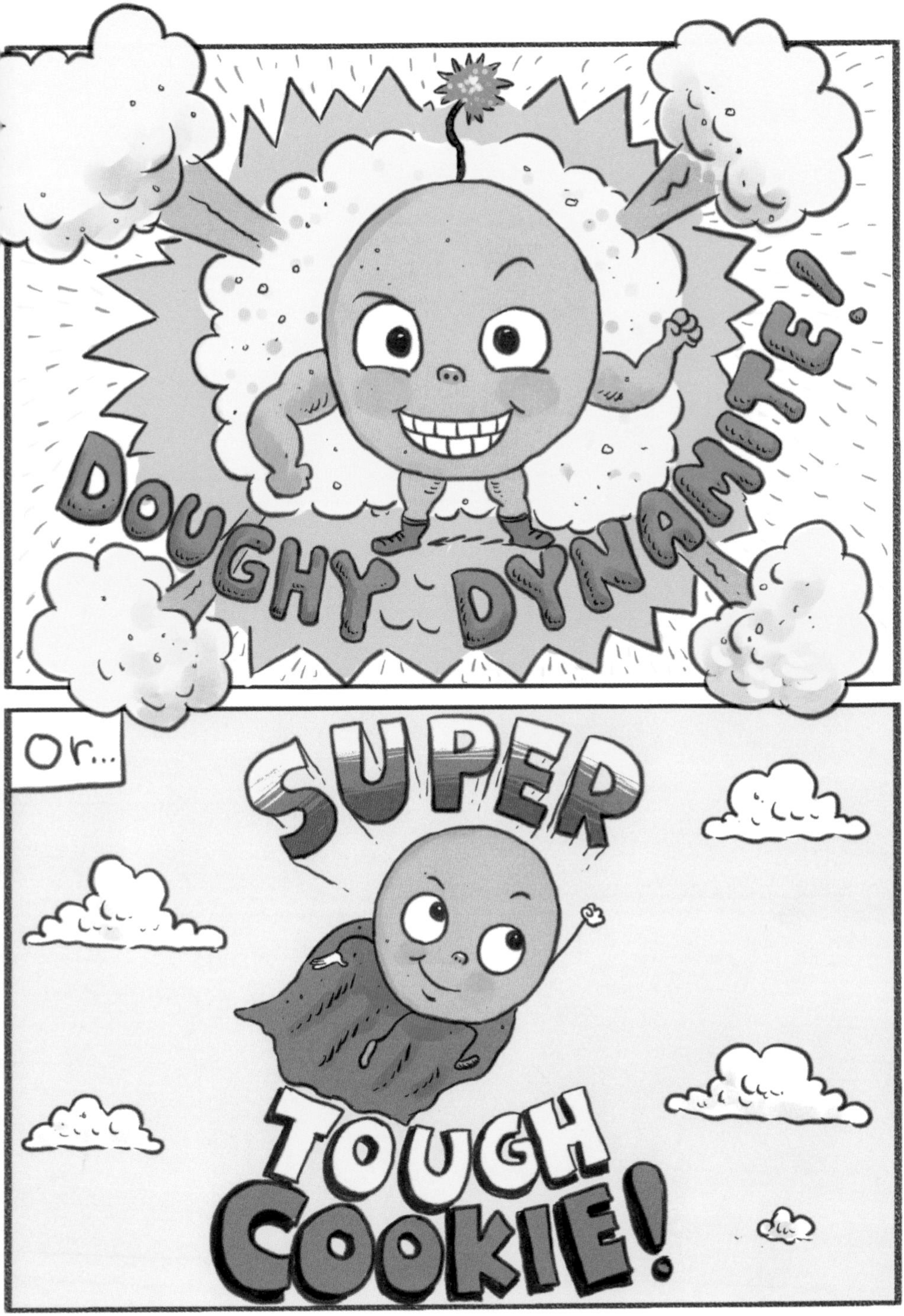
DOUGHY DYNAMITE!
Or...
SUPER
TOUGH
COOKIE!

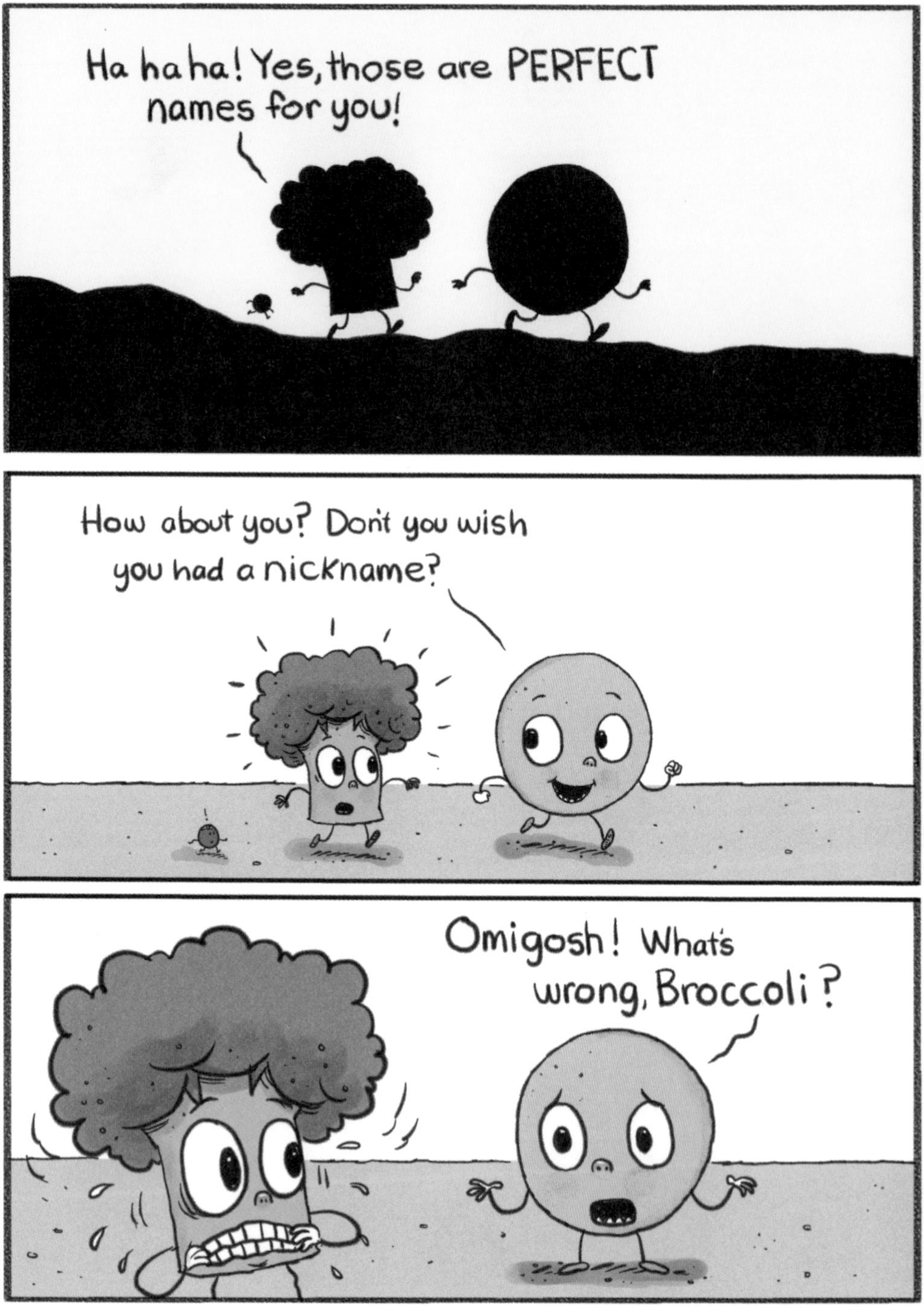
Ha ha ha! Yes, those are PERFECT names for you!
How about you? Don't you wish you had a nickname?
Omigosh! What's wrong, Broccoli?

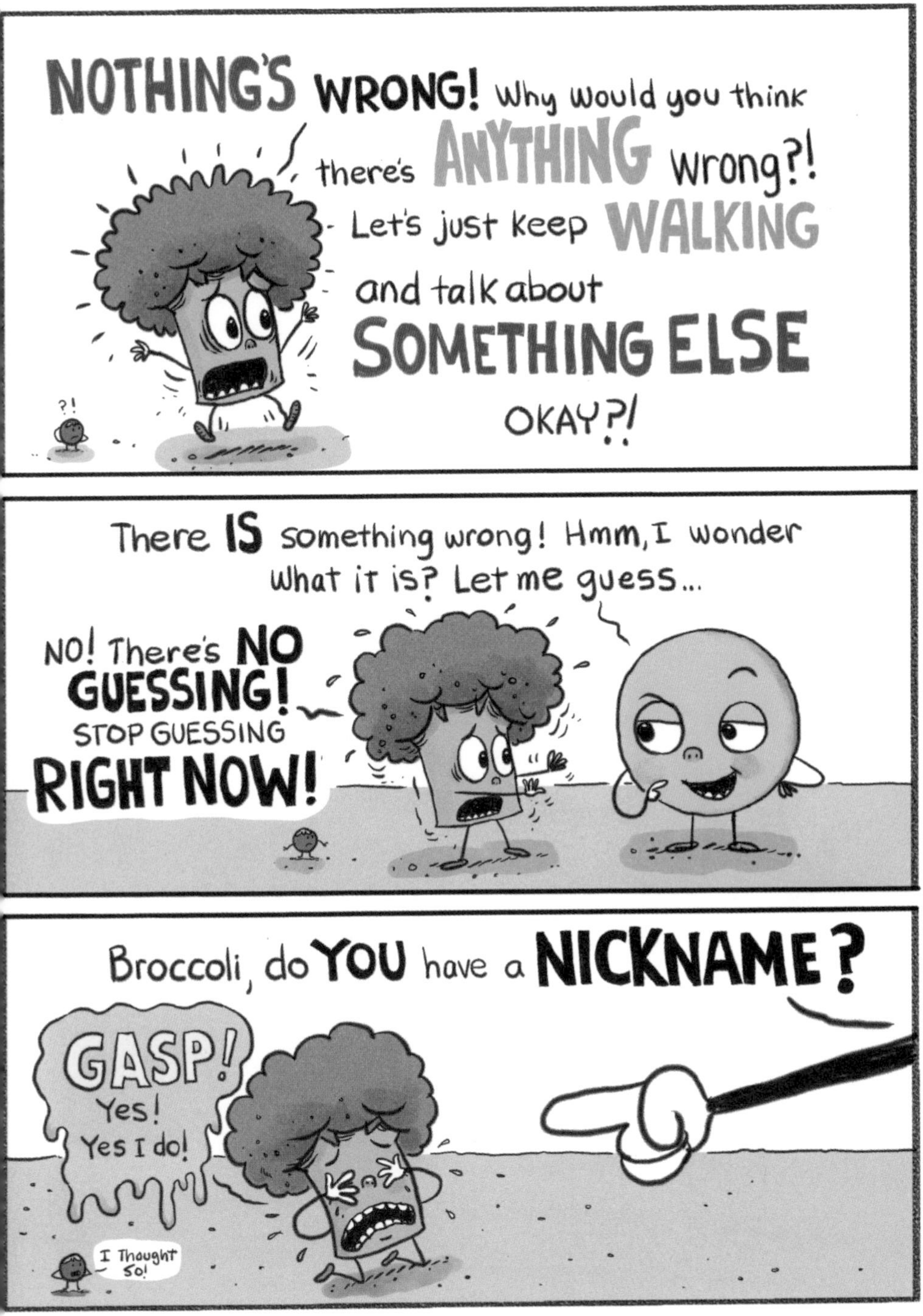
NOTHING'S WRONG! Why would you think there's ANYTHING wrong?! Let's just keep WALKING and talk about SOMETHING ELSE OKAY?!
?!
There IS something wrong! Hmm, I wonder what it is? Let me guess...
NO! There's NO GUESSING! STOP GUESSING RIGHT NOW!
Broccoli, do YOU have a NICKNAME?
GASP! Yes! Yes I do!
I Thought so!

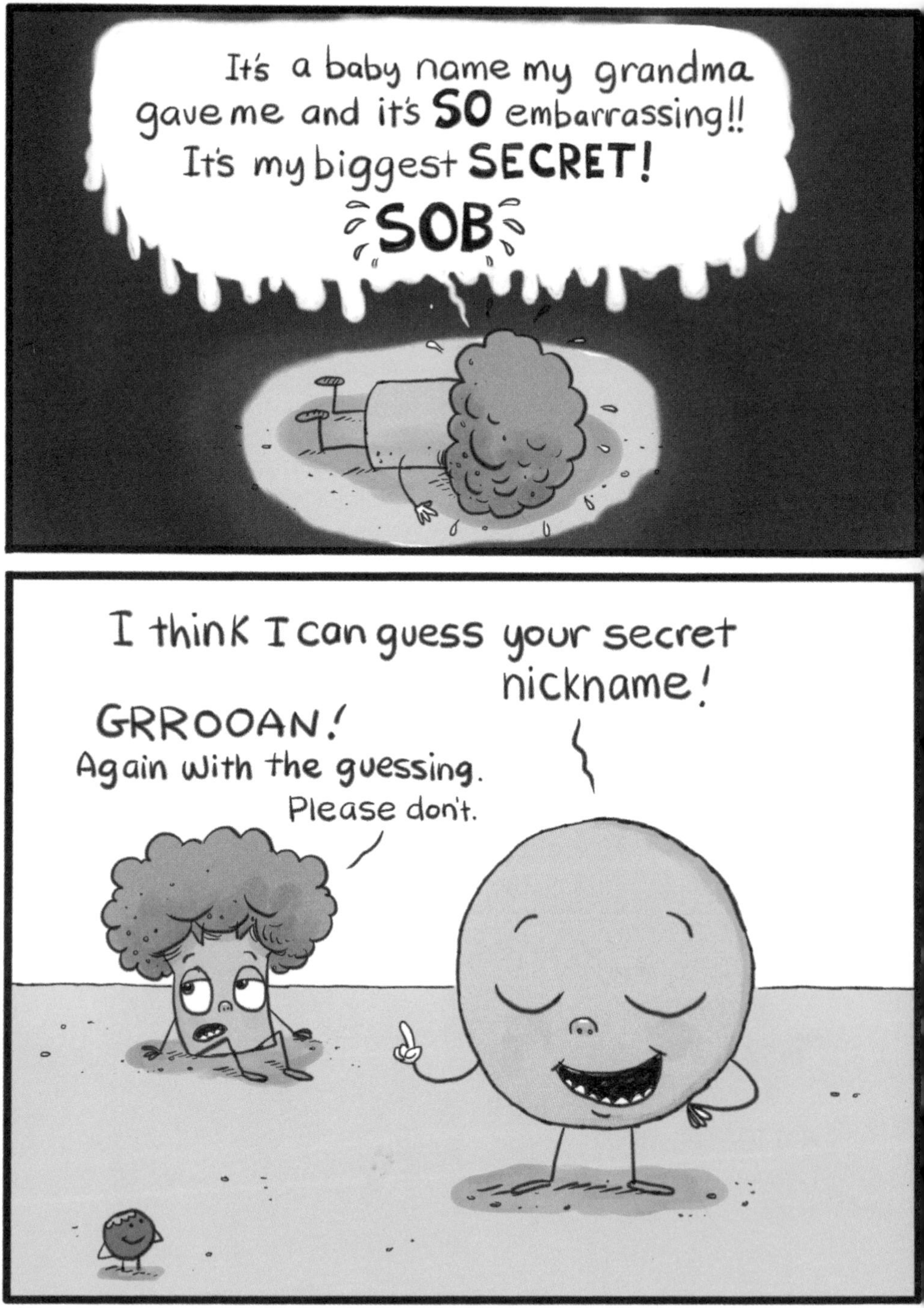
It's a baby name my grandma gave me and it's SO embarrassing!! It's my biggest SECRET!
SOB
I think I can guess your secret nickname!
GRROOAN! Again with the guessing. Please don't.

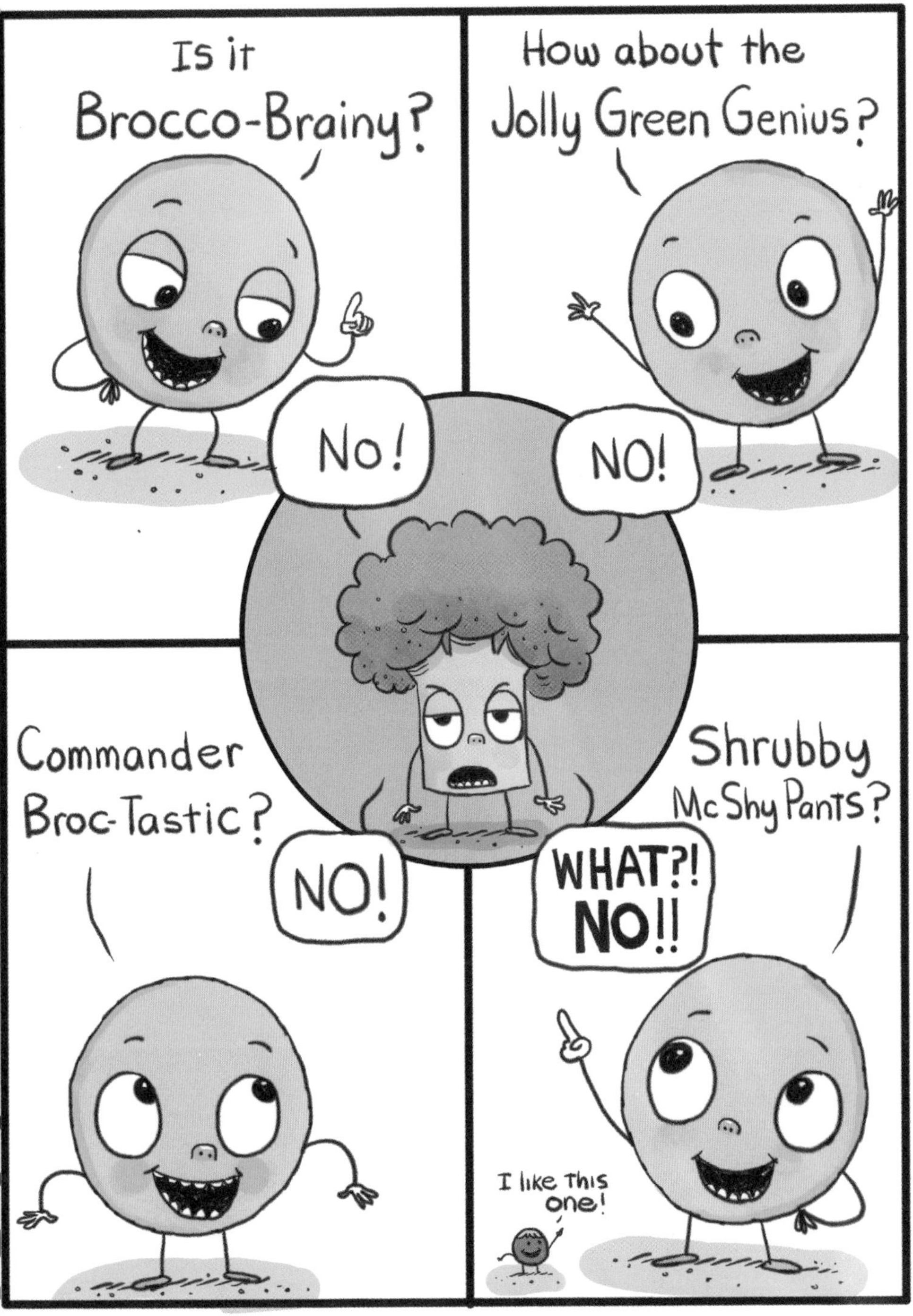
Is it Brocco-Brainy?
No!
How about the Jolly Green Genius?
NO!
Commander Broc-Tastic?
NO!
Shrubby McShyPants?
WHAT?! NO!!
I like This one!

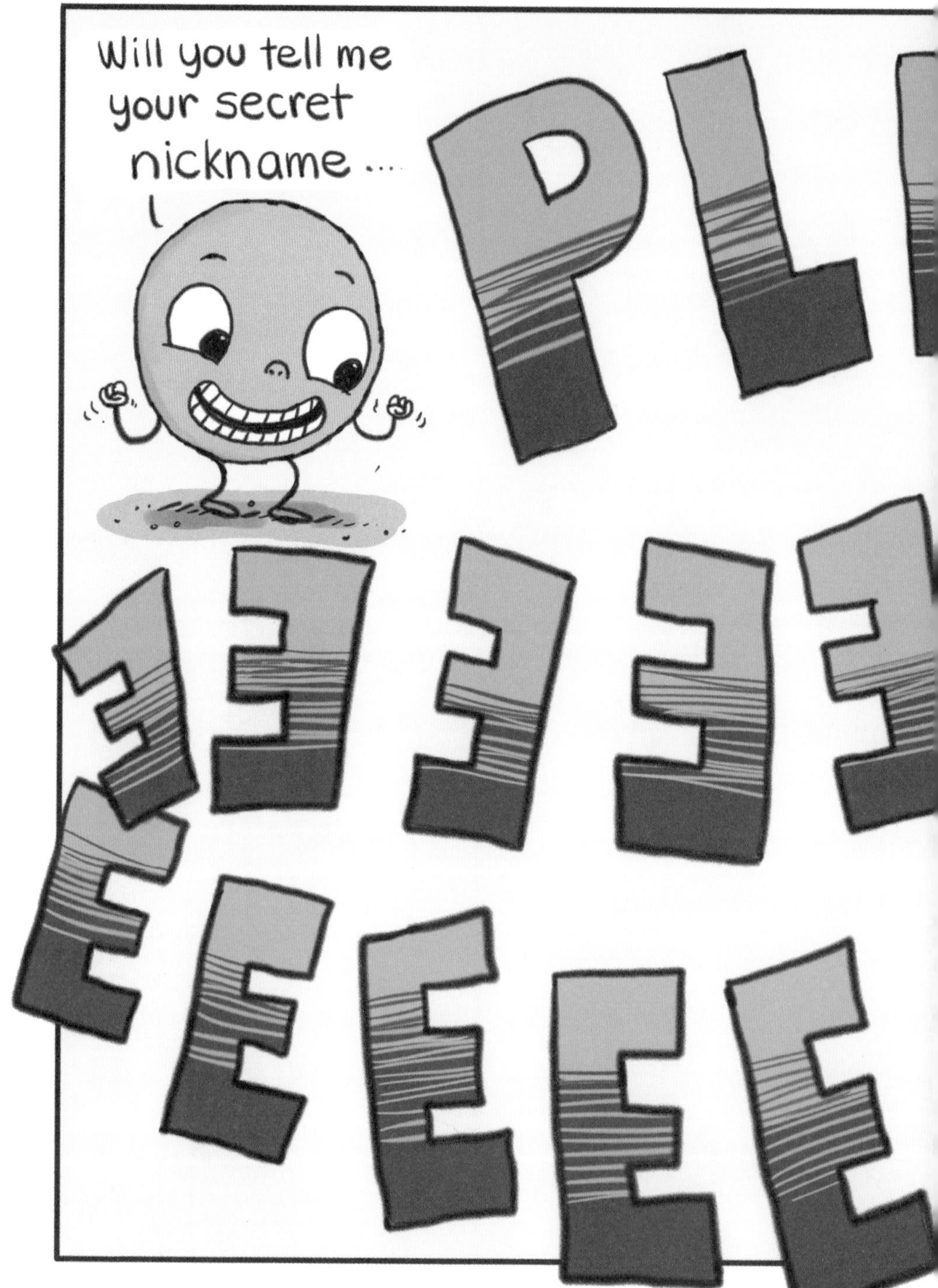
Will you tell me your secret nickname . . .
PLEEEEEEEE

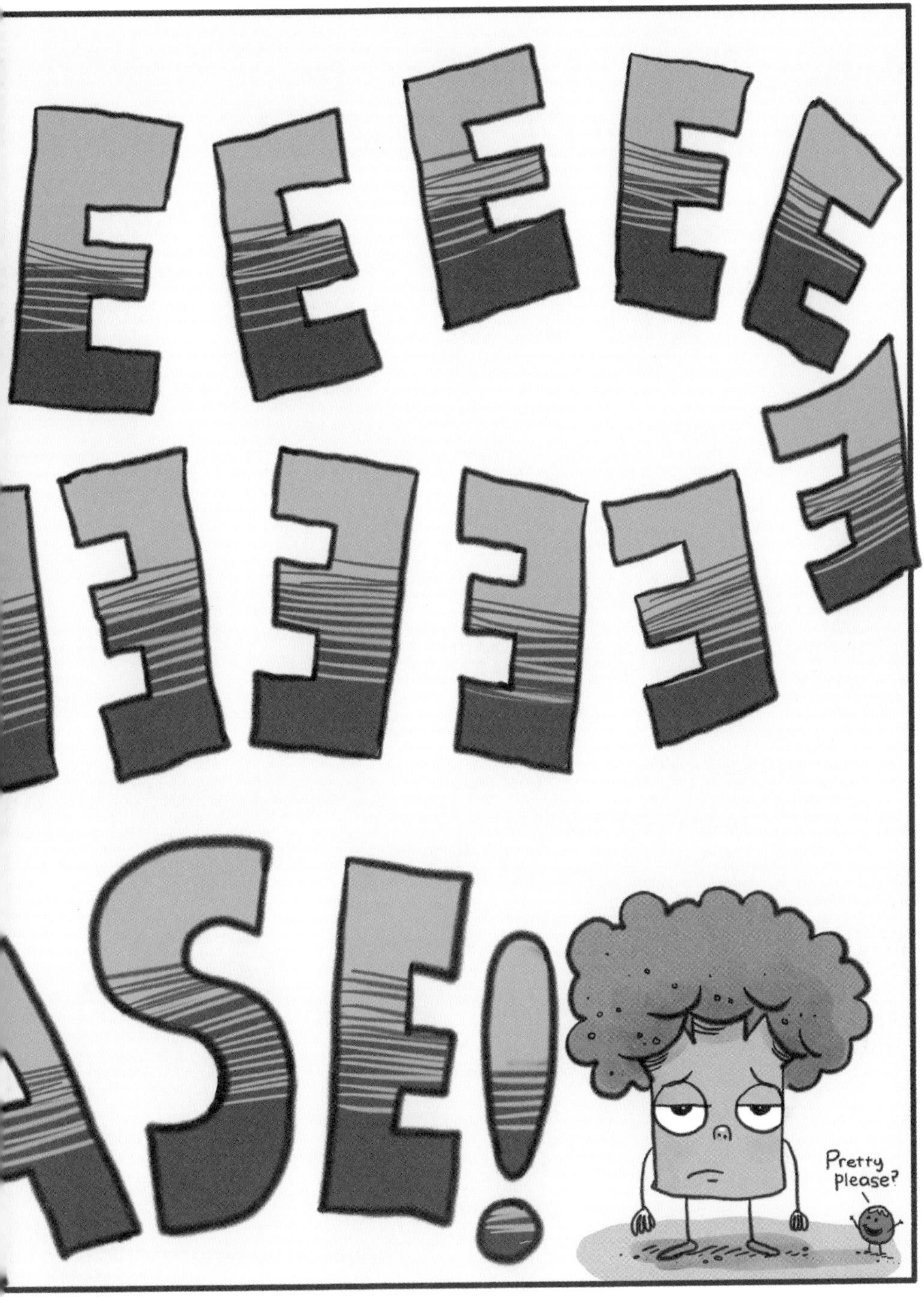
EEEEE
EEEEEE
ASE!
Pretty please?

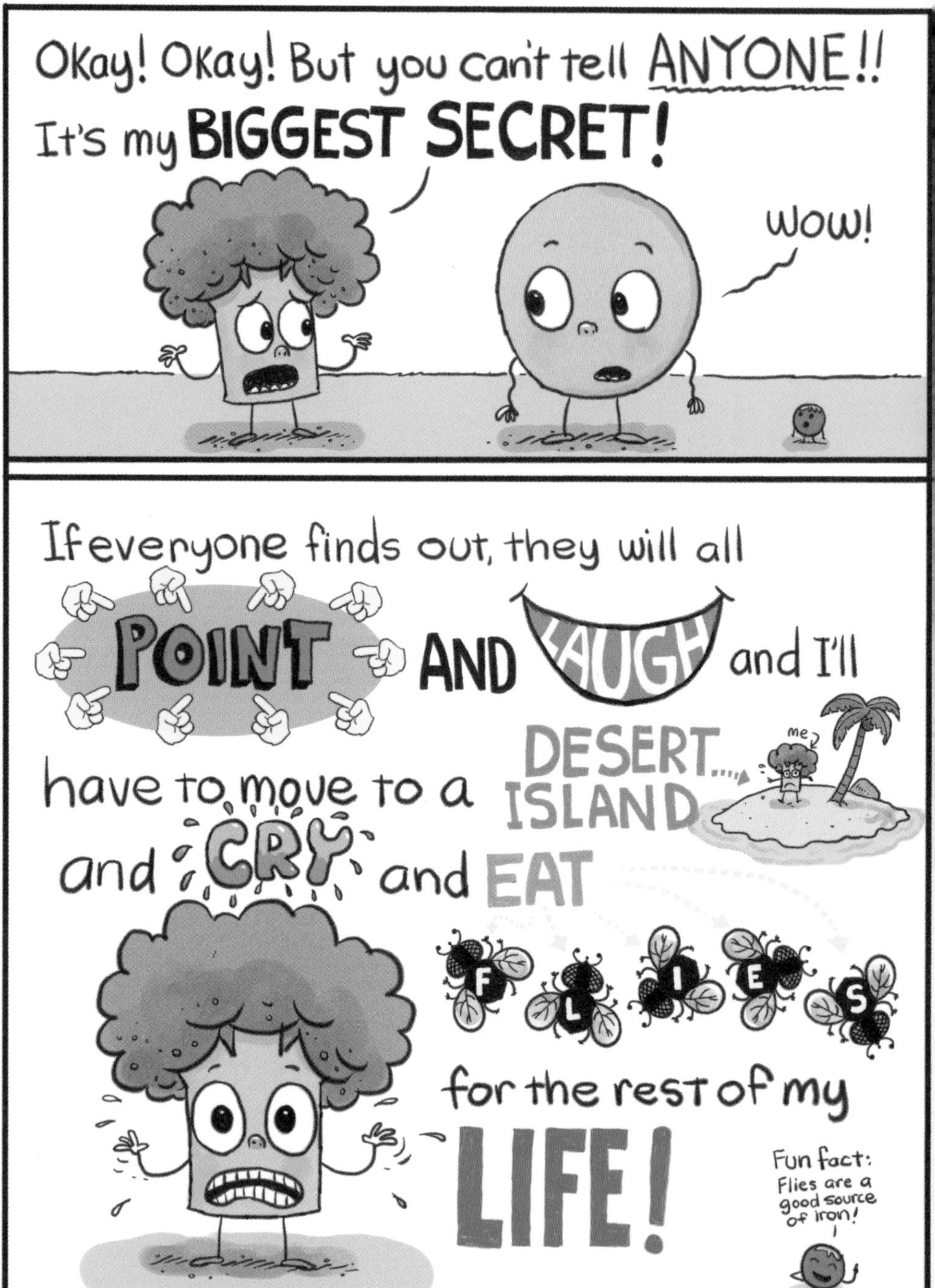
Okay! Okay! But you can't tell ANYONE!!
It's my BIGGEST SECRET!
WOW!
If everyone finds out, they will all
POINT AND LAUGH and I'll
have to move to a DESERT ISLAND
me
and CRY and EAT
FLIES
for the rest of my
LIFE!
Fun fact: Flies are a good source of iron!

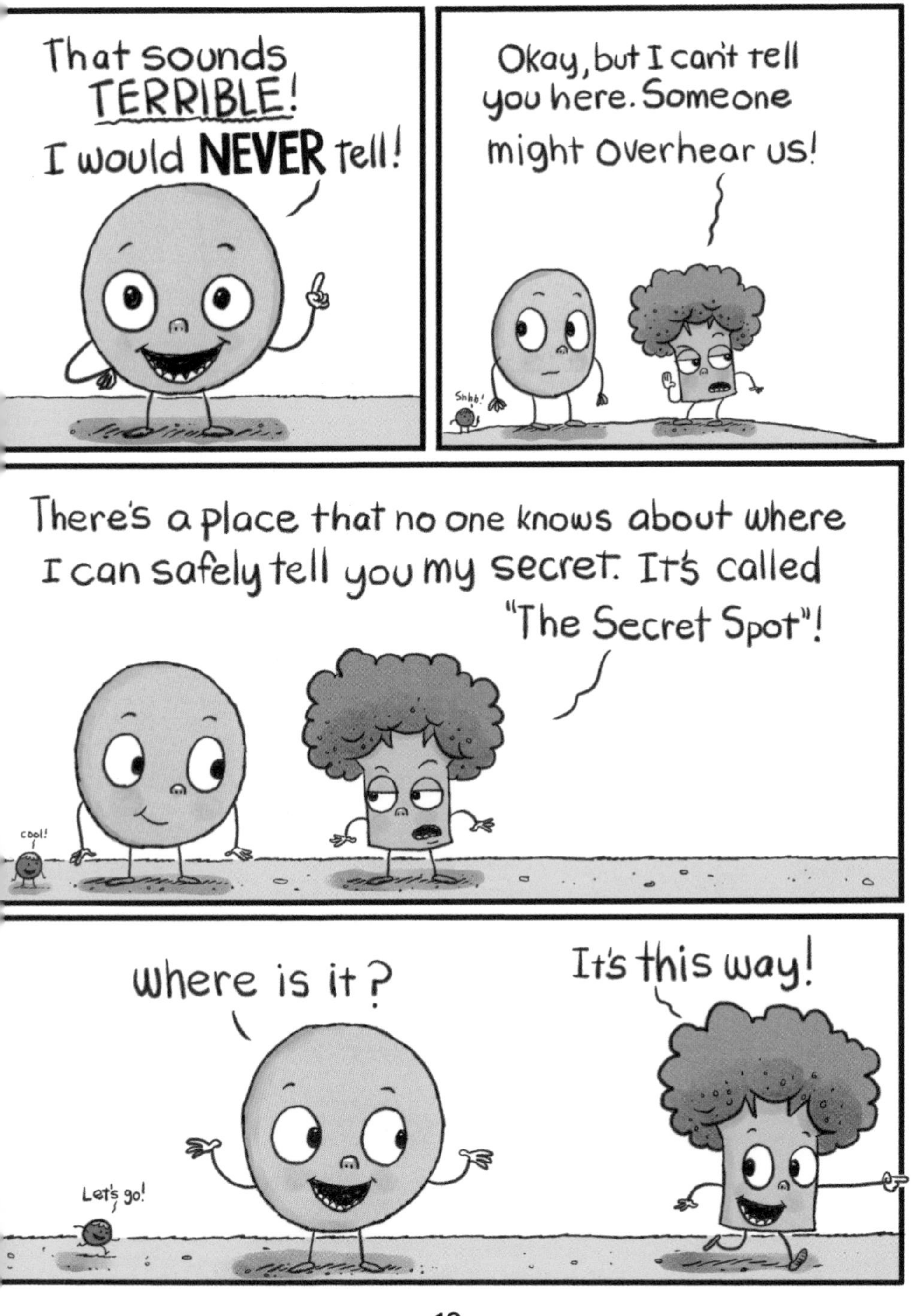
That sounds TERRIBLE! I would NEVER tell!
Okay, but I can't tell you here. Someone might overhear us!
Shhh!
There's a place that no one knows about where I can safely tell you my secret. It's called "The Secret Spot"!
cool!
Where is it?
It's this way!
Let's go!

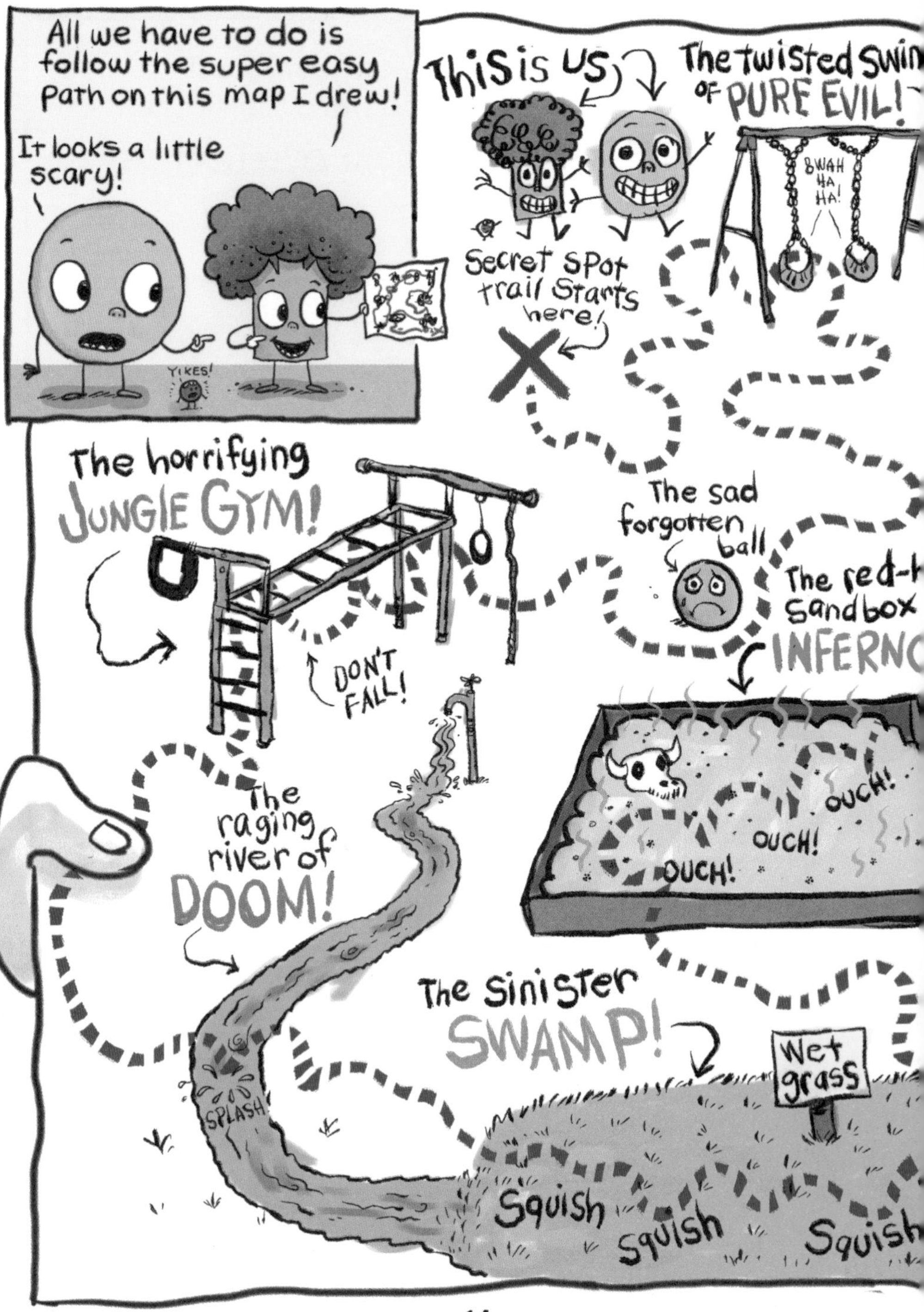

All we have to do is follow the super easy path on this map I drew!
It looks a little scary!
YIKES!
This is US
The twisted swin
of PURE EVIL!
BWAH HA HA!
Secret spot trail starts here!
The horrifying JUNGLE GYM!
DON'T FALL!
The sad forgotten ball
The red-h
sandbox
INFERNO
OUCH!
OUCH!
OUCH!
The raging river of DOOM!
SPLASH
The sinister SWAMP!
Wet grass
Squish
Squish
Squish

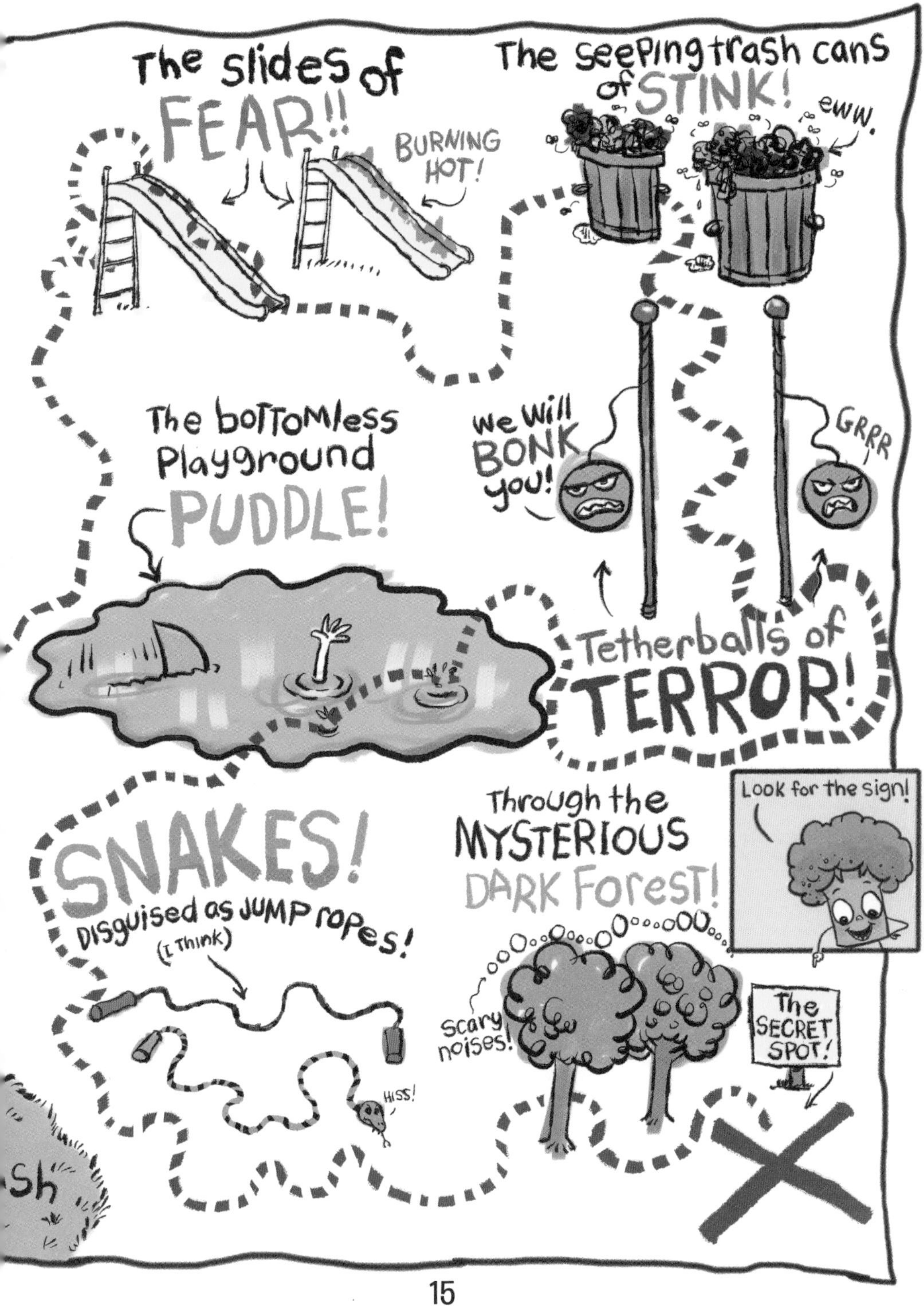
The slides of FEAR!!
BURNING HOT!
The seeping trash cans of STINK!
eww.
The bottomless Playground PUDDLE!
We will BONK you!
GRRR
Tetherballs of TERROR!
SNAKES!
Disguised as JUMP ropes!
(I Think)
HISS!
Through the MYSTERIOUS DARK Forest!
Look for the sign!
scary noises!
The SECRET SPOT!
Sh

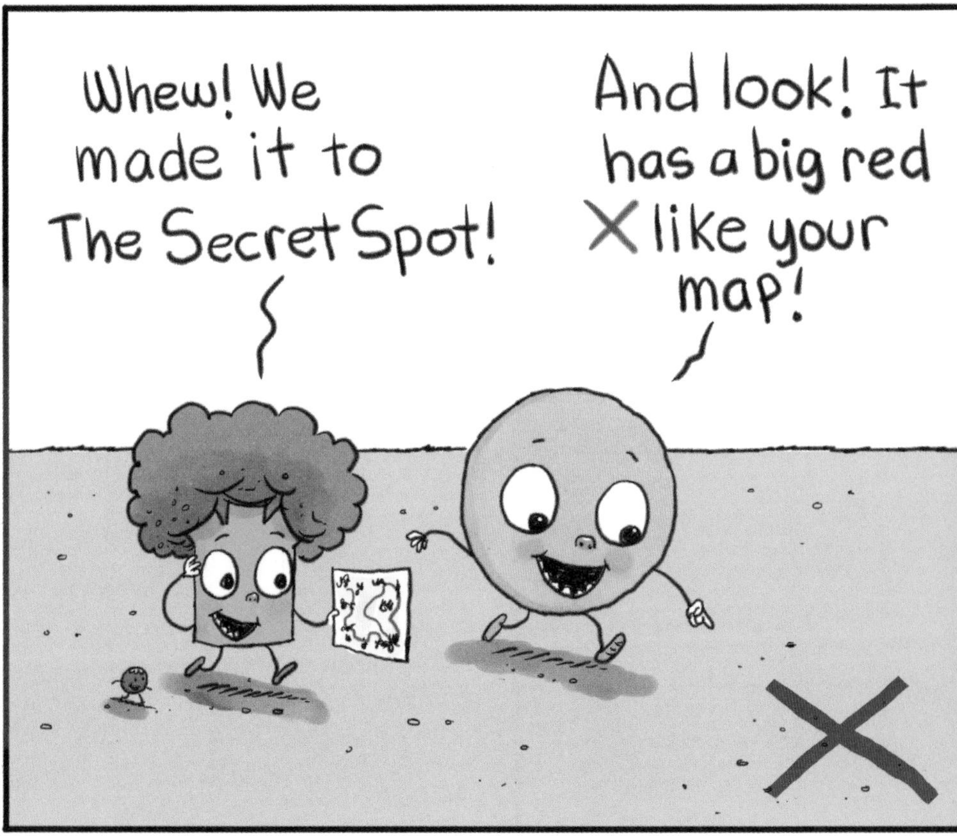
Whew! We made it to The Secret Spot!
And look! It has a big red X like your map!

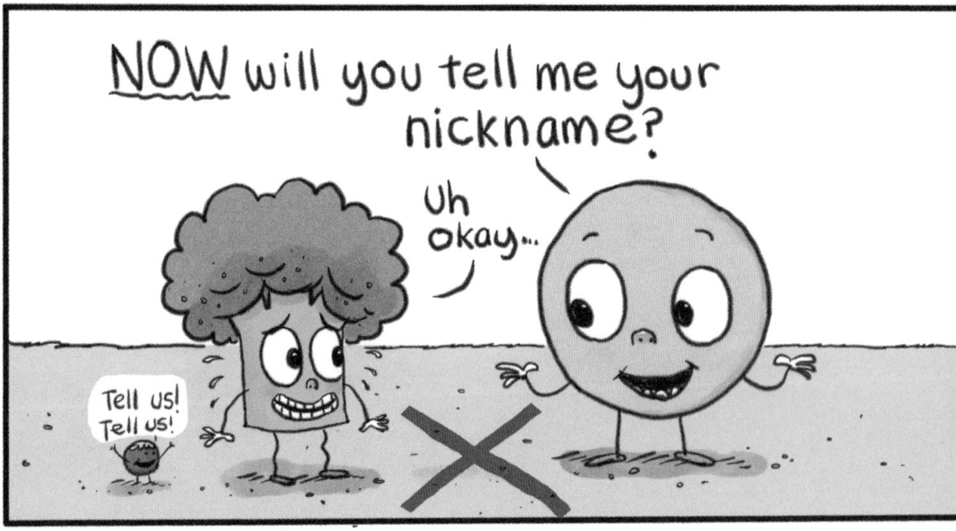
NOW will you tell me your nickname?
Uh okay...
Tell us! Tell us!

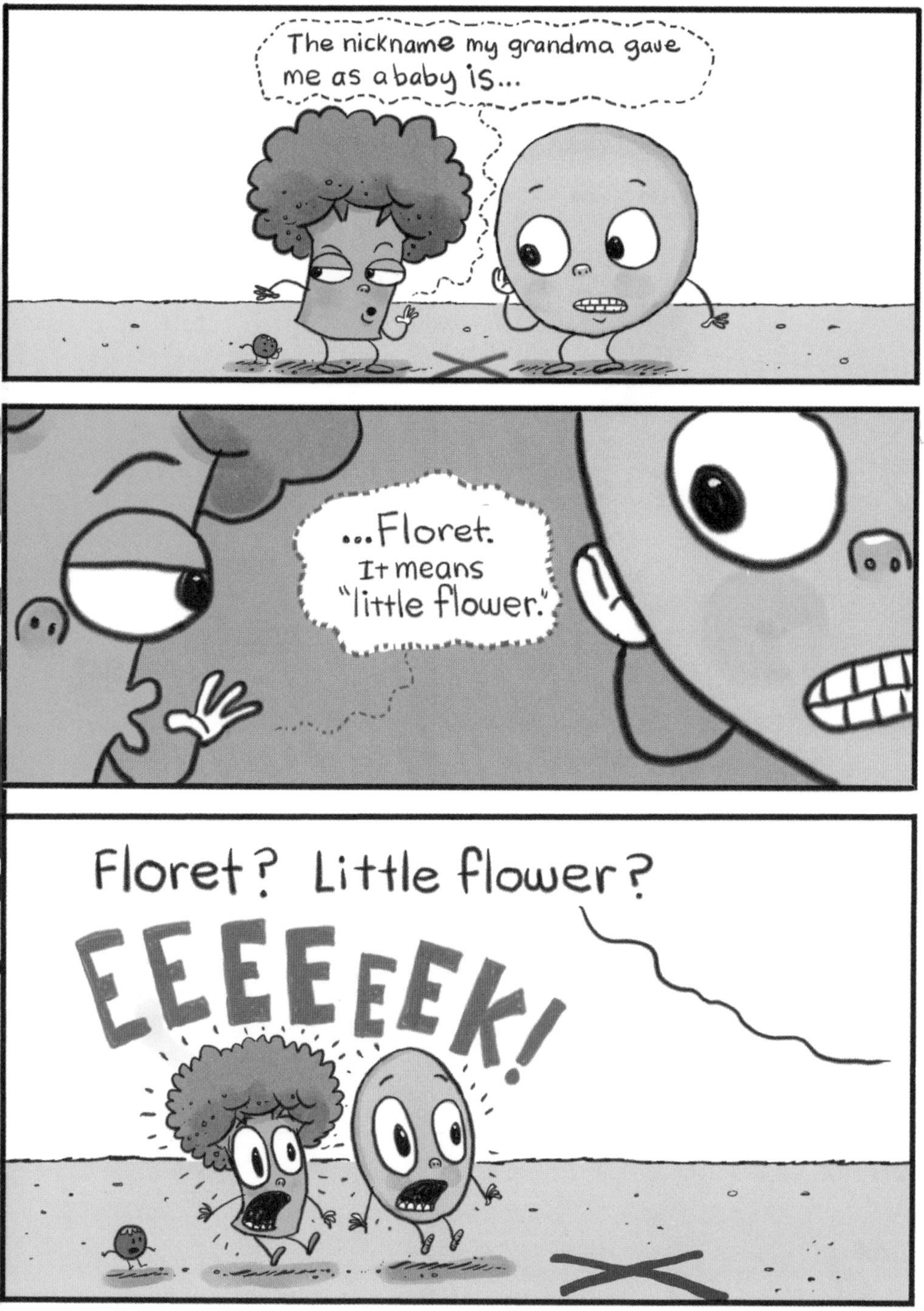
The nickname my grandma gave me as a baby is...
...Floret. It means "little flower."
Floret? Little flower?
EEEEEEK!

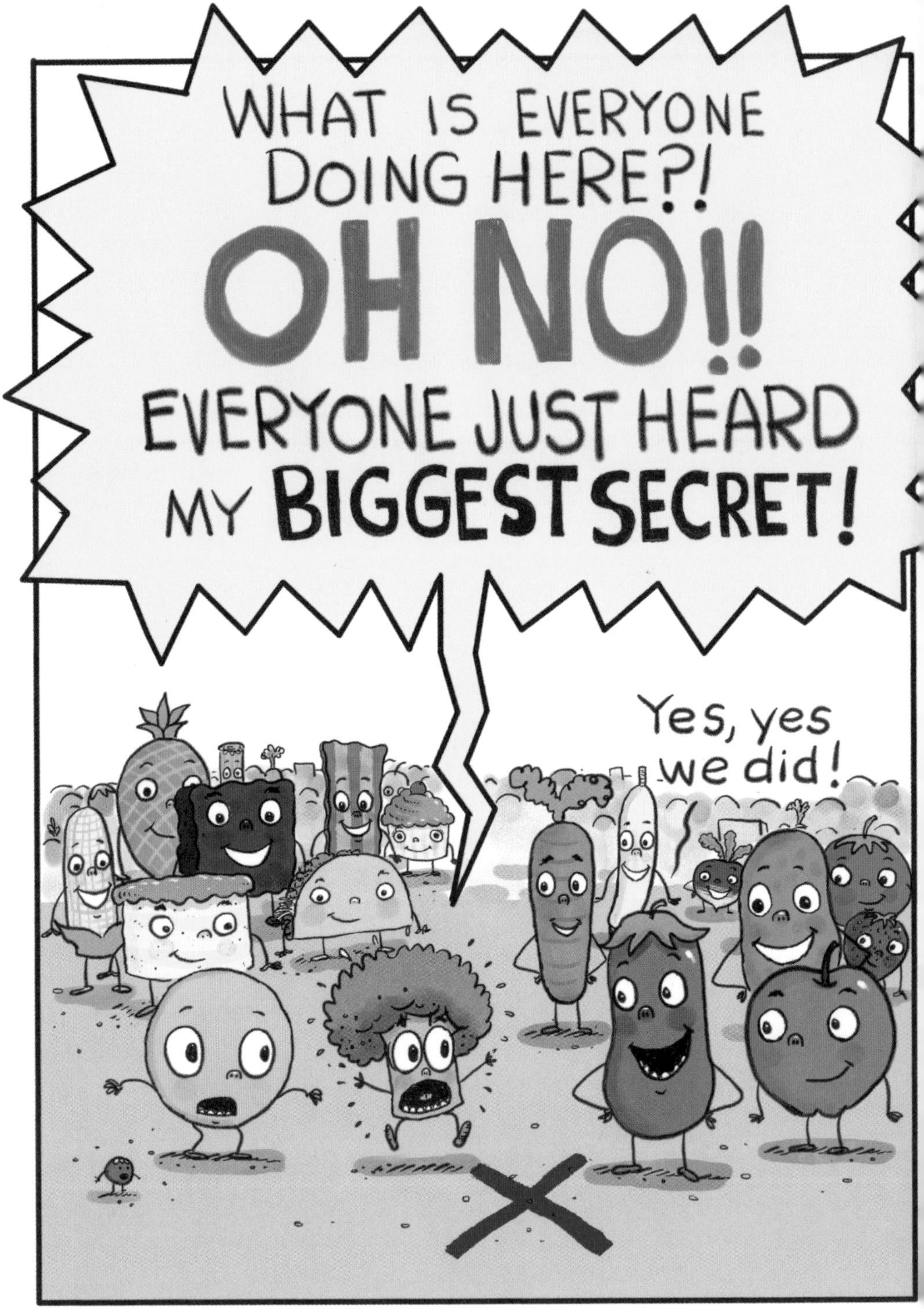
WHAT IS EVERYONE DOING HERE?!
OH NO!!
EVERYONE JUST HEARD MY BIGGEST SECRET!
Yes, yes we did!

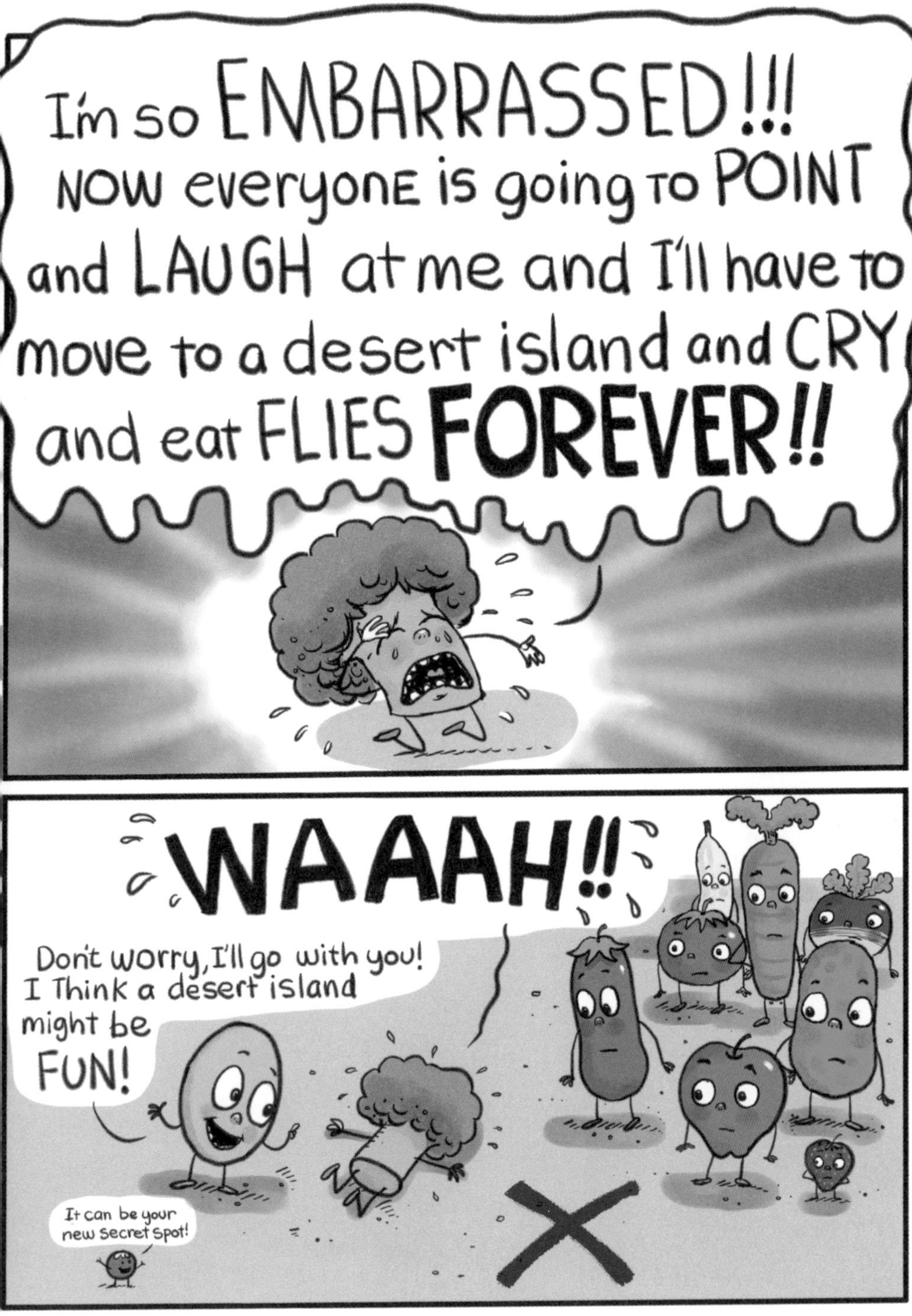
I'm so EMBARRASSED!!! NOW everyone is going to POINT and LAUGH at me and I'll have to move to a desert island and CRY and eat FLIES FOREVER!!
WAAAH!!
Don't worry, I'll go with you! I Think a desert island might be FUN!
It can be your new Secret Spot!

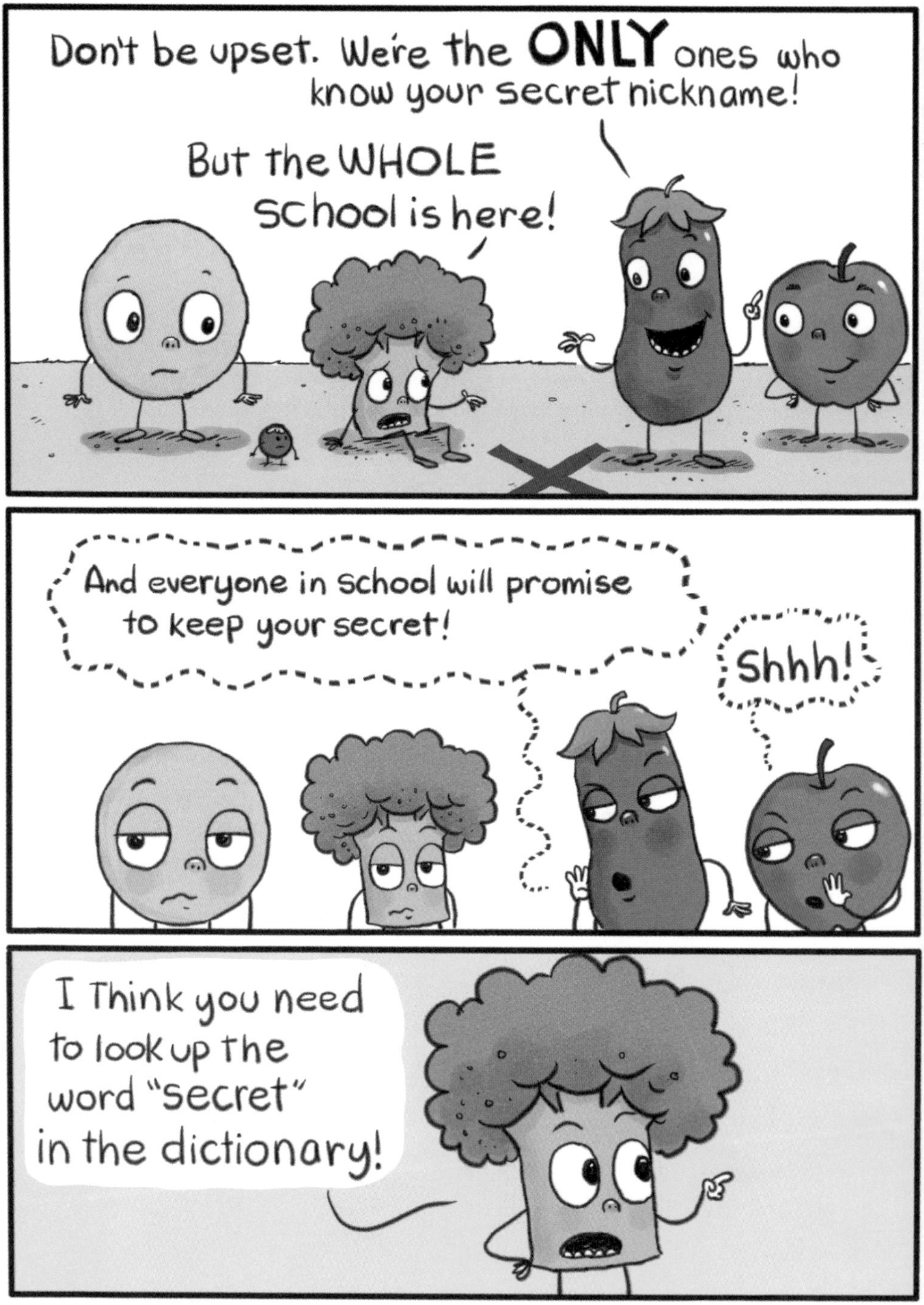
Don't be upset. We're the ONLY ones who know your secret nickname!
But the WHOLE school is here!
And everyone in school will promise to keep your secret!
Shhh!
I Think you need to look up the word "secret" in the dictionary!

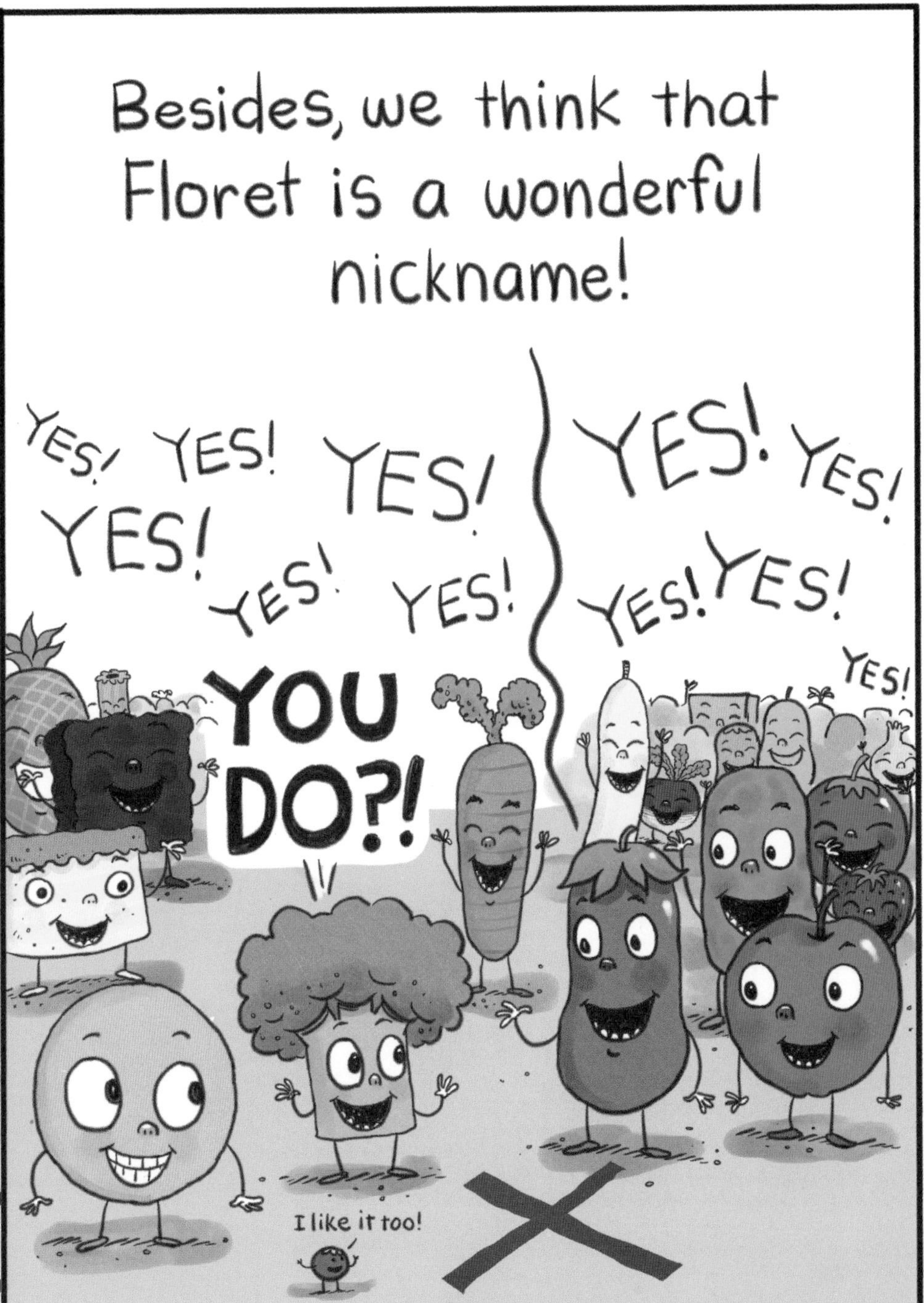
Besides, we think that Floret is a wonderful nickname!
YES! YES! YES!
YES!
YES! YES!
YES! YES!
YES! YES!
YES!
YOU DO?!
I like it too!

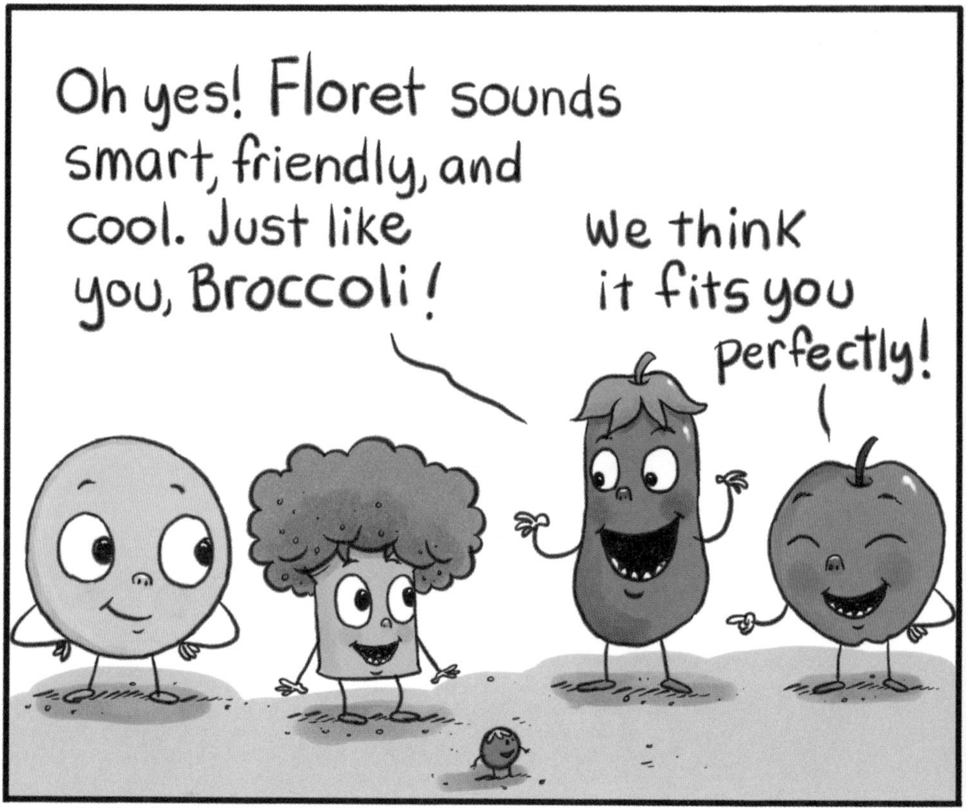
Oh yes! Floret sounds smart, friendly, and cool. Just like you, Broccoli!
We think it fits you perfectly!

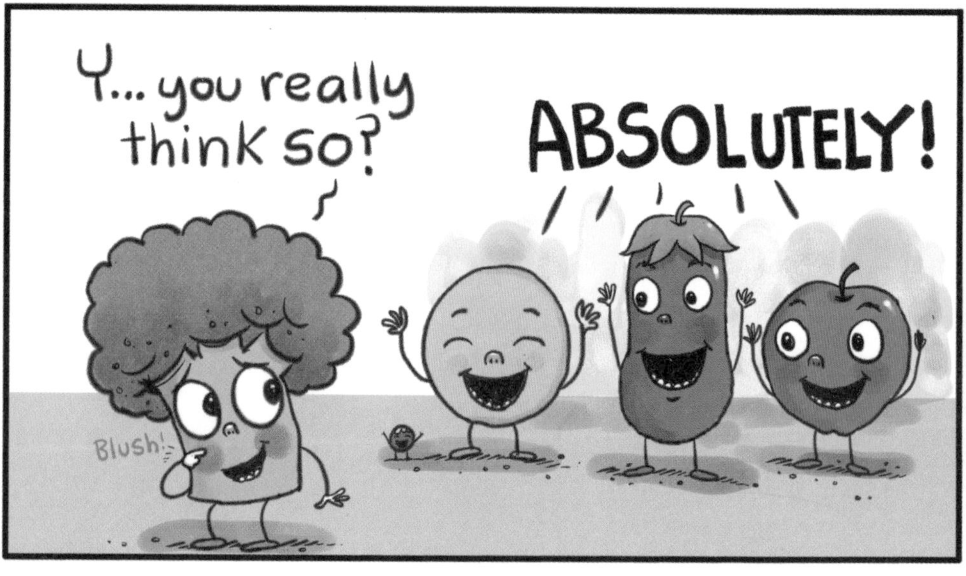
Y... you really think so?
ABSOLUTELY!
Blush!

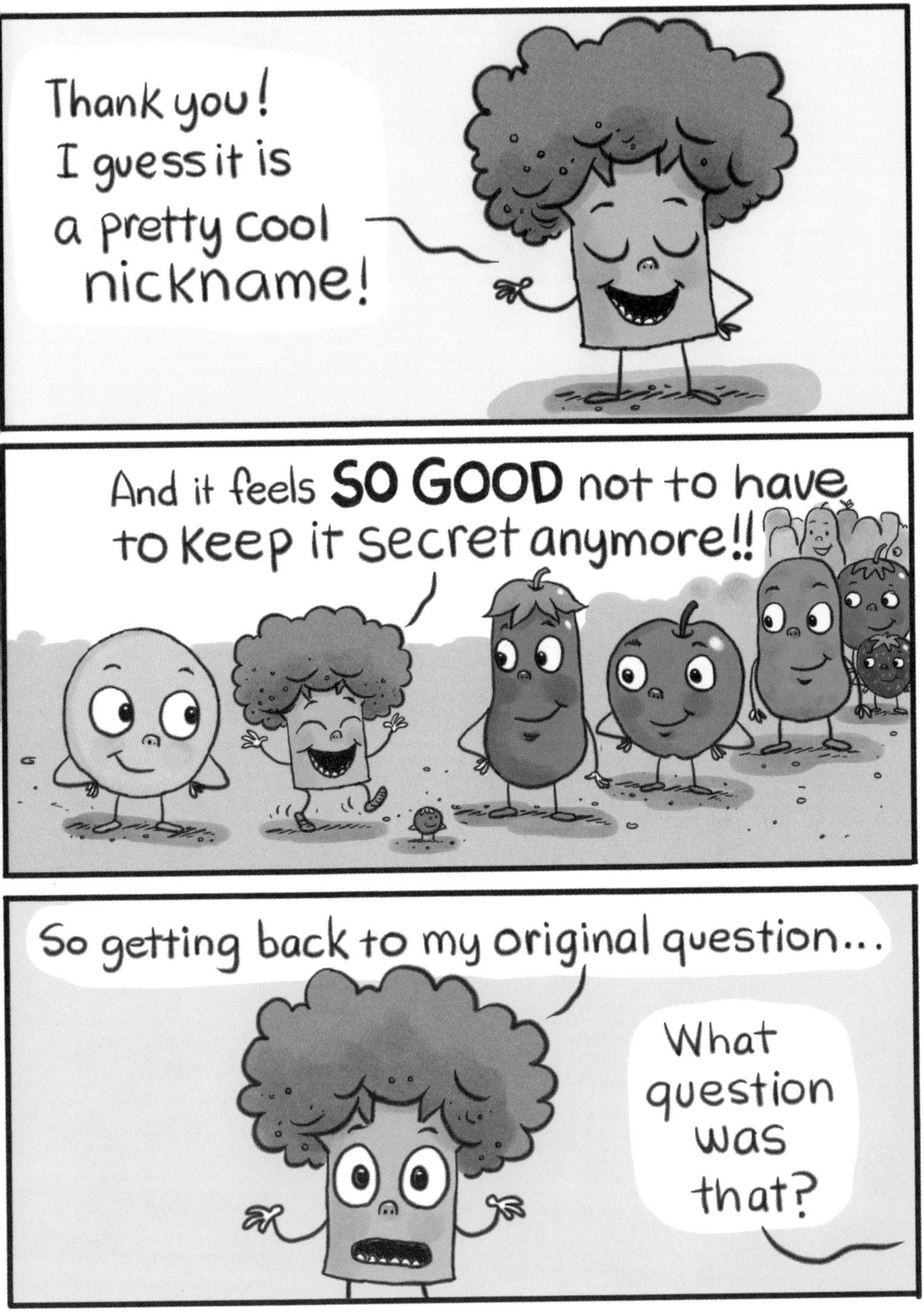
Thank you! I guess it is a pretty cool nickname!
And it feels **SO GOOD** not to have to keep it secret anymore!!
So getting back to my original question...
What question was that?

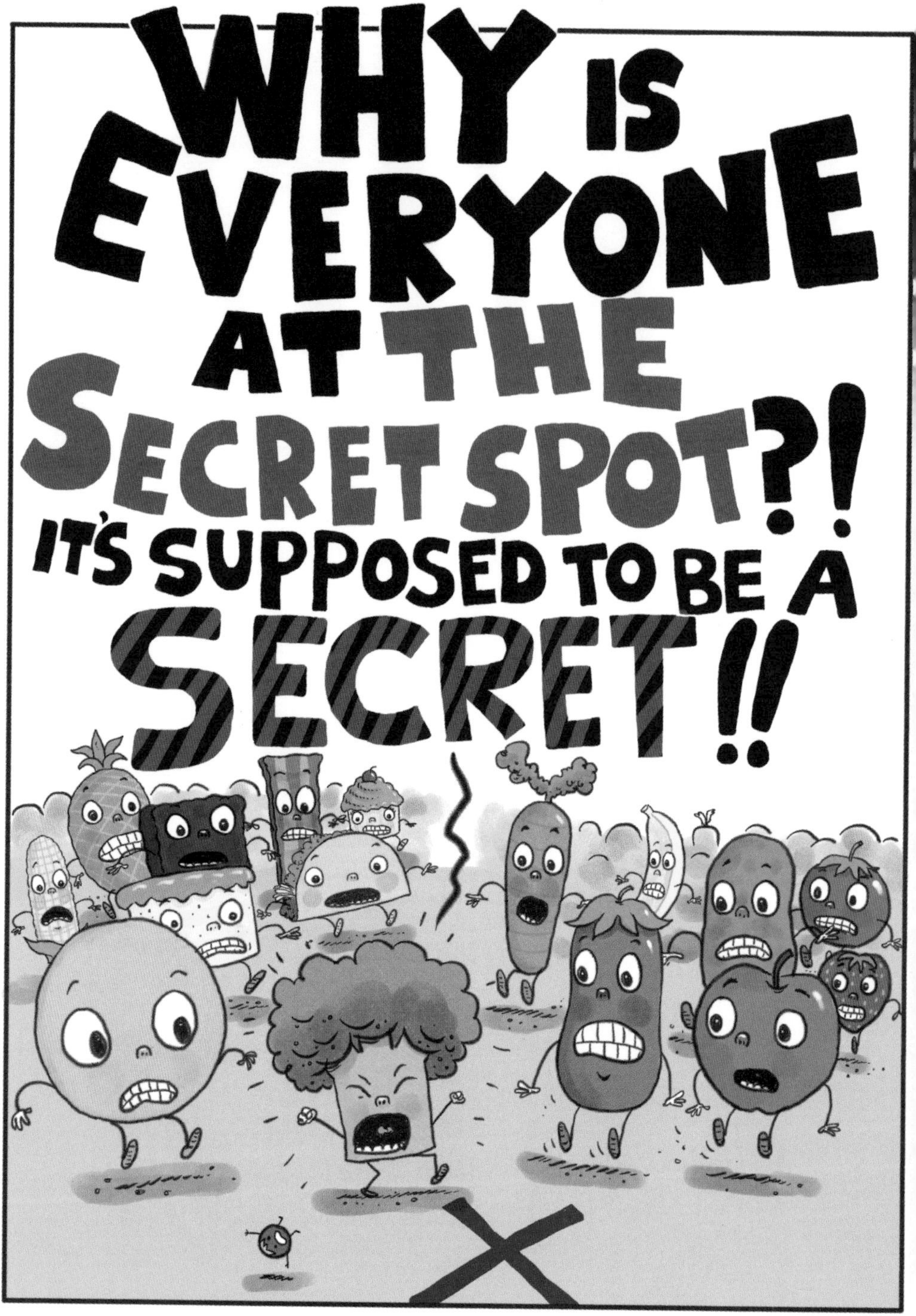
WHY IS EVERYONE AT THE SECRET SPOT?!
IT'S SUPPOSED TO BE A SECRET!!

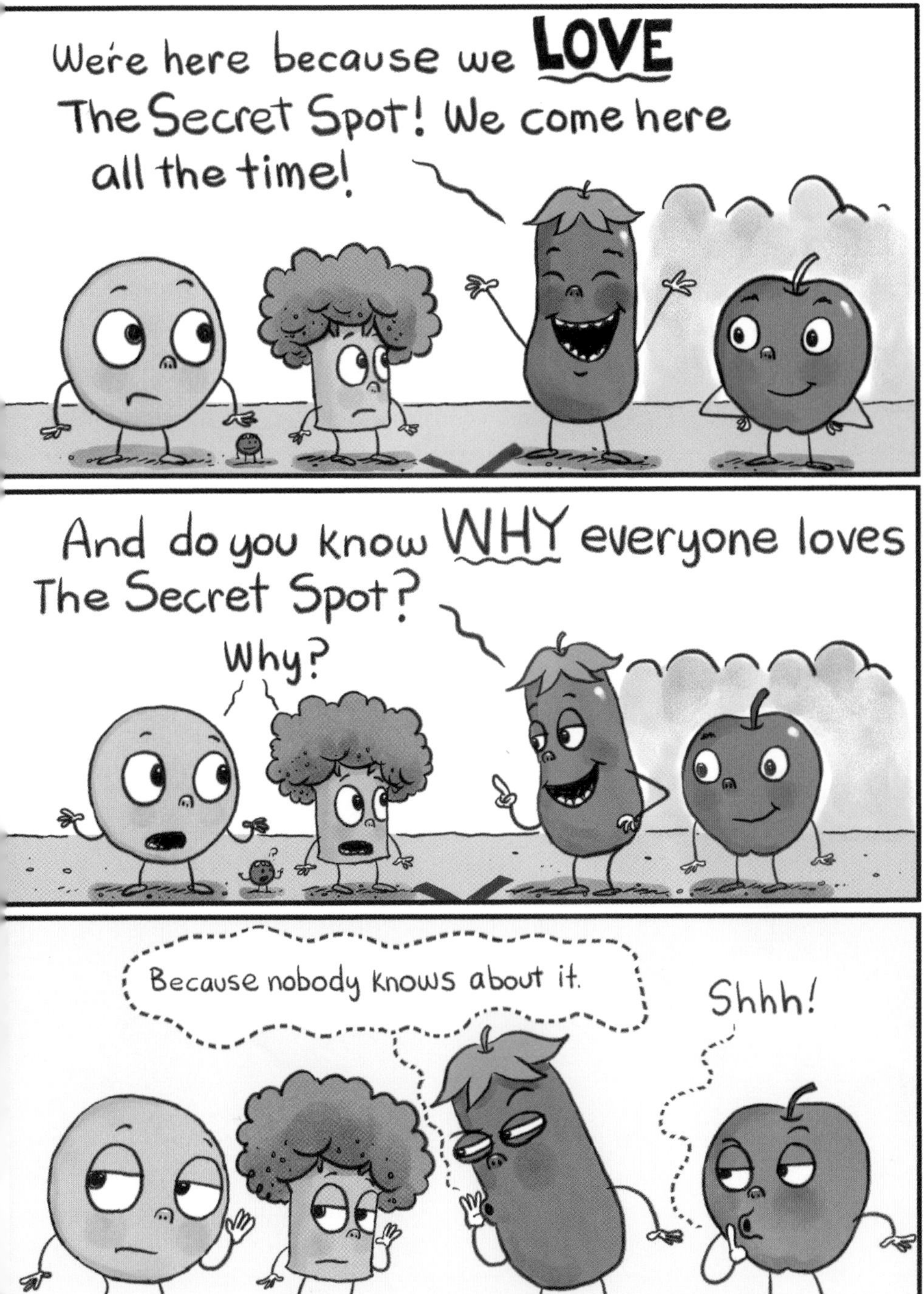
We're here because we LOVE The Secret Spot! We come here all the time!
And do you know WHY everyone loves The Secret Spot?
Why?
Because nobody knows about it.
Shhh!

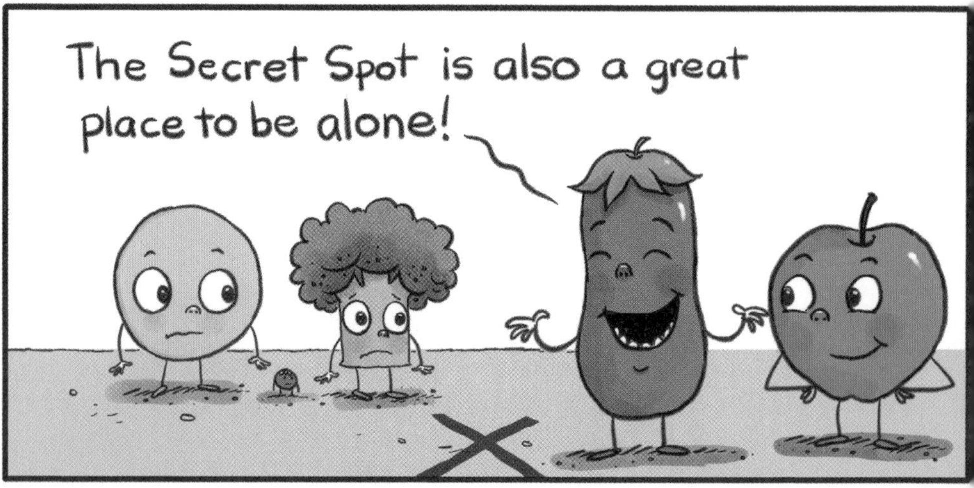
The Secret Spot is also a great place to be alone!

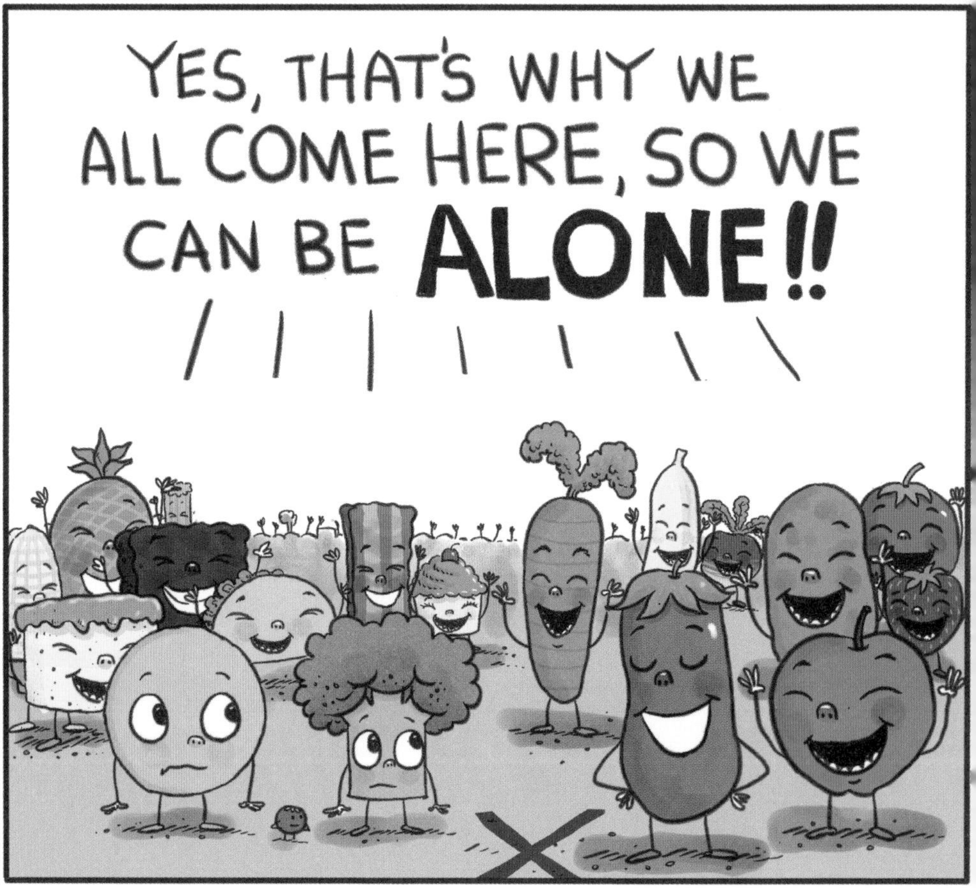
YES, THAT'S WHY WE ALL COME HERE, SO WE CAN BE ALONE!!

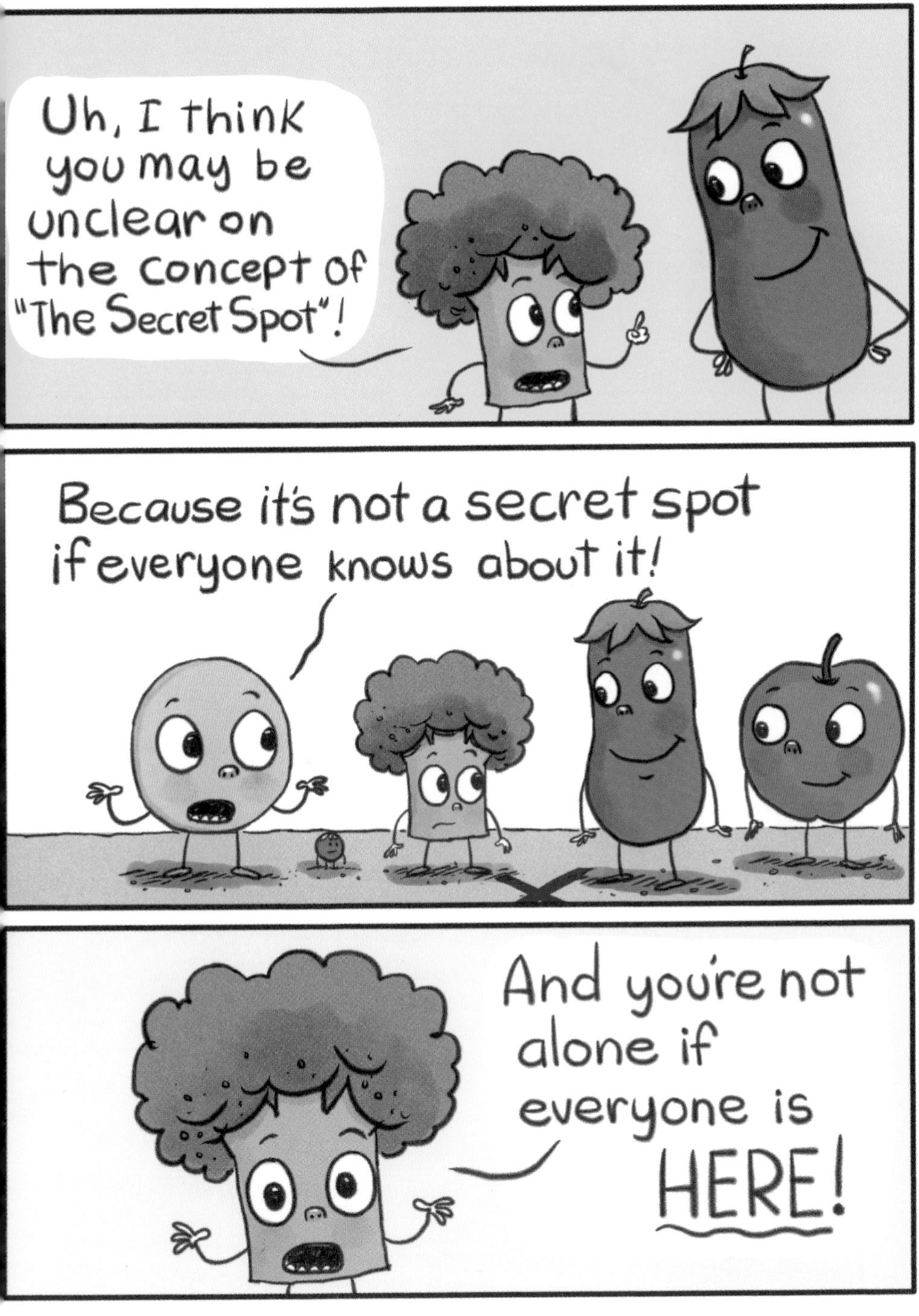
Uh, I think you may be unclear on the concept of "The Secret Spot"!
Because it's not a secret spot if everyone knows about it!
And you're not alone if everyone is HERE!

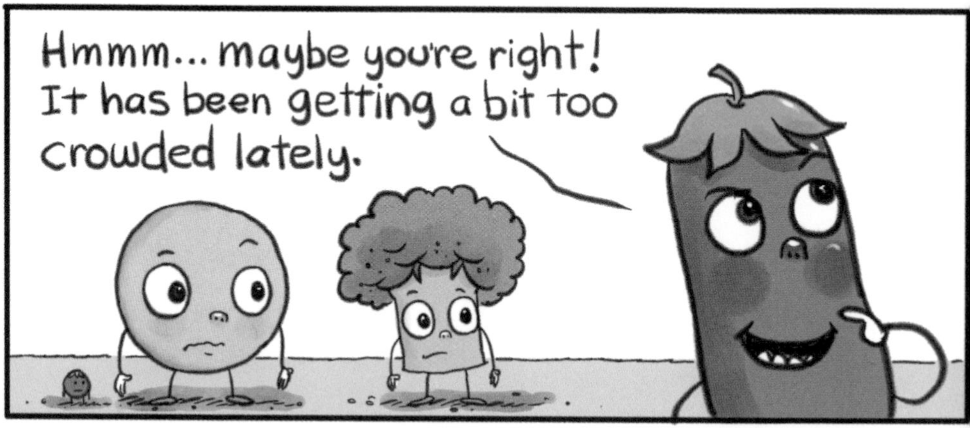
Hmmm... maybe you're right! It has been getting a bit too crowded lately.

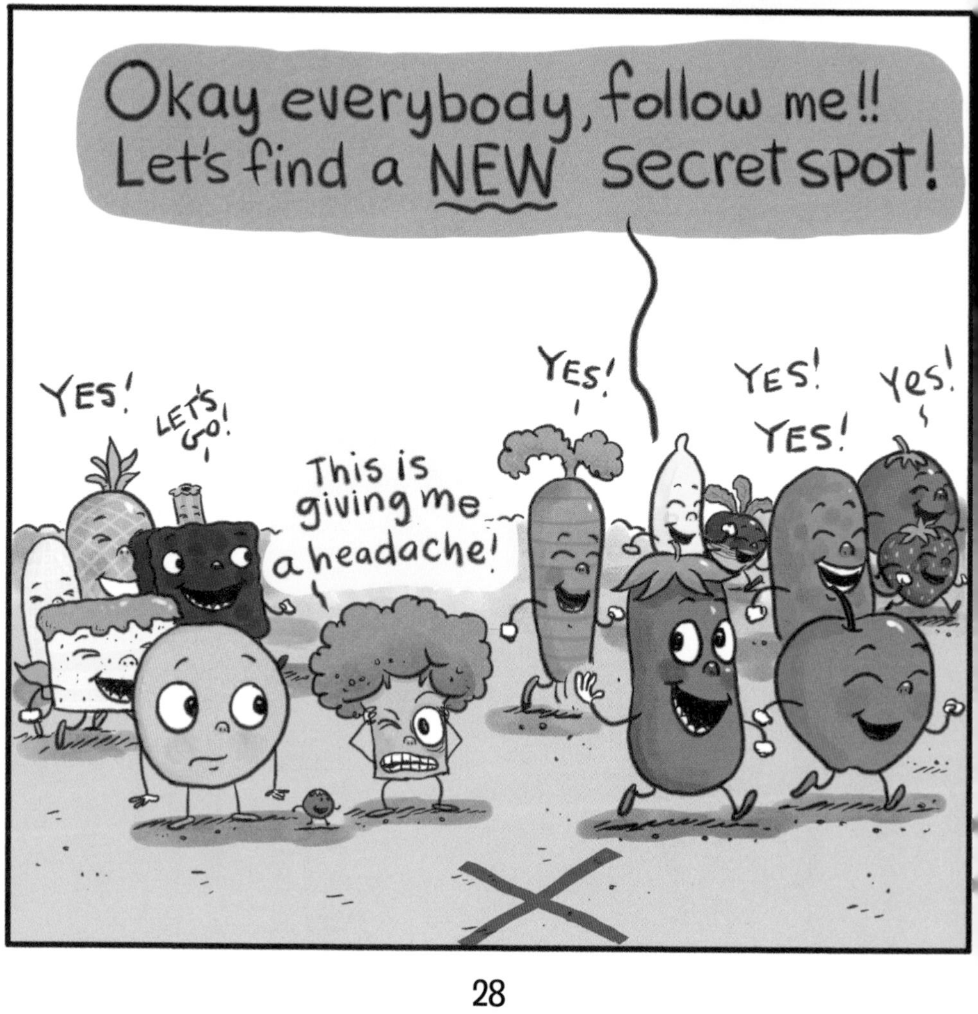
Okay everybody, follow me!! Let's find a NEW secret spot!
YES!
LET'S GO!
This is giving me a headache!
YES!
YES!
Yes!
YES!

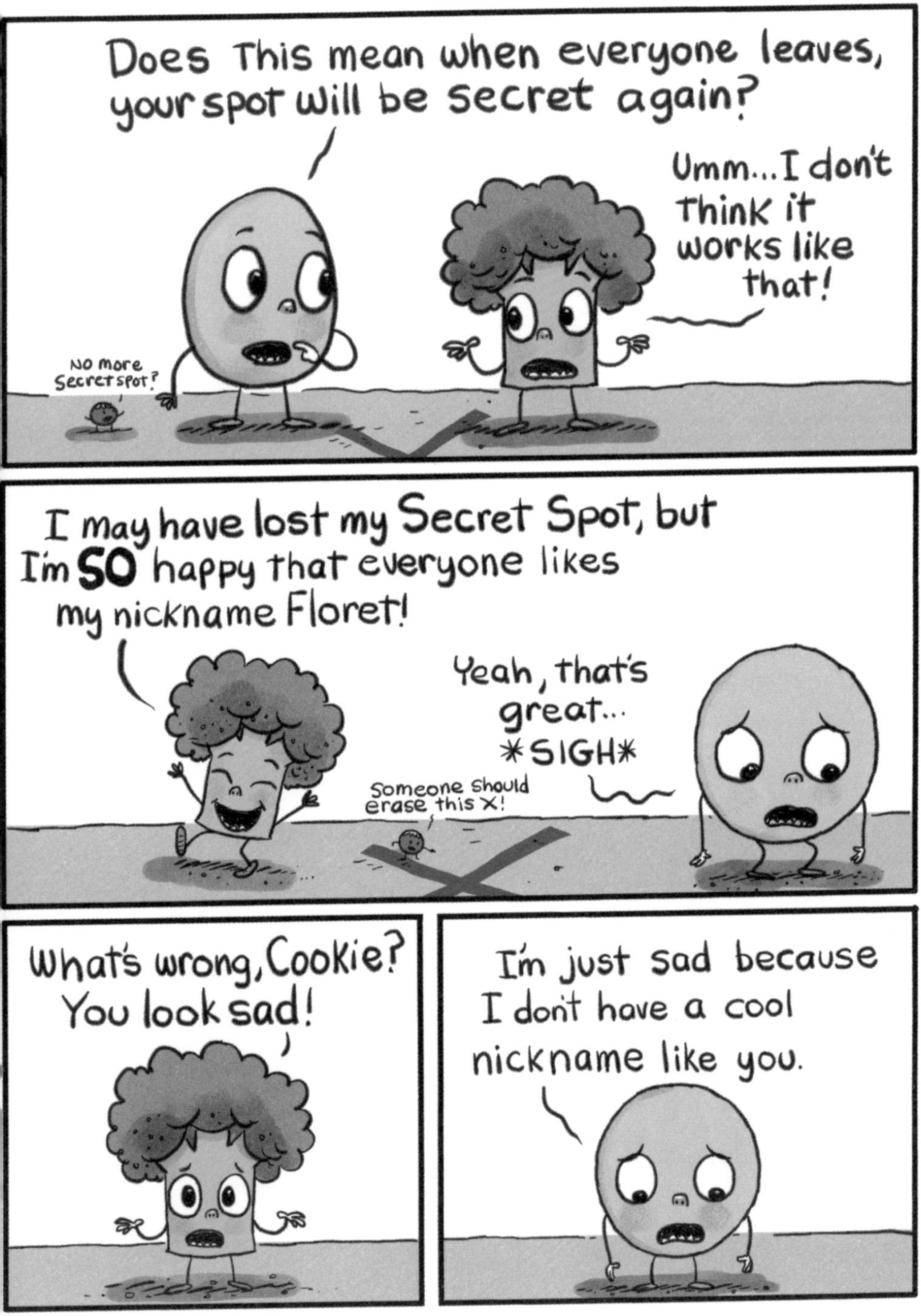
Does This mean when everyone leaves, your spot will be secret again?
Umm...I don't Think it works like that!
No more Secret spot?
I may have lost my Secret Spot, but I'm SO happy that everyone likes my nickname Floret!
Yeah, that's great... *SIGH*
Someone should erase this X!
What's wrong, Cookie? You look sad!
I'm just sad because I don't have a cool nickname like you.

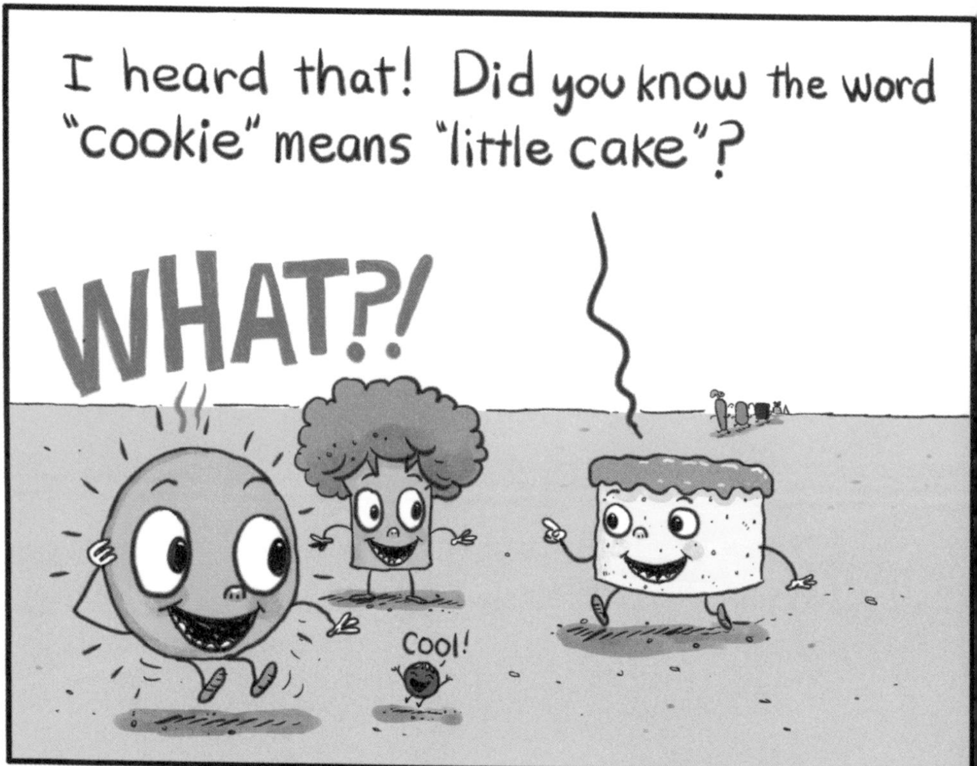
I heard that! Did you know the word "cookie" means "little cake"?
WHAT?!
COOL!

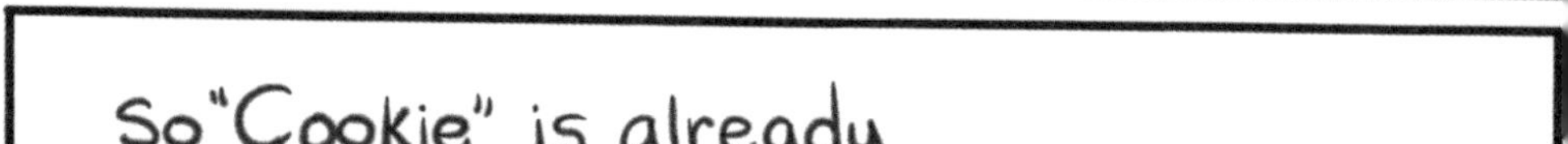
So "Cookie" is already a NICKNAME?!
Yes!

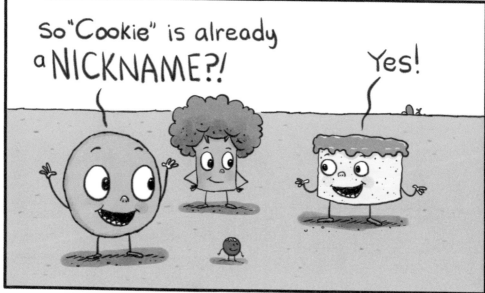

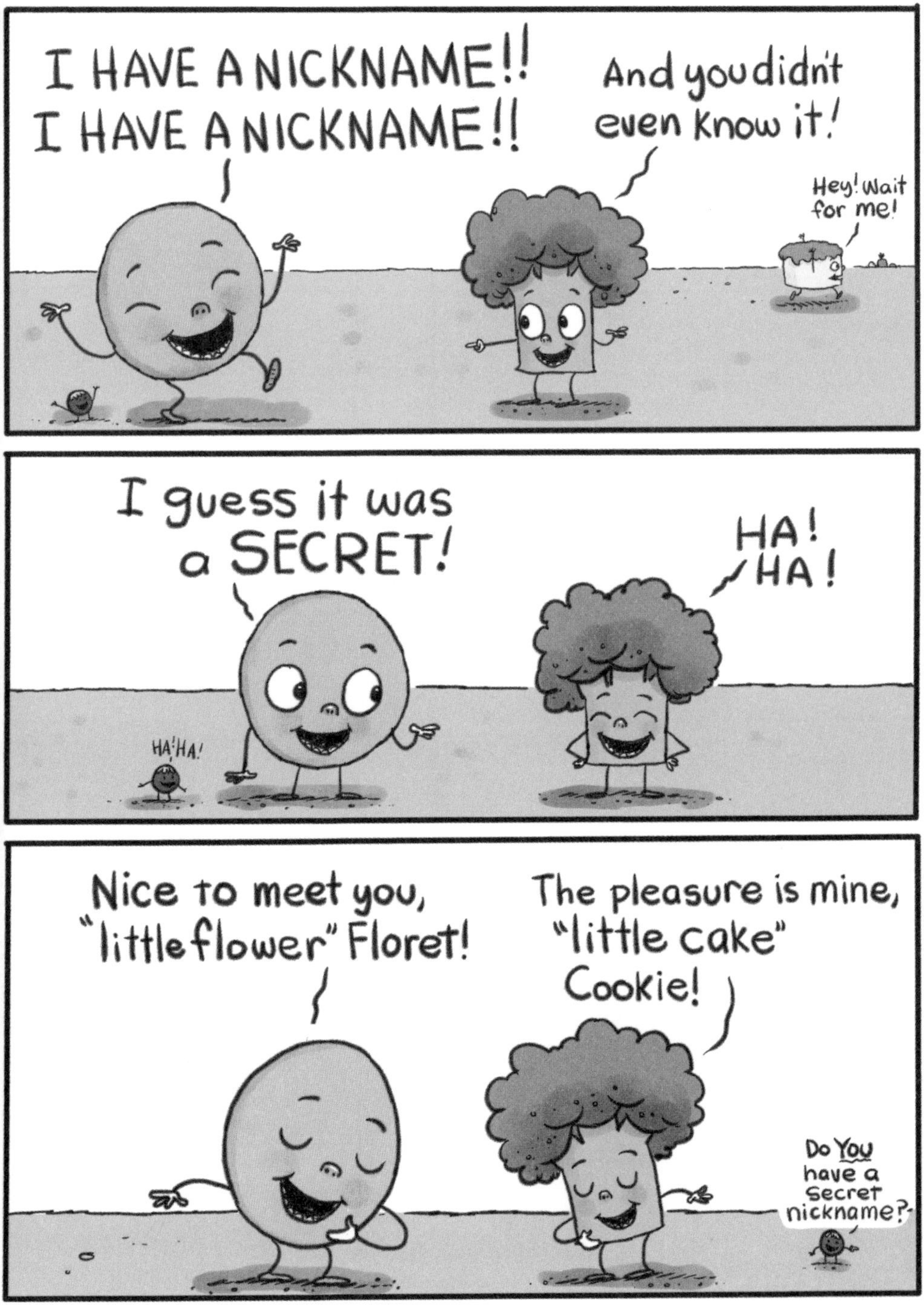
I HAVE A NICKNAME!!
I HAVE A NICKNAME!!
And you didn't even know it!
Hey! Wait for me!
I guess it was a SECRET!
HA! HA!
HA! HA!
Nice to meet you, "little flower" Floret!
The pleasure is mine, "little cake" Cookie!
Do You have a secret nickname?

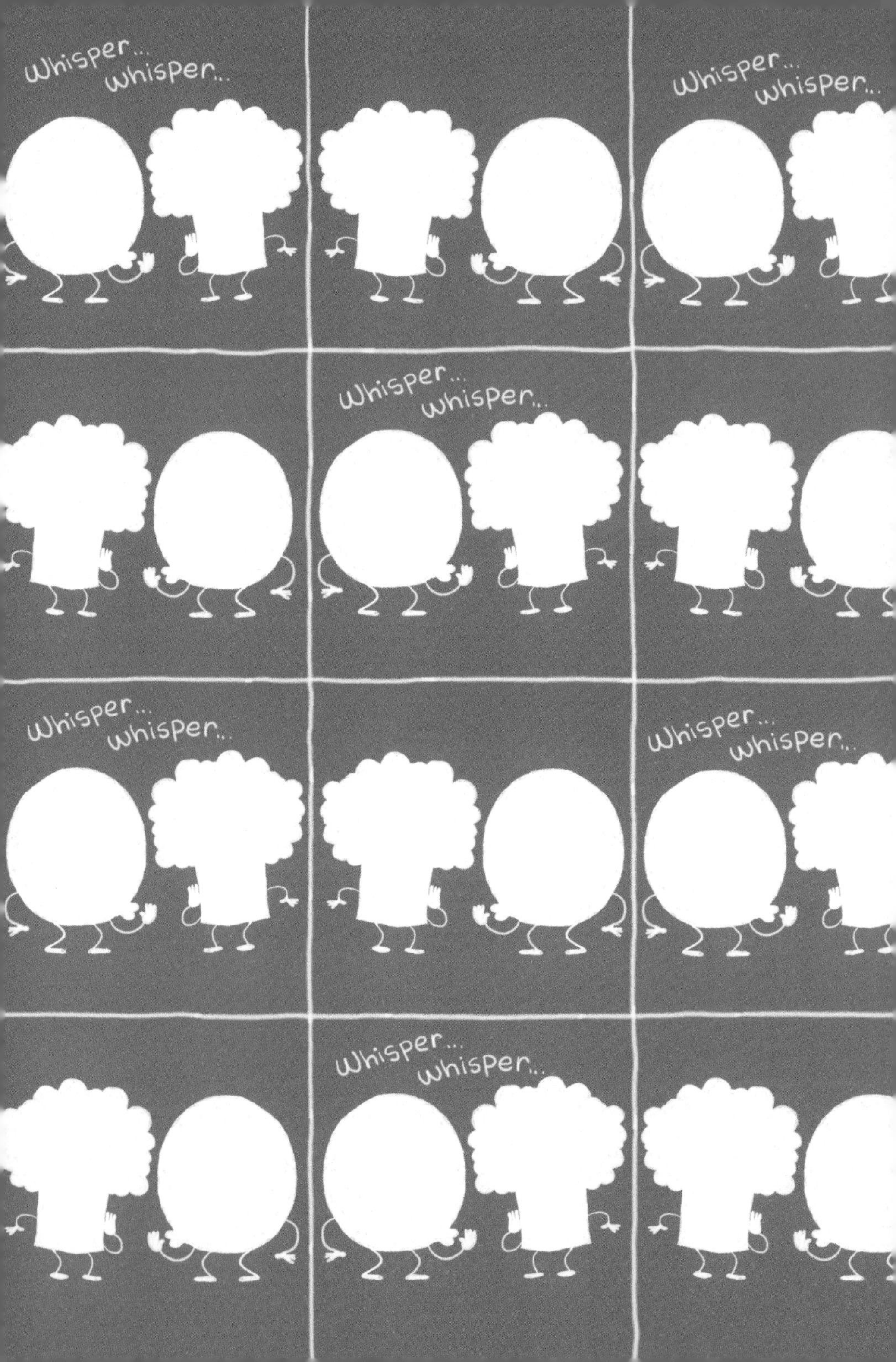
Whisper... whisper...
Whisper... whisper...
Whisper... whisper...
Whisper... whisper...
Whisper... whisper...
Whisper... whisper...

Chapter 2

THE SECRET CURE FOR BOREDOM!

You will be AMAZED!

It's pure GENIUS!

And it works 100% of the time!

Guaranteed!

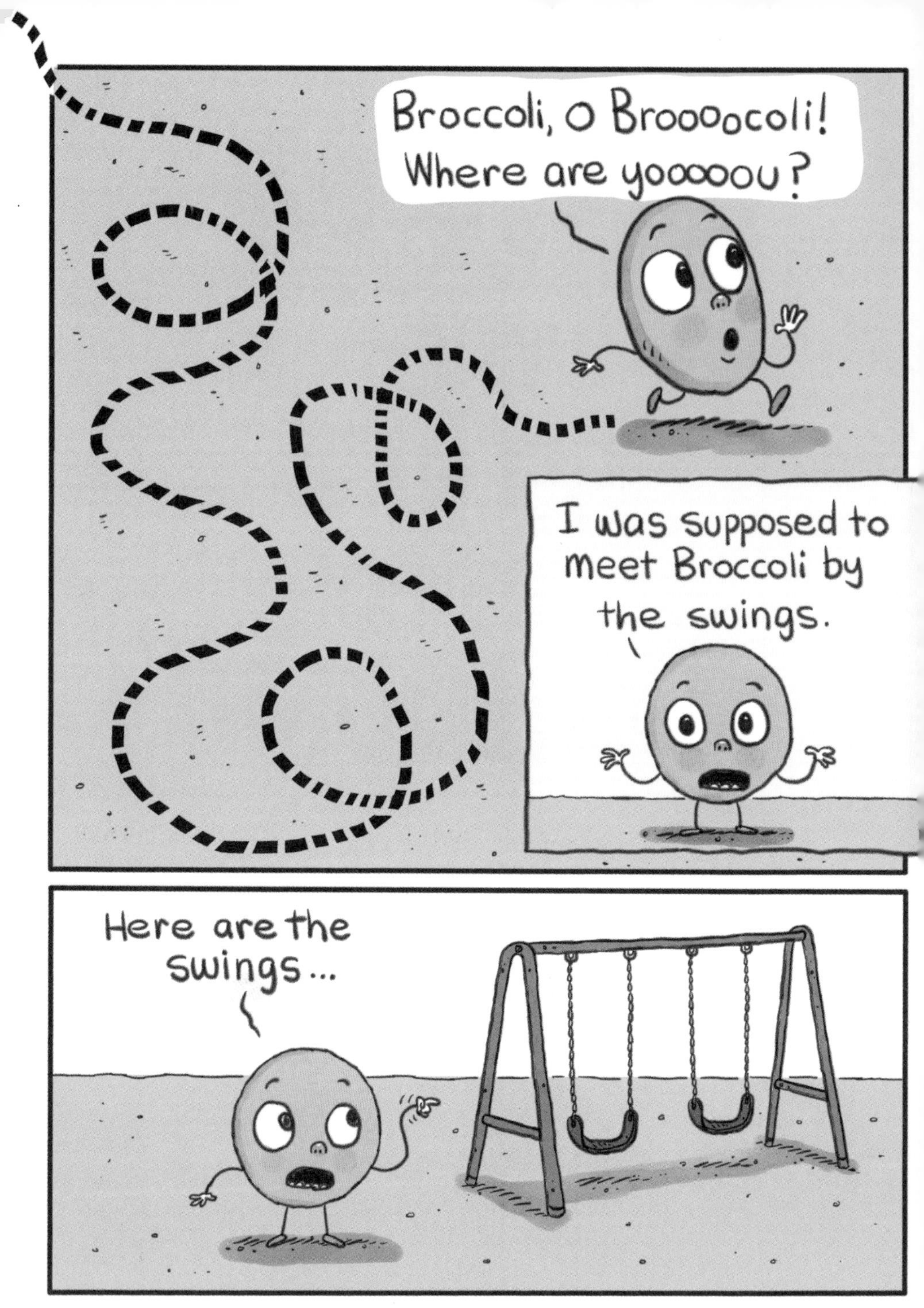
Broccoli, O Broooocoli! Where are yoooou?
I was supposed to meet Broccoli by the swings.
Here are the swings...

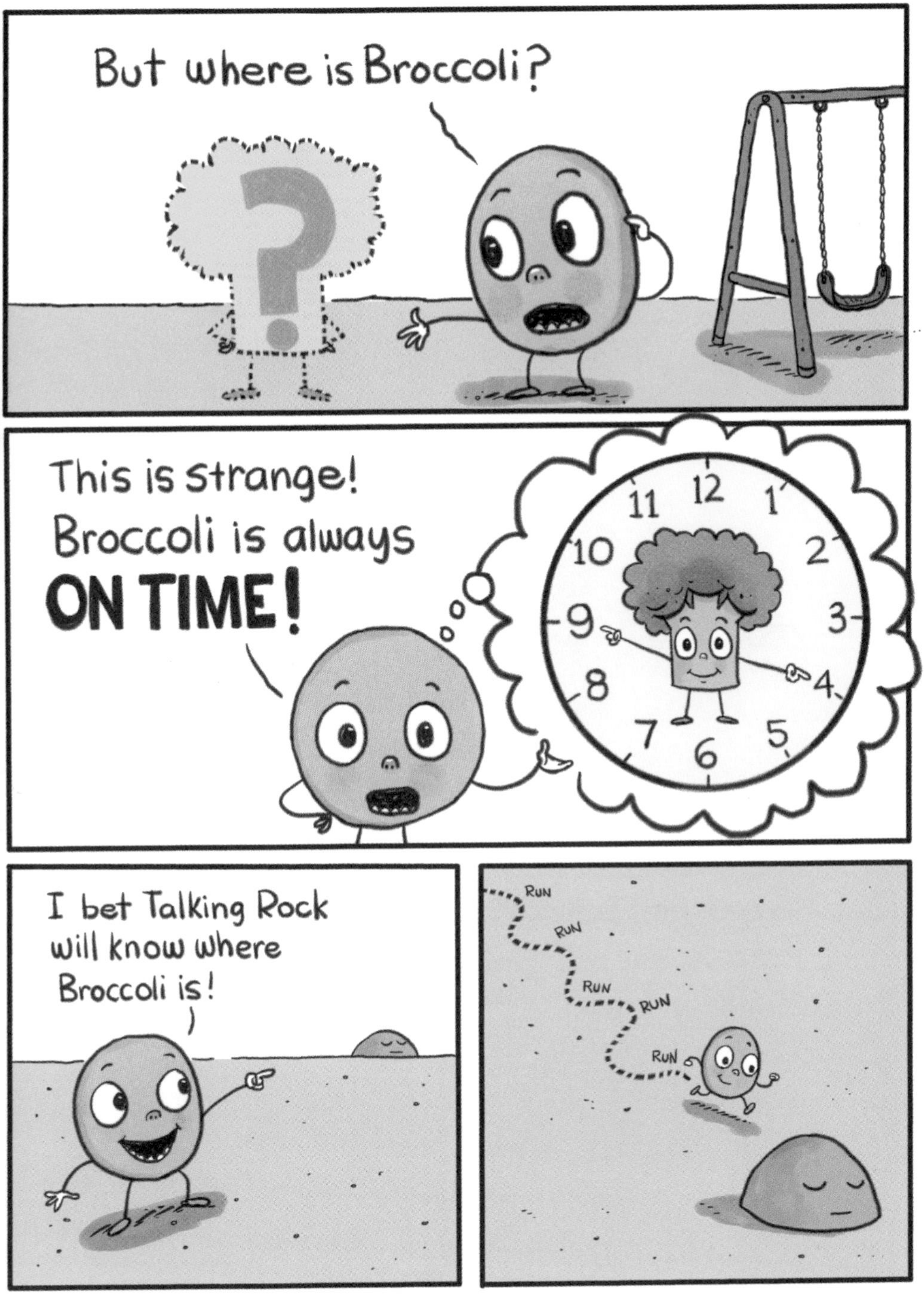
But where is Broccoli?
This is strange! Broccoli is always ON TIME!
11 12 1 10 2 9 3 8 4 7 6 5
I bet Talking Rock will know where Broccoli is!
RUN
RUN
RUN
RUN
RUN

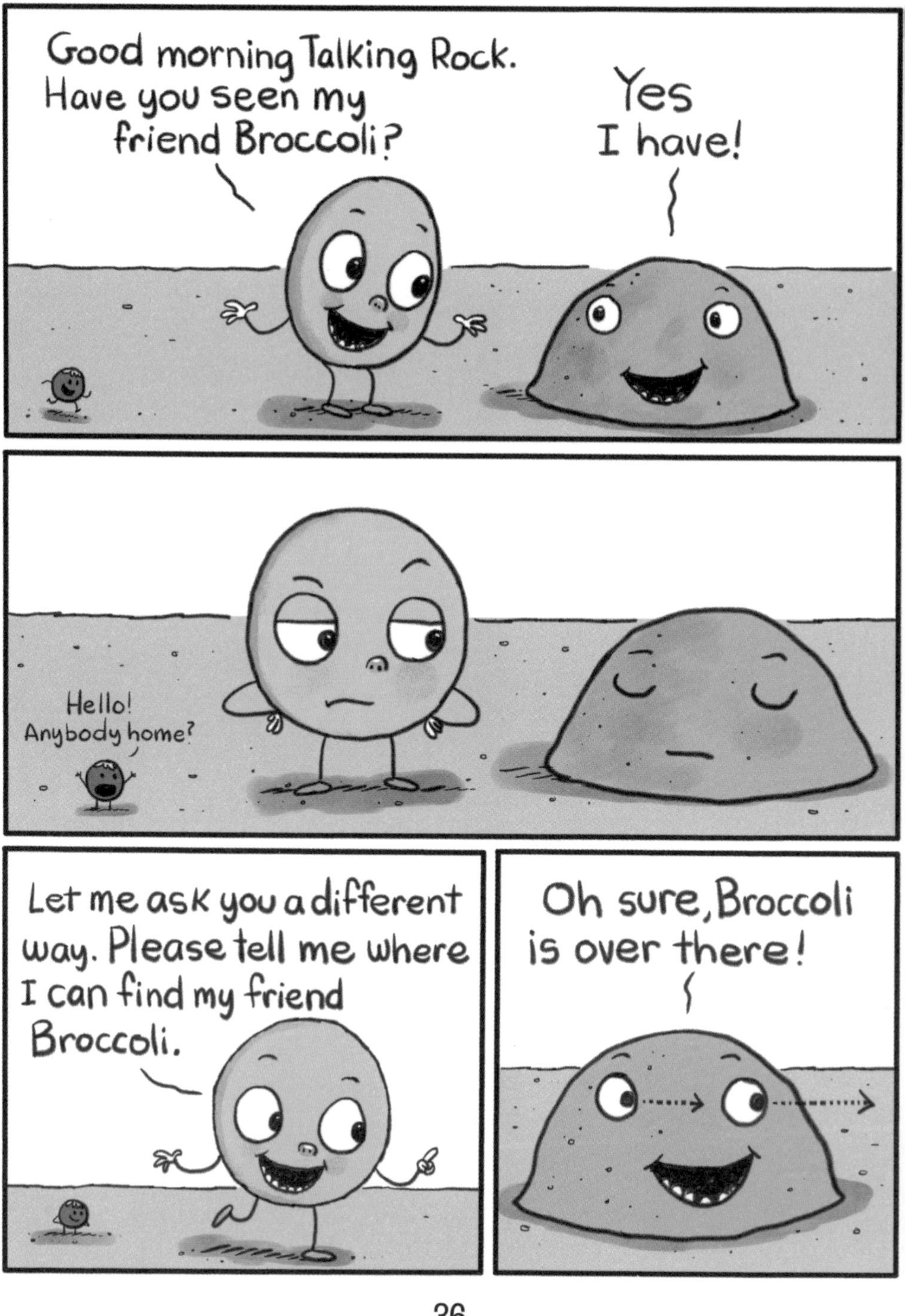
Good morning Talking Rock. Have you seen my friend Broccoli?
Yes I have!
Hello! Anybody home?
Let me ask you a different way. Please tell me where I can find my friend Broccoli.
Oh sure, Broccoli is over there!

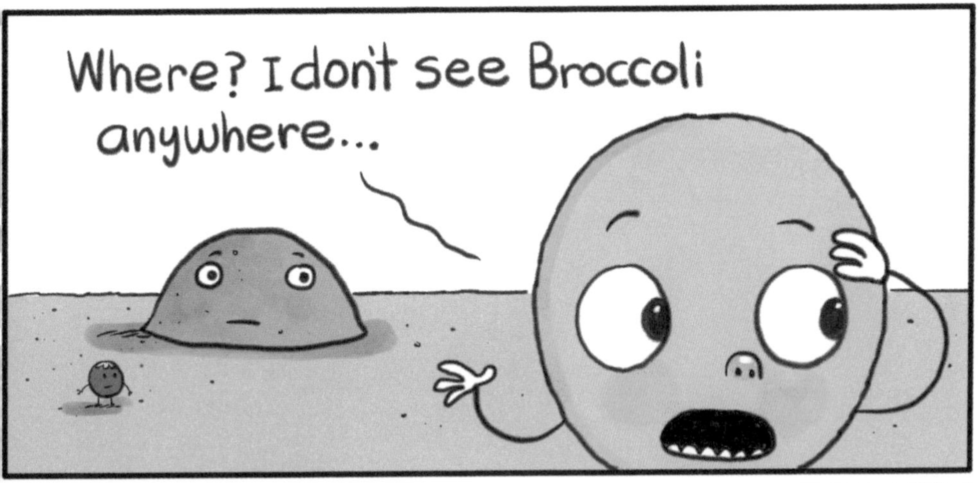
Where? I don't see Broccoli anywhere...

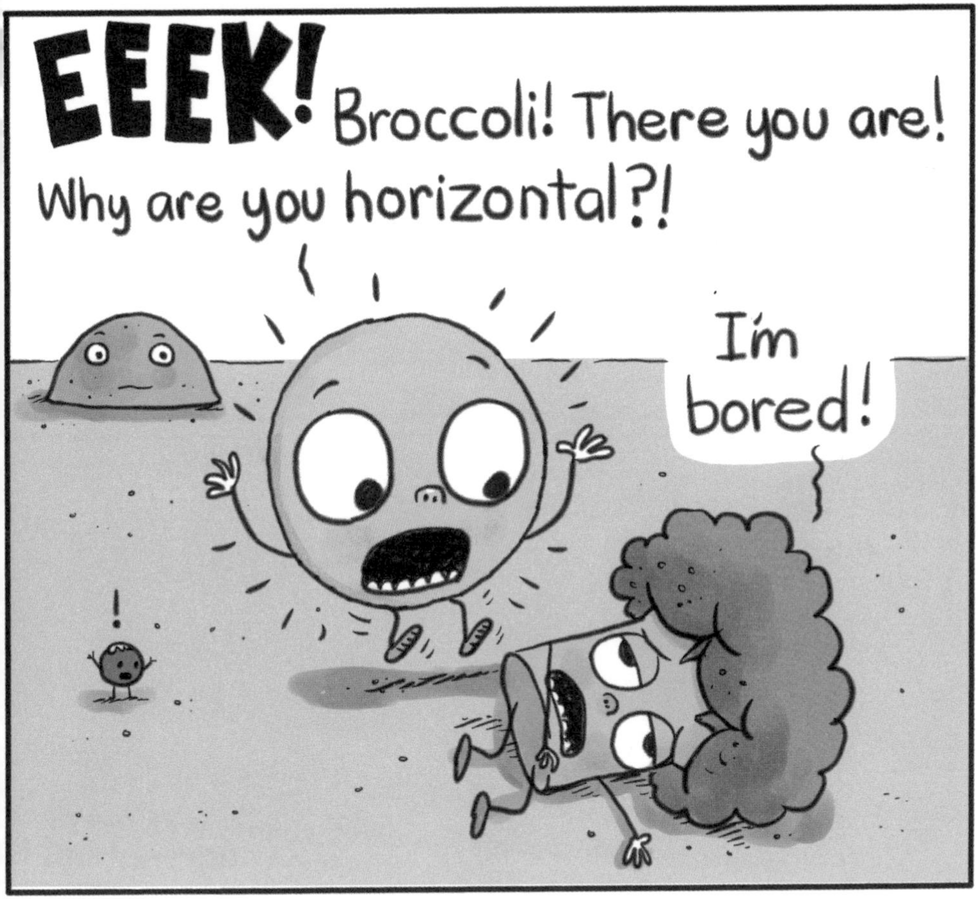
EEEK! Broccoli! There you are! Why are you horizontal?!
I'm bored!

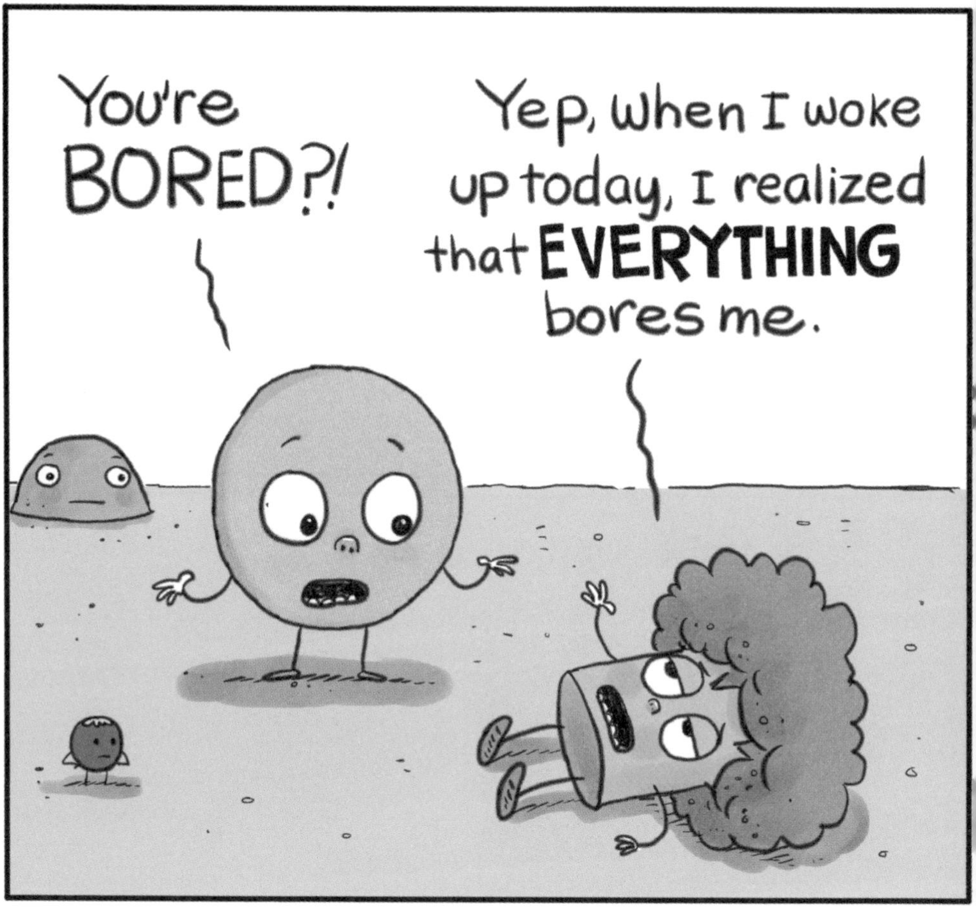
You're BORED?!
Yep, when I woke up today, I realized that EVERYTHING bores me.

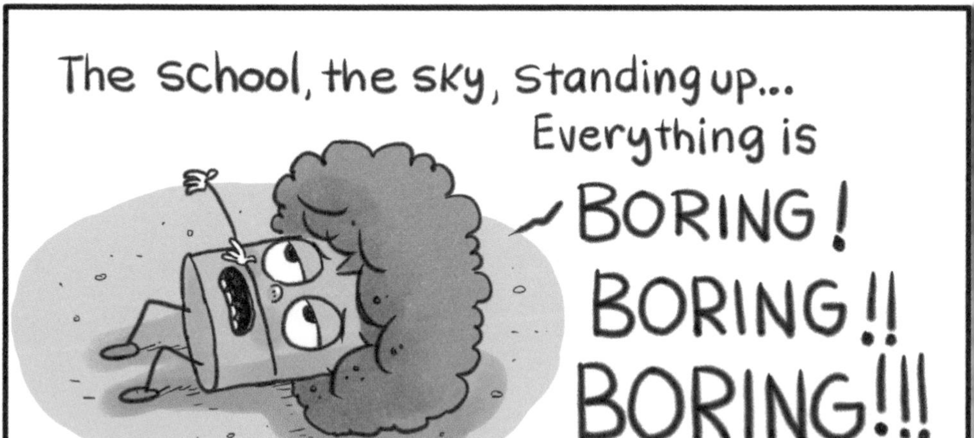
The school, the sky, standing up...
Everything is BORING! BORING!! BORING!!!

Everything?! Even MATH?! You LOVE math!
Adding .... +
Subtracting ..... −
Multiplying .... ×
Dividing .... ÷
= BORING!
How about your favorite dance, THE HOKEY POKEY?
I love this dance!
All that putting your feet IN and OUT and shaking them all about makes me BORED!

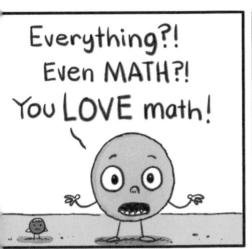

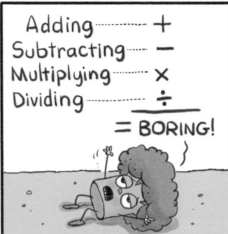

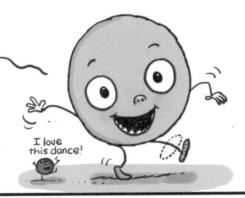

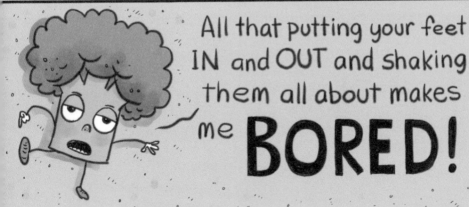

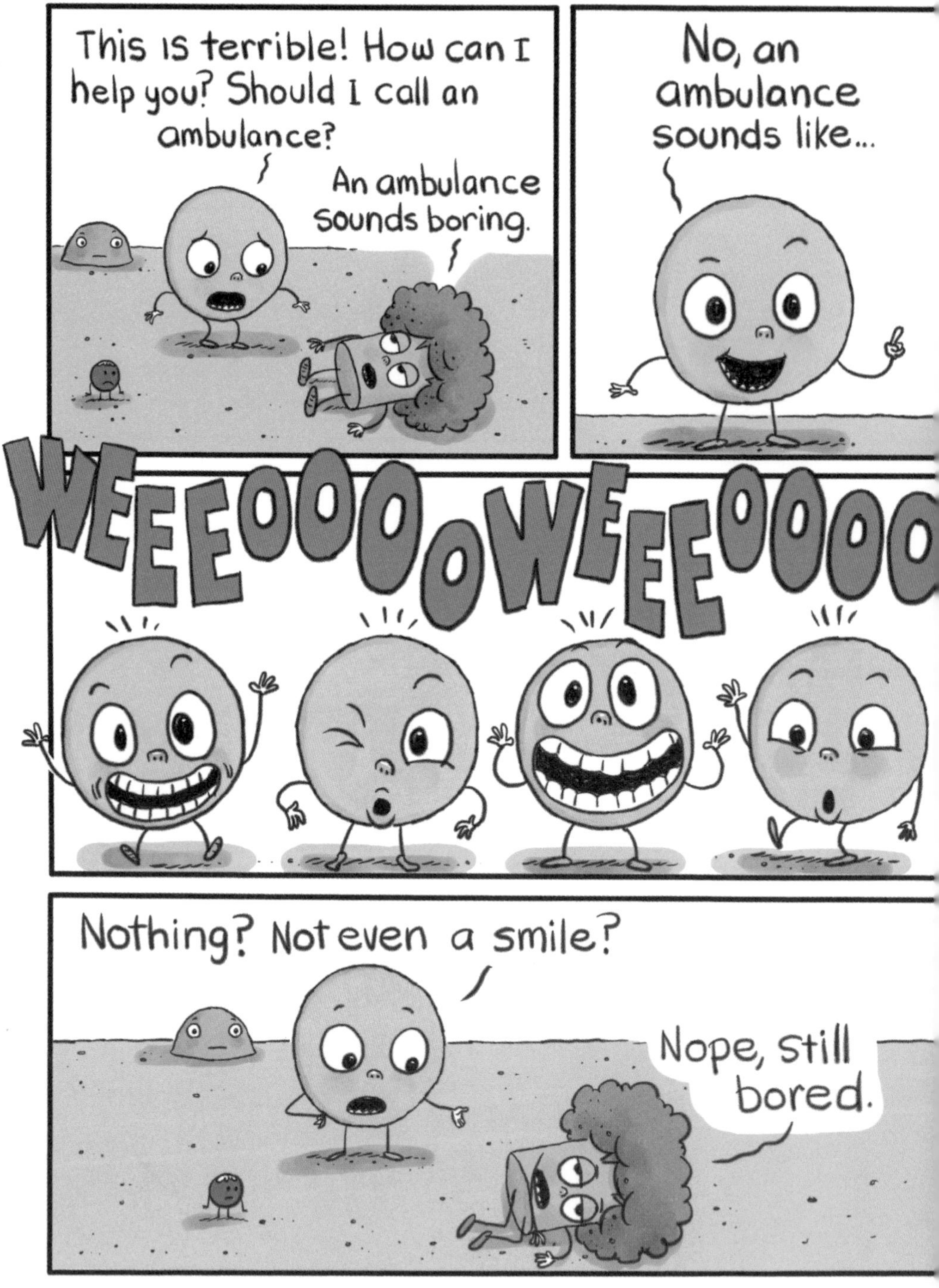
This is terrible! How can I help you? Should I call an ambulance?
An ambulance sounds boring.
No, an ambulance sounds like...
WEEEOOOOWEEEOOOO
Nothing? Not even a smile?
Nope, still bored.

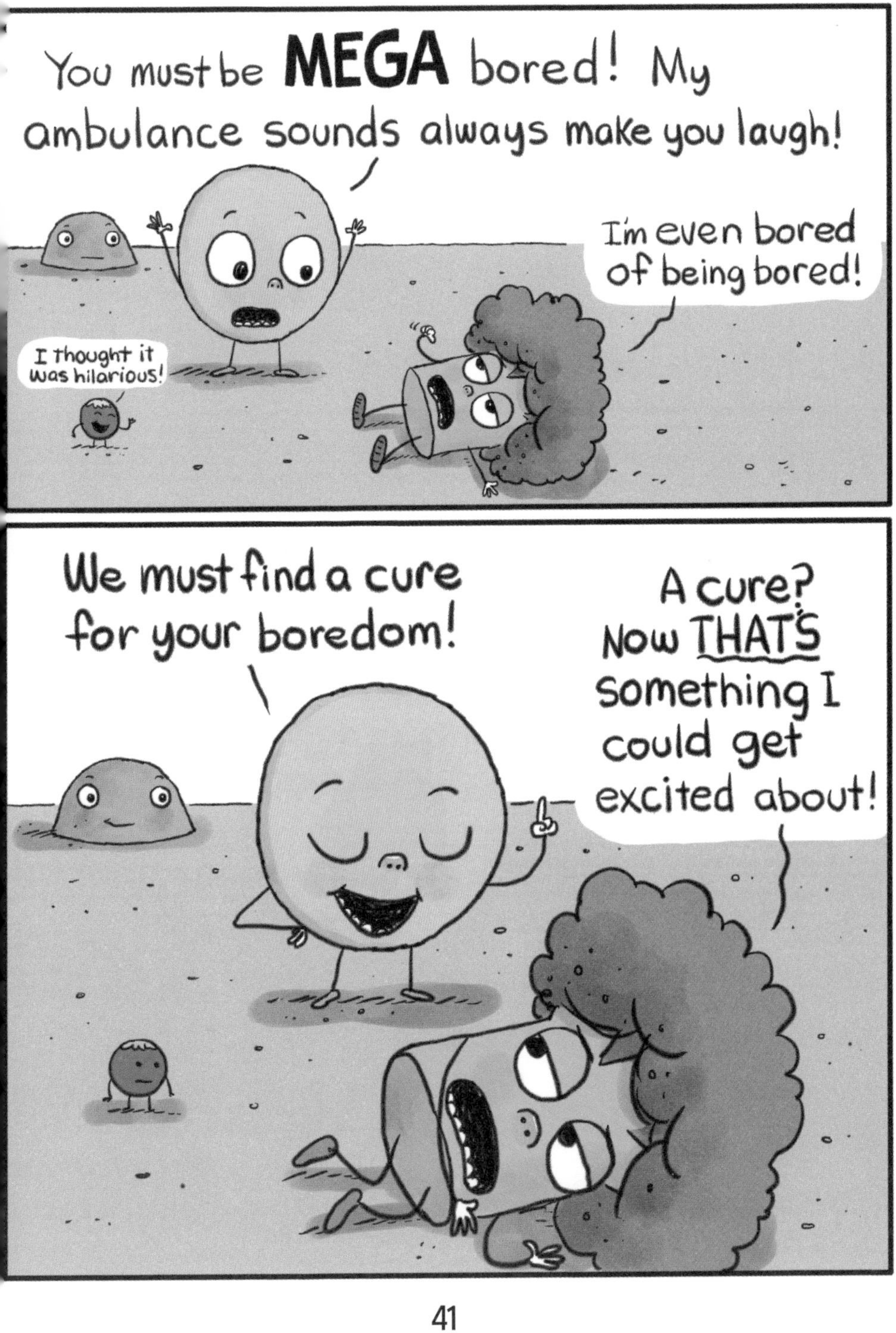
You must be MEGA bored! My ambulance sounds always make you laugh!
I'm even bored of being bored!
I thought it was hilarious!
We must find a cure for your boredom!
A cure? Now THAT'S something I could get excited about!

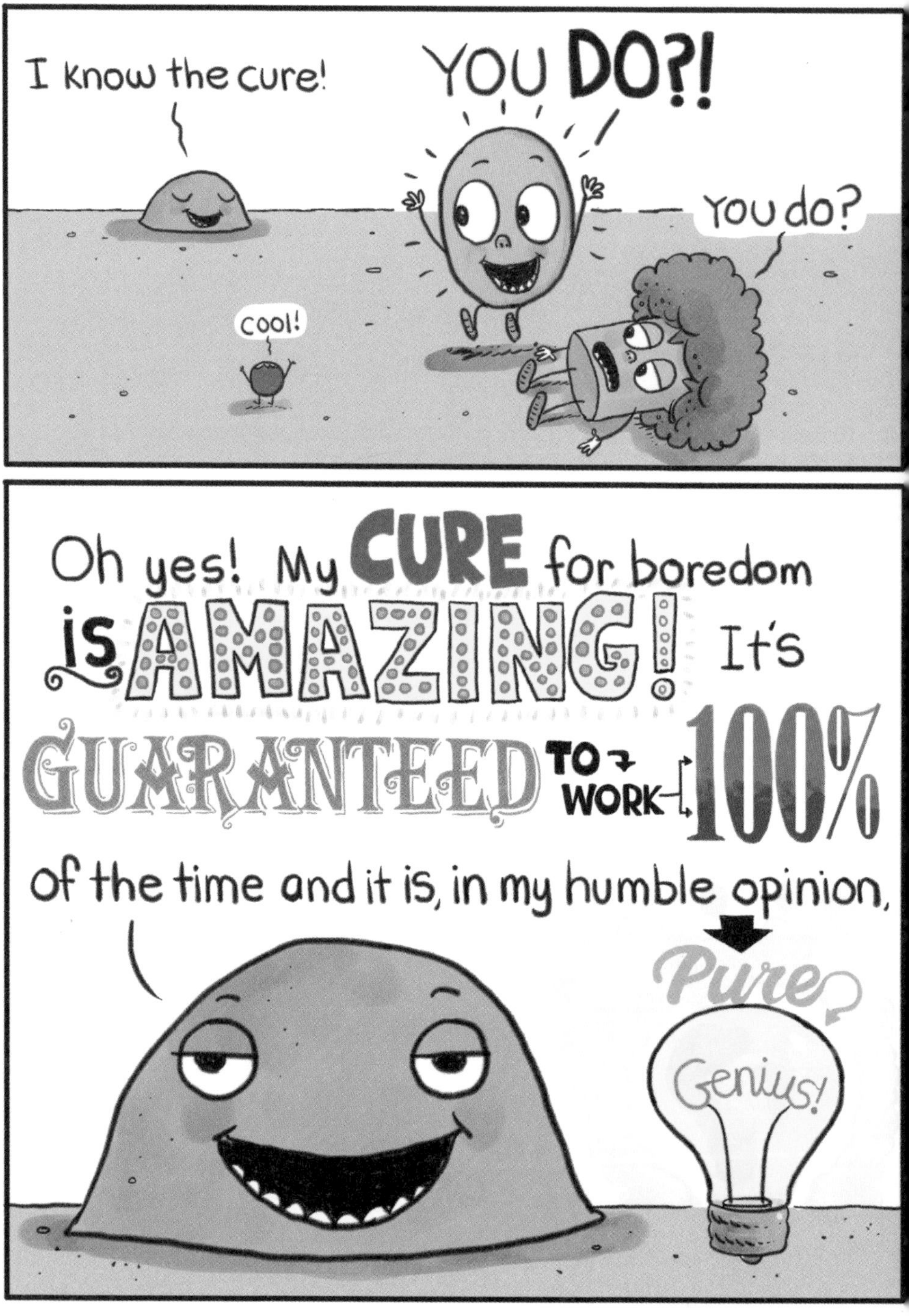
I know the cure!
YOU DO?!
You do?
cool!
Oh yes! My CURE for boredom is AMAZING! It's GUARANTEED TO WORK 100% of the time and it is, in my humble opinion,
Pure
Genius!

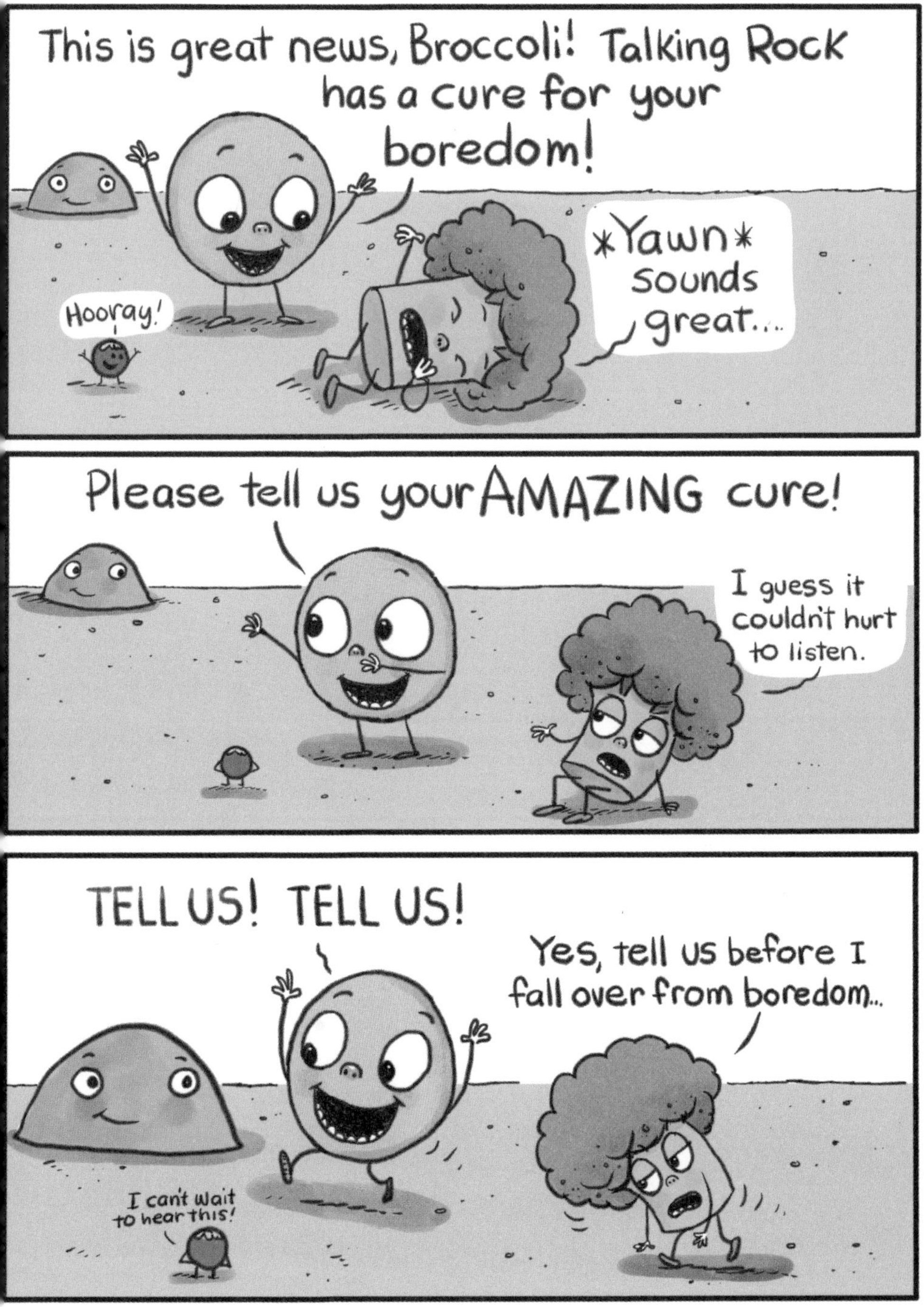
This is great news, Broccoli! Talking Rock has a cure for your boredom!
Hooray!
Yawn sounds great....
Please tell us your AMAZING cure!
I guess it couldn't hurt to listen.
TELL US! TELL US!
Yes, tell us before I fall over from boredom...
I can't wait to hear this!

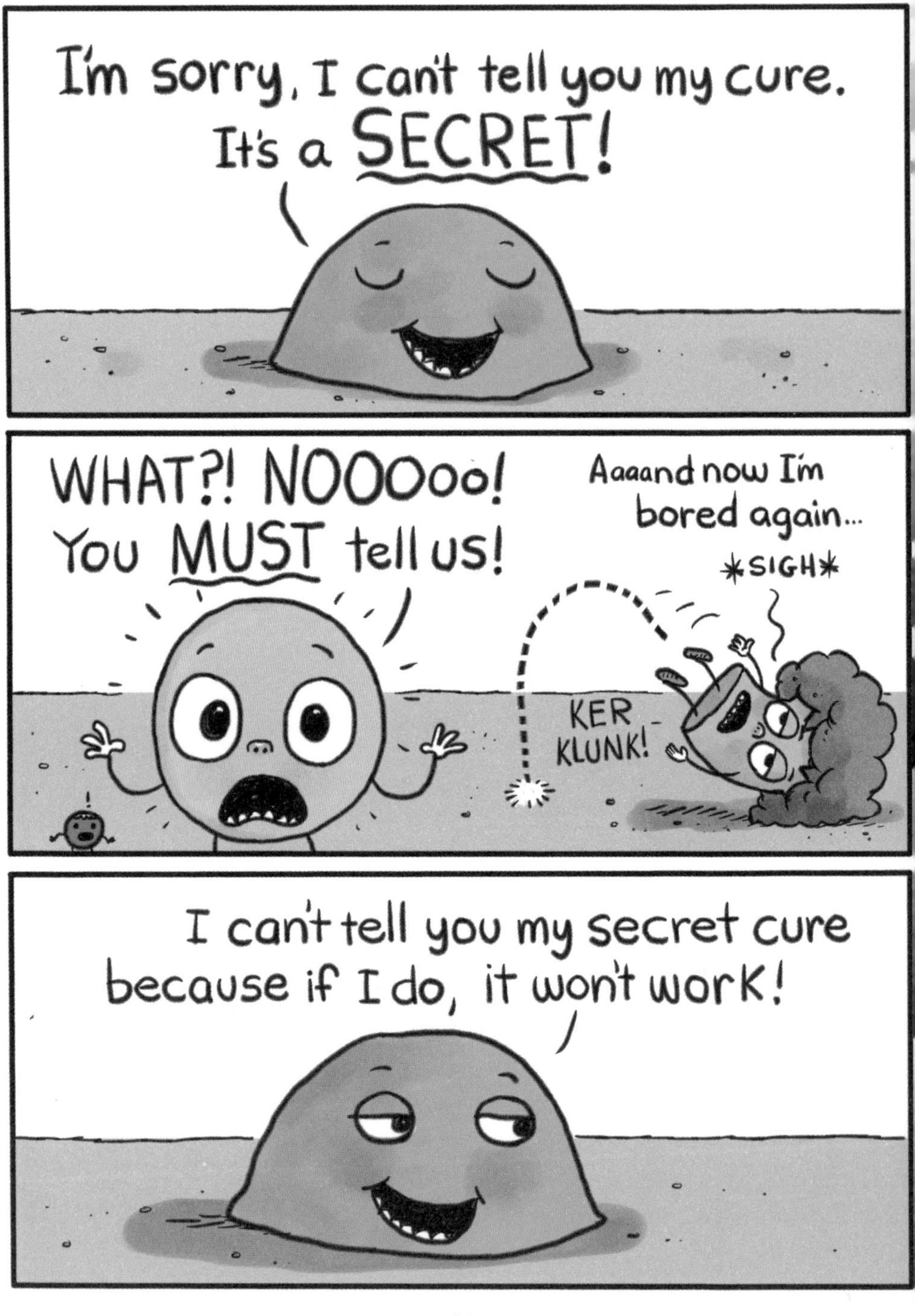
I'm sorry, I can't tell you my cure. It's a SECRET!
WHAT?! NOOOoo! You MUST tell us!
Aaaand now I'm bored again...
SIGH
KER KLUNK!
I can't tell you my secret cure because if I do, it won't work!

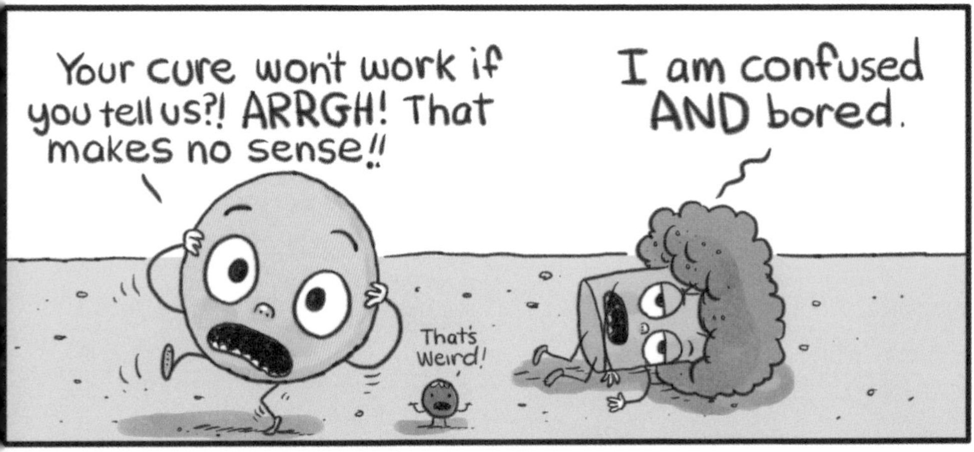
Your cure won't work if you tell us?! ARRGH! That makes no sense!!
I am confused AND bored.
That's Weird!

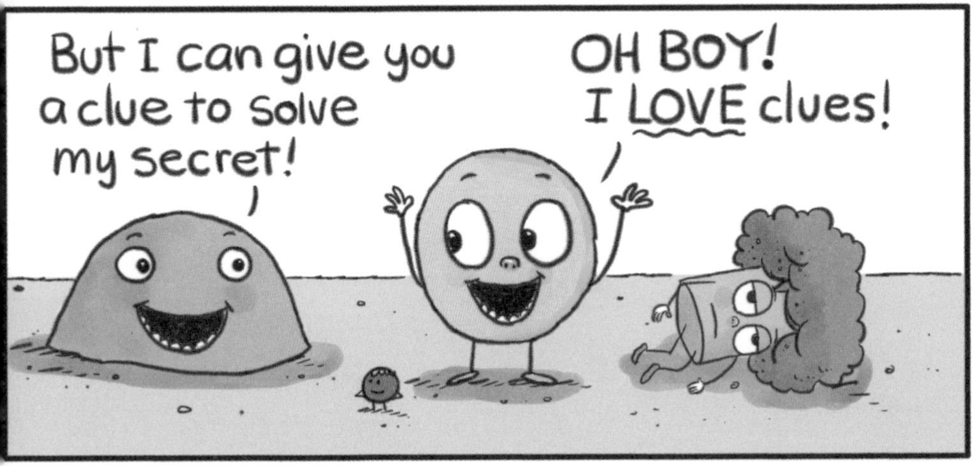
But I can give you a clue to solve my secret!
OH BOY! I LOVE clues!

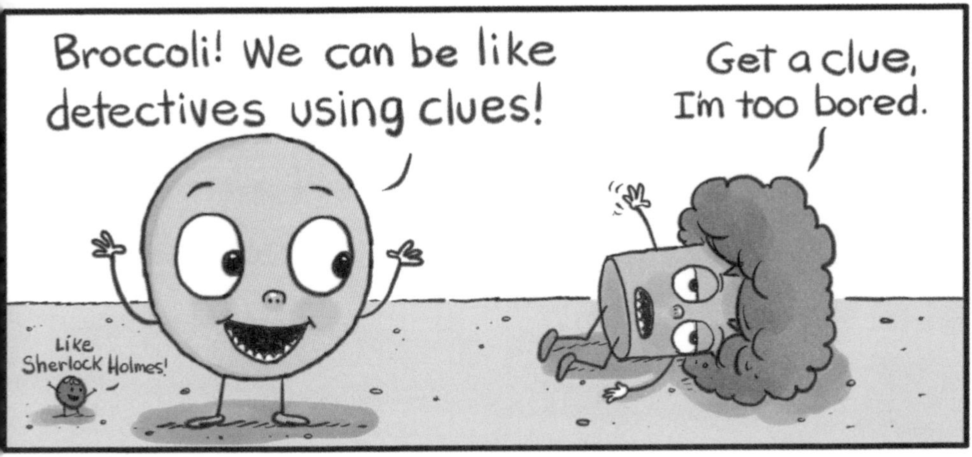
Broccoli! We can be like detectives using clues!
Get a clue, I'm too bored.
Like Sherlock Holmes!

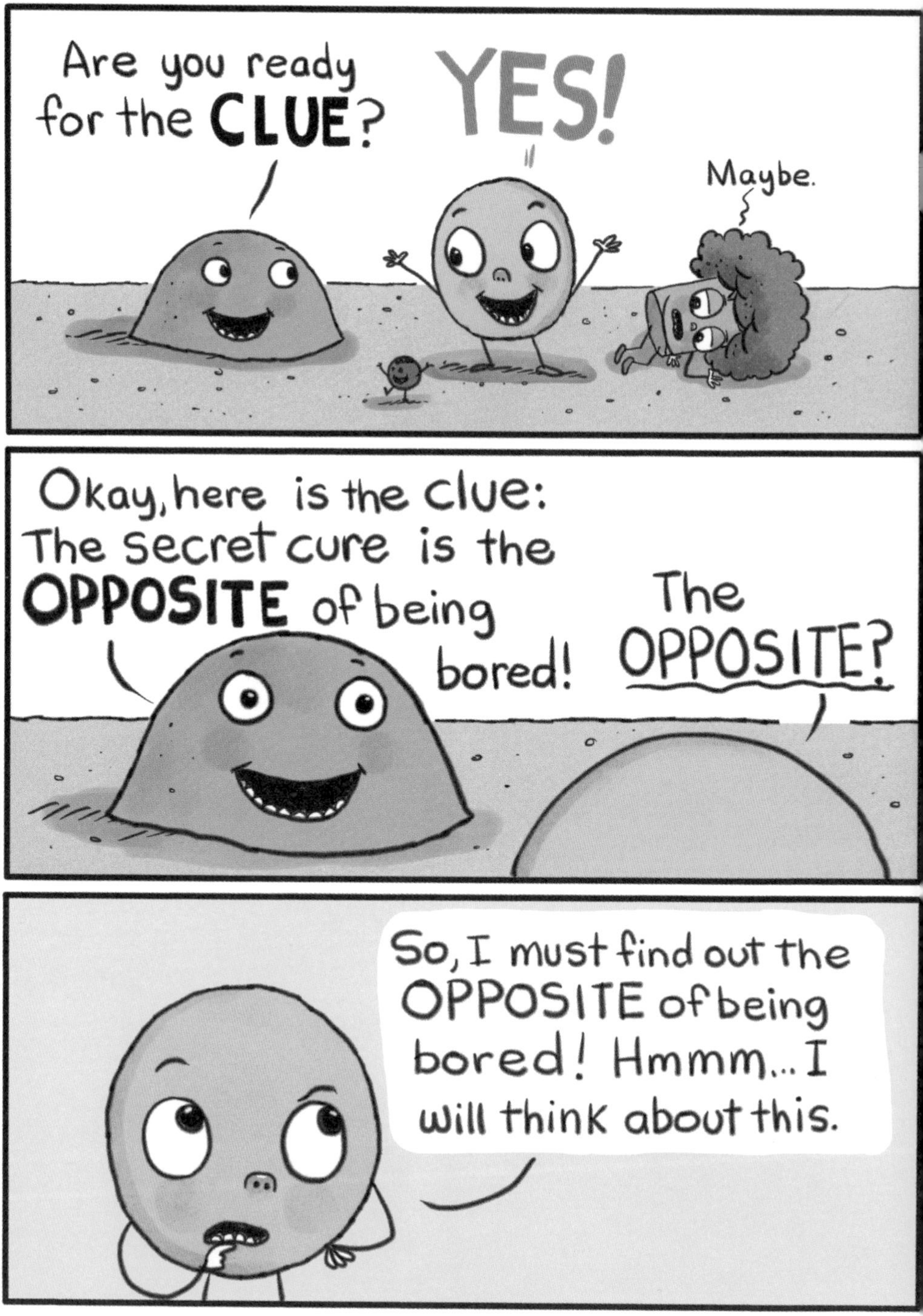
Are you ready for the CLUE?
YES!
Maybe.
Okay, here is the clue: The secret cure is the OPPOSITE of being bored!
The OPPOSITE?
So, I must find out the OPPOSITE of being bored! Hmmm... I will think about this.

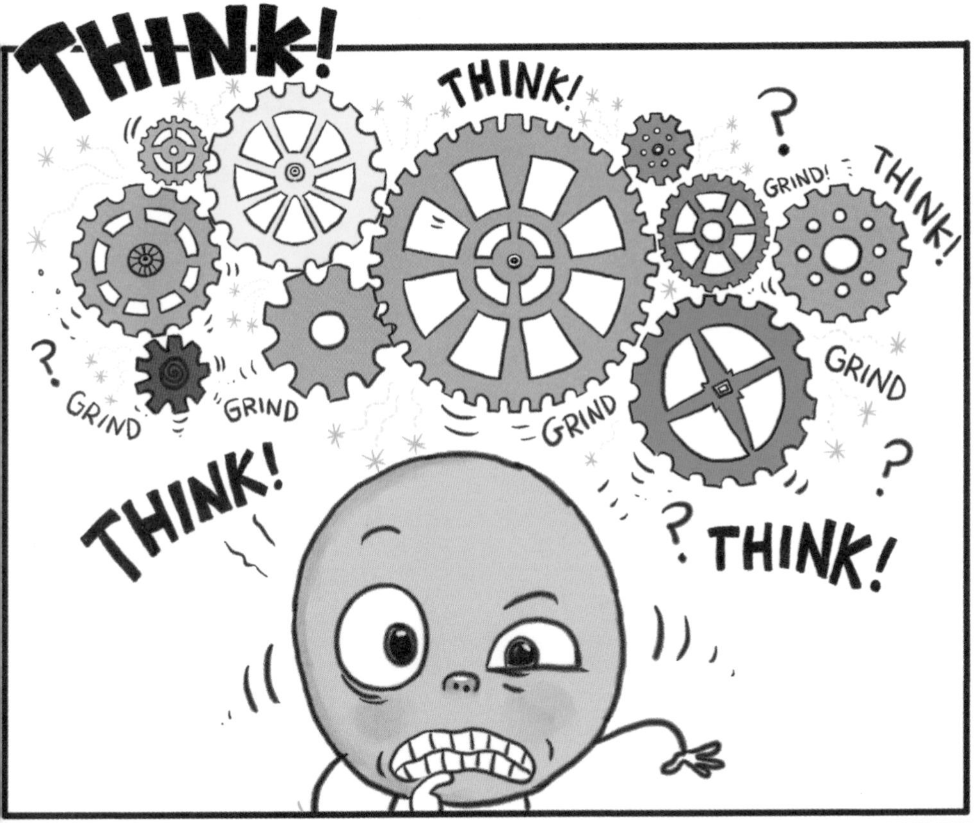
THINK!
THINK!
?
GRIND!
THINK!
?
GRIND
GRIND
GRIND
GRIND
?
THINK!
?
THINK!

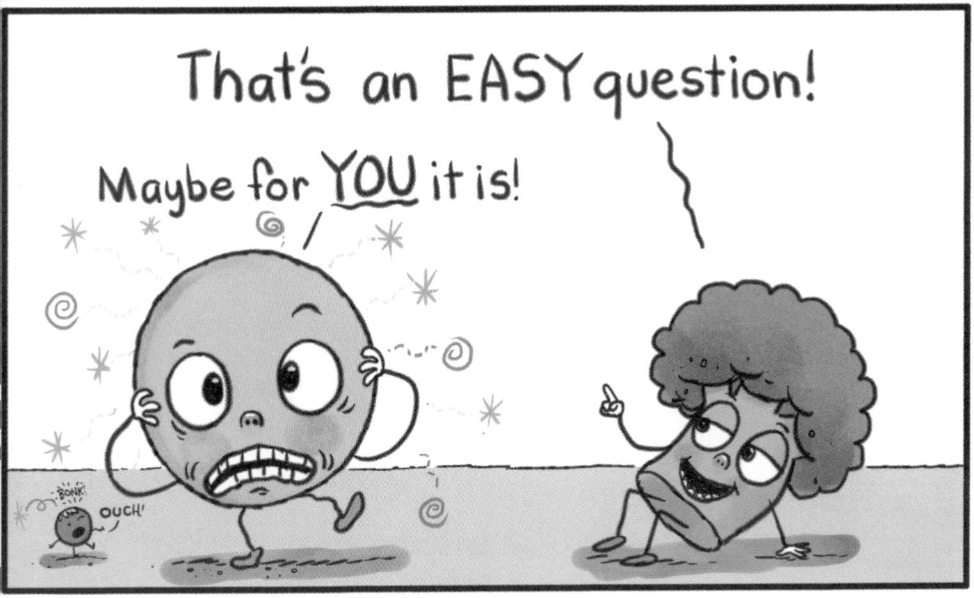
That's an EASY question!
Maybe for YOU it is!
BONK!
OUCH!

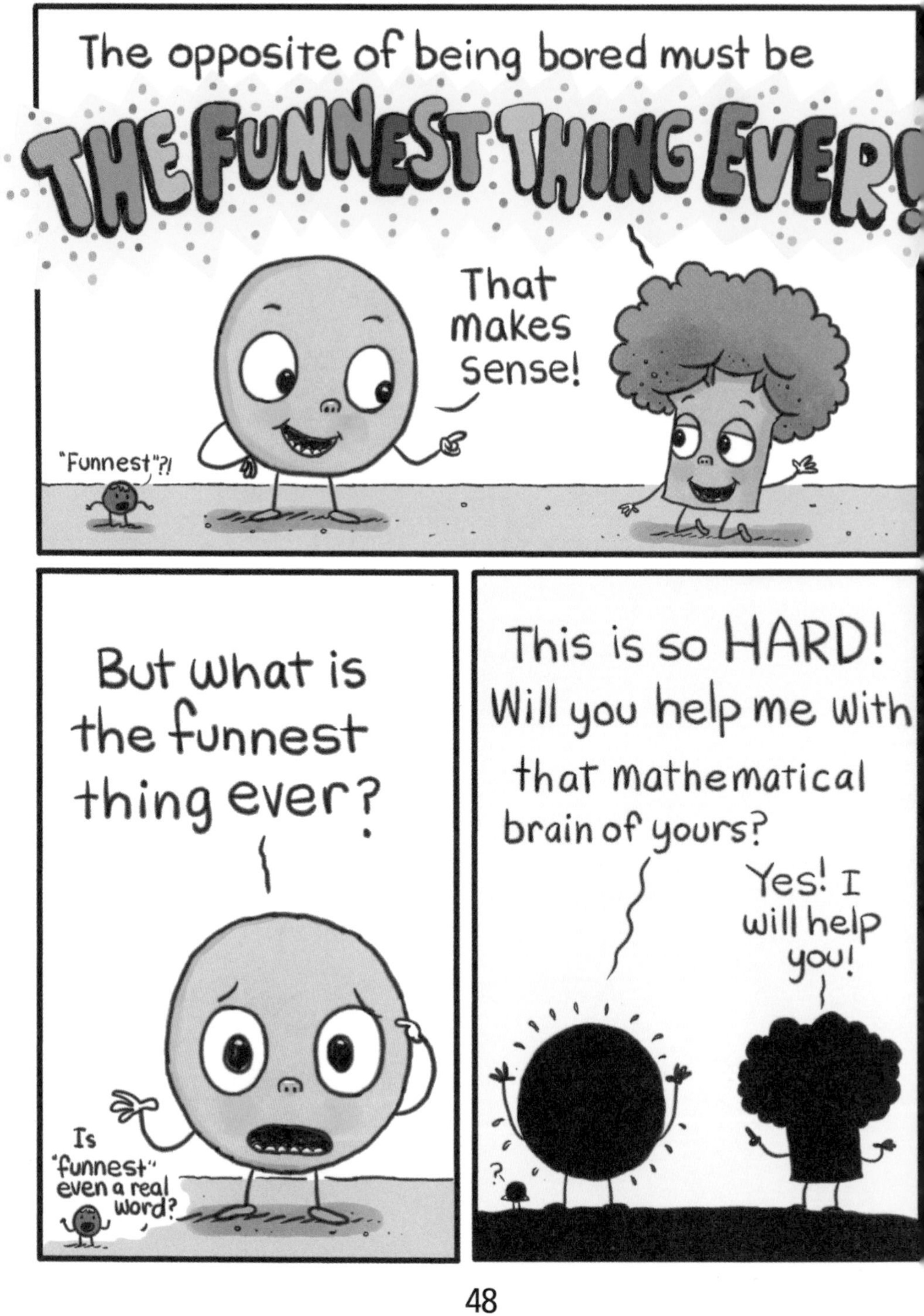
The opposite of being bored must be
THE FUNNEST THING EVER!
That makes sense!
"Funnest"?!
But what is the funnest thing ever?
Is "funnest" even a real word?
This is so HARD! Will you help me with that mathematical brain of yours?
Yes! I will help you!
?

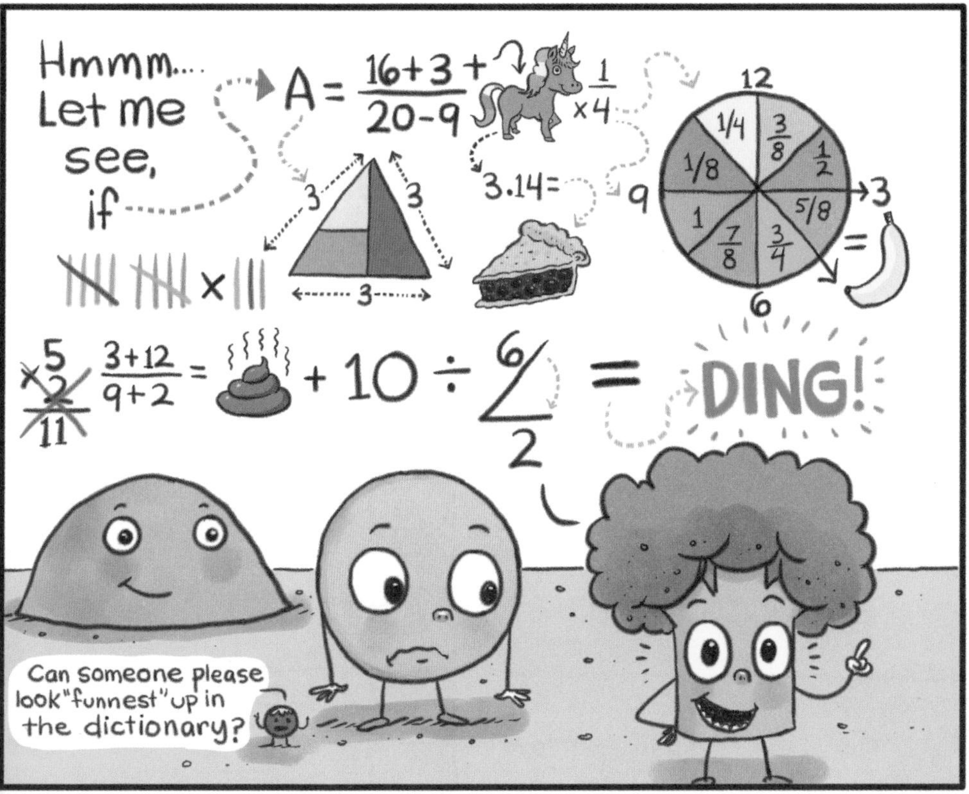
Hmmm... Let me see, if
A = 16+3+ / 20-9
1 / x4
3.14=
9
3
3
3
x
12
1/4
3/8
1/2
1/8
1
7/8
3/4
5/8
3
6
=
5 / 2 / 11
3+12 / 9+2 =
+ 10 ÷ 6 / 2
=
DING!
Can someone please look "funnest" up in the dictionary?

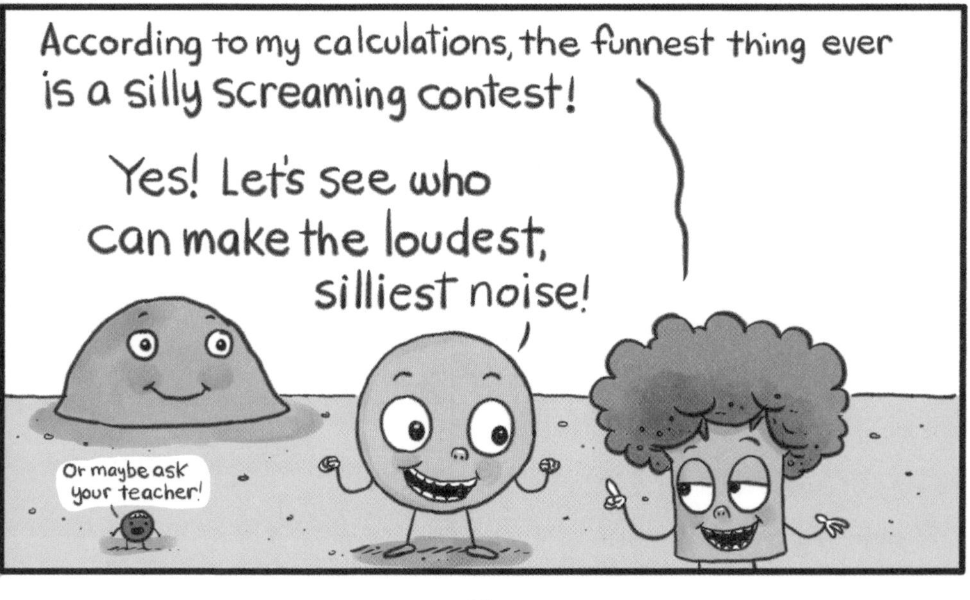
According to my calculations, the funnest thing ever is a silly screaming contest!
Yes! Let's see who can make the loudest, silliest noise!
Or maybe ask your teacher!

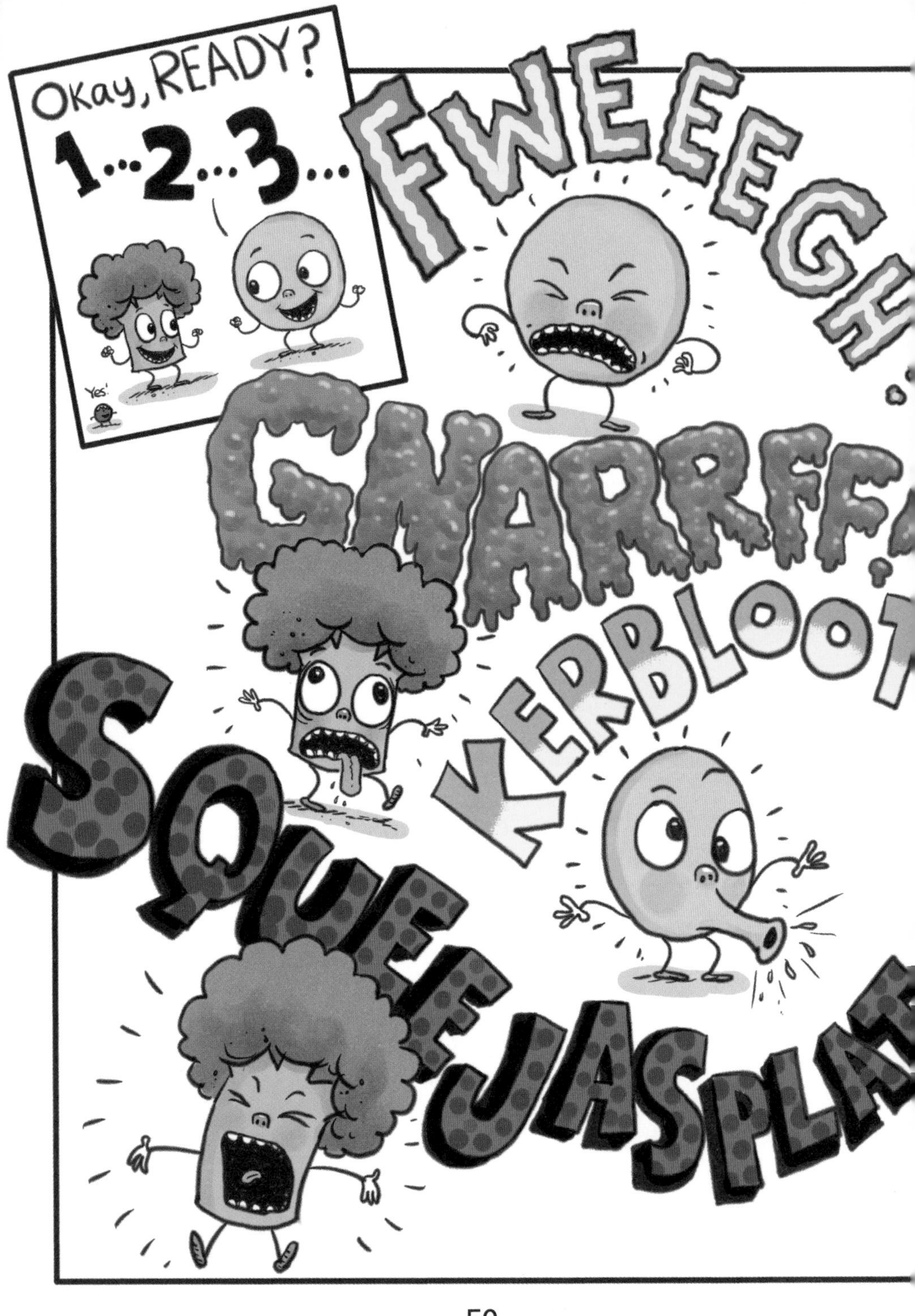
Okay, READY?
1...2...3...
Yes!
FWEEEGH
GNARFF
KERBLOOT
SQUEEF
JASPLAT

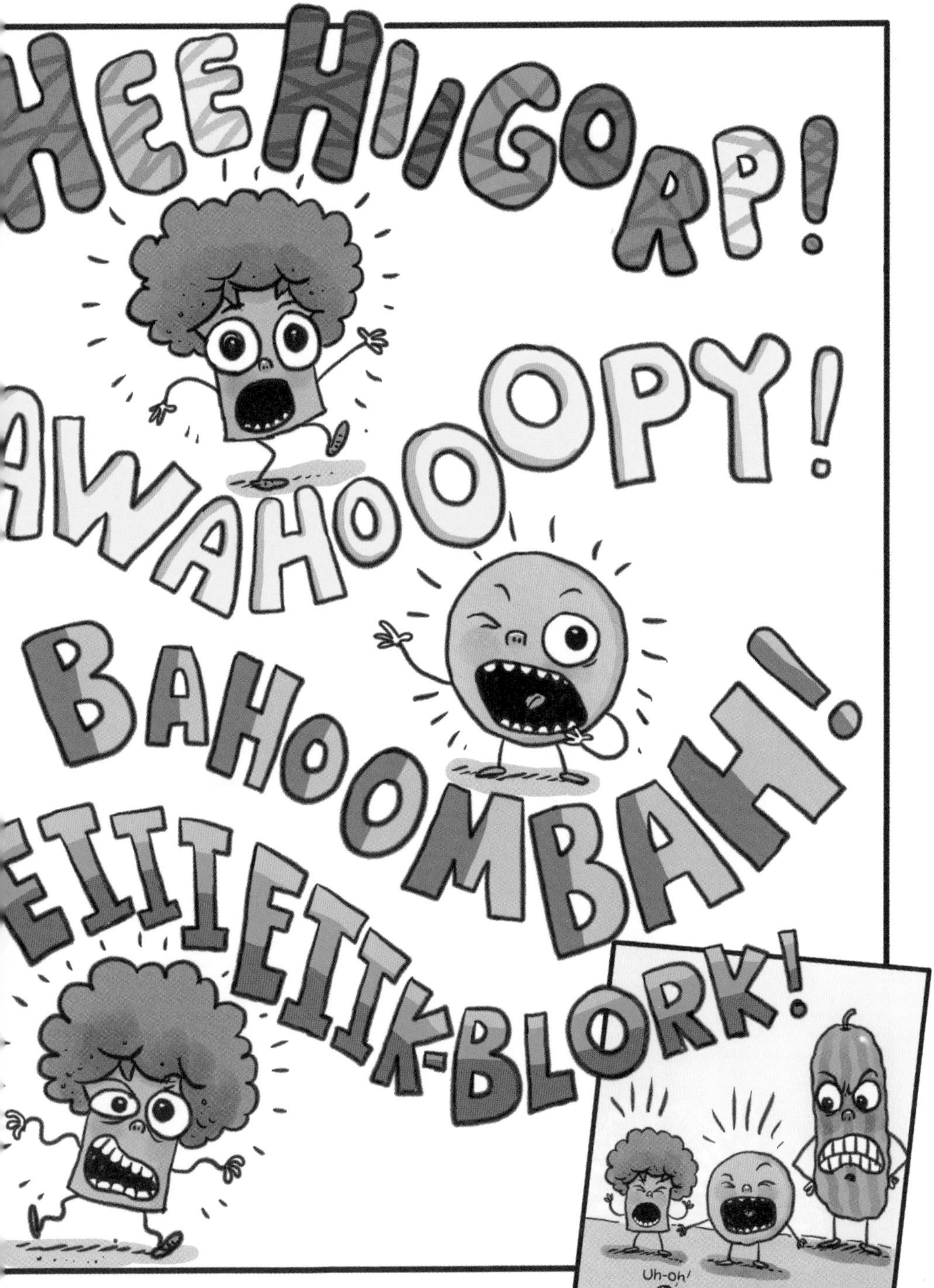
HEEHIIGORP!
AWAHOOOOPY!
BAHOOOMBAH!
EIIIEIIK-BLORK!
Uh-oh!

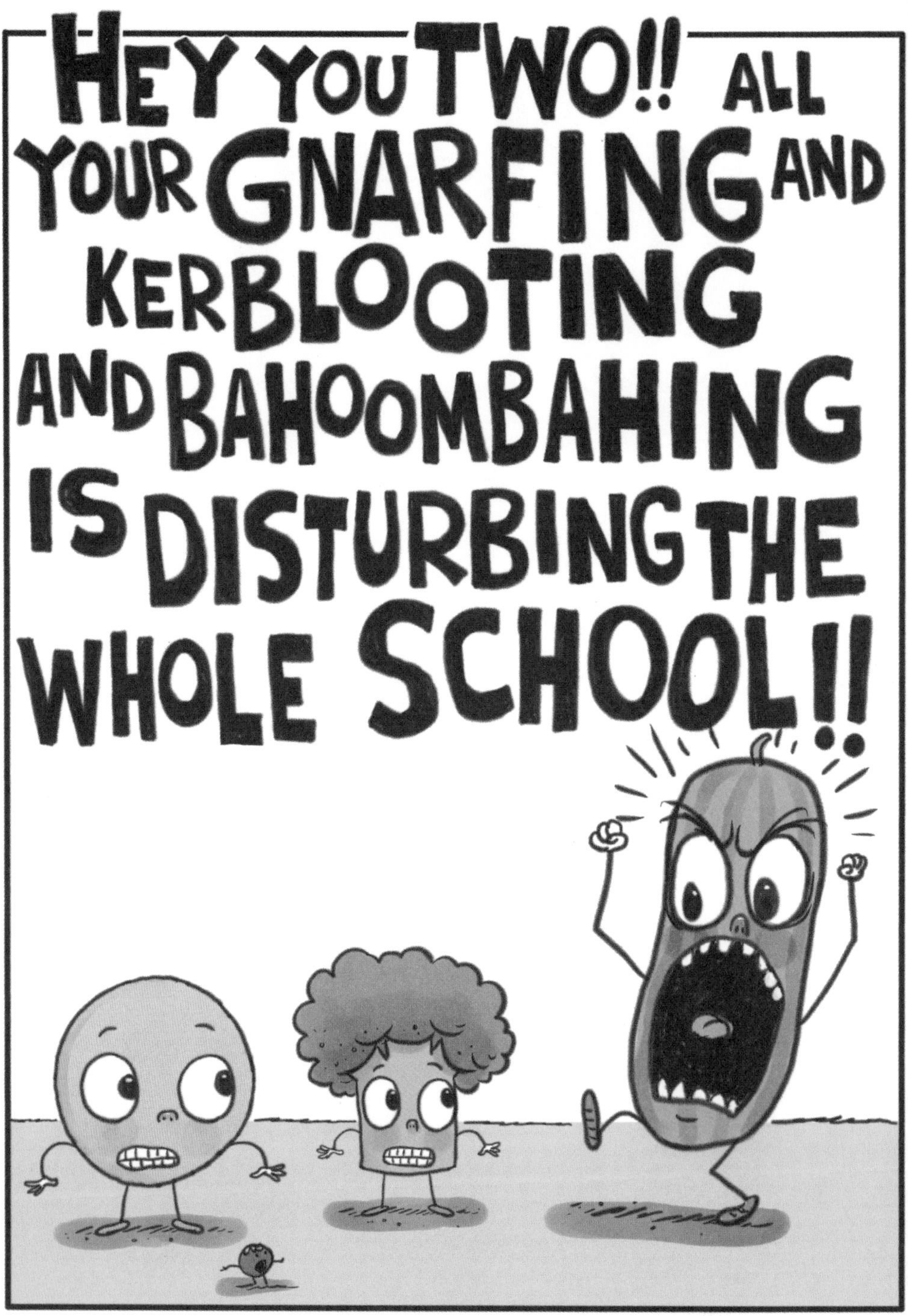
HEY YOU TWO!! ALL YOUR GNARFING AND KERBLOOTING AND BAHOOMBAHING IS DISTURBING THE WHOLE SCHOOL!!

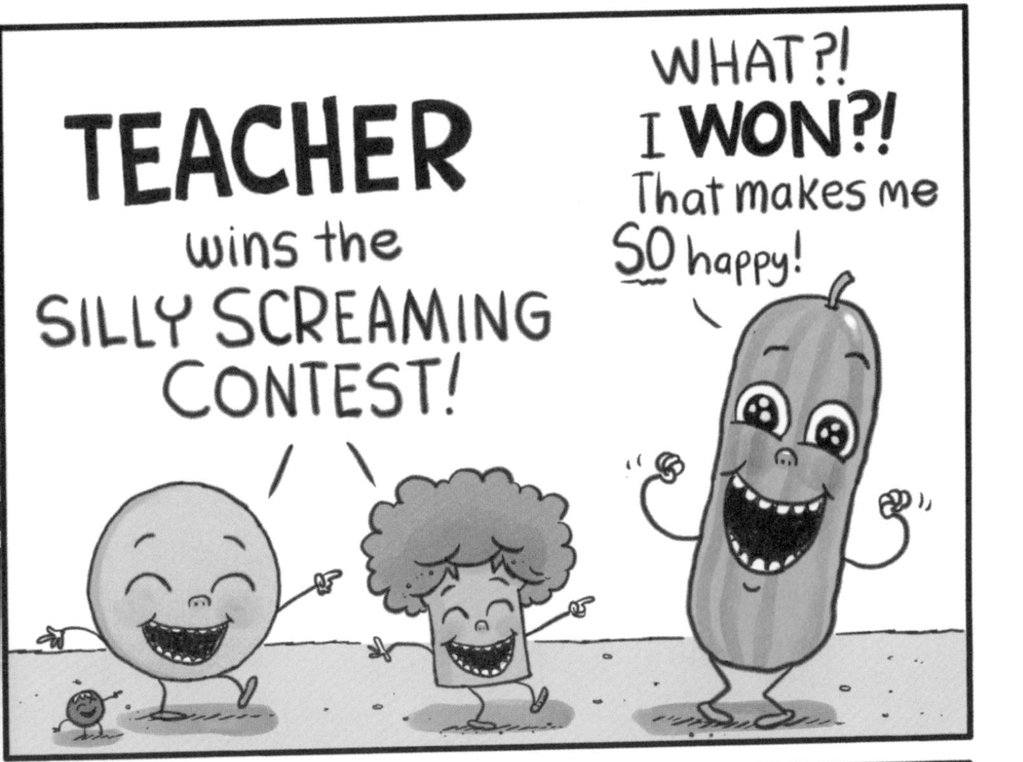
TEACHER wins the SILLY SCREAMING CONTEST!
WHAT?! I WON?! That makes me SO happy!

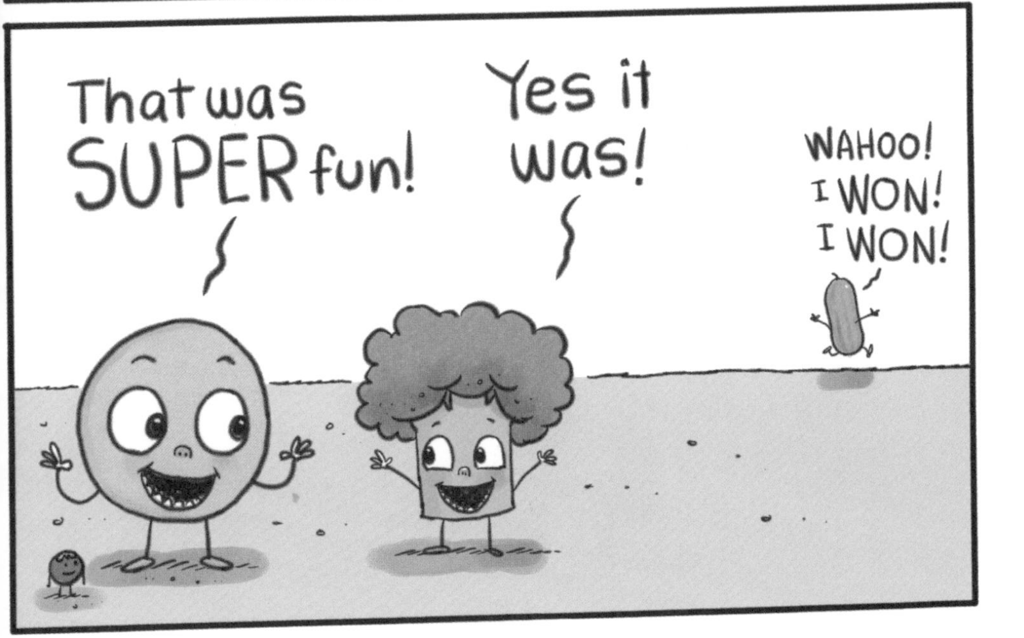
That was SUPER fun!
Yes it was!
WAHOO! I WON! I WON!

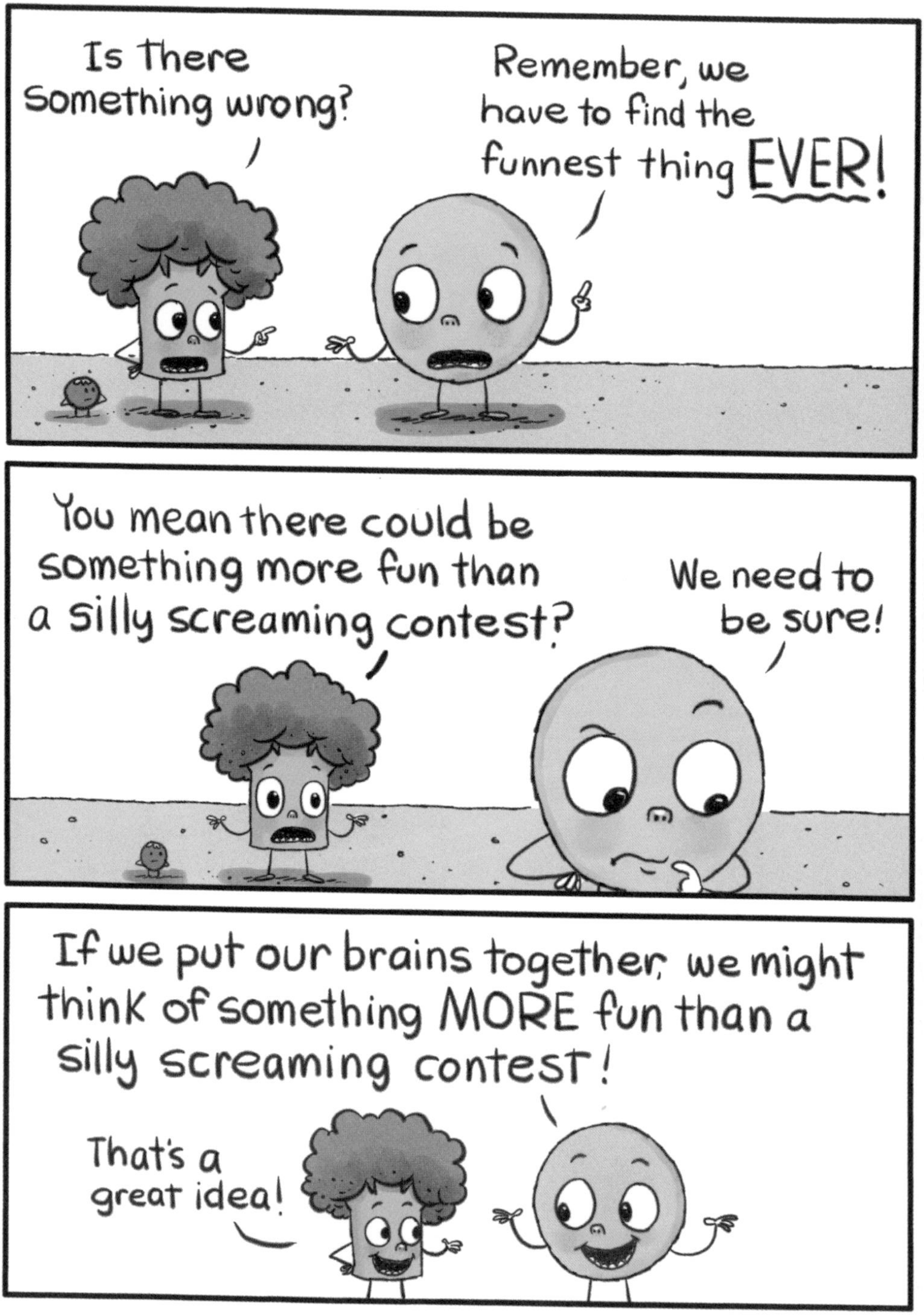
Is there something wrong?
Remember, we have to find the funnest thing EVER!
You mean there could be something more fun than a silly screaming contest?
We need to be sure!
If we put our brains together, we might think of something MORE fun than a silly screaming contest!
That's a great idea!

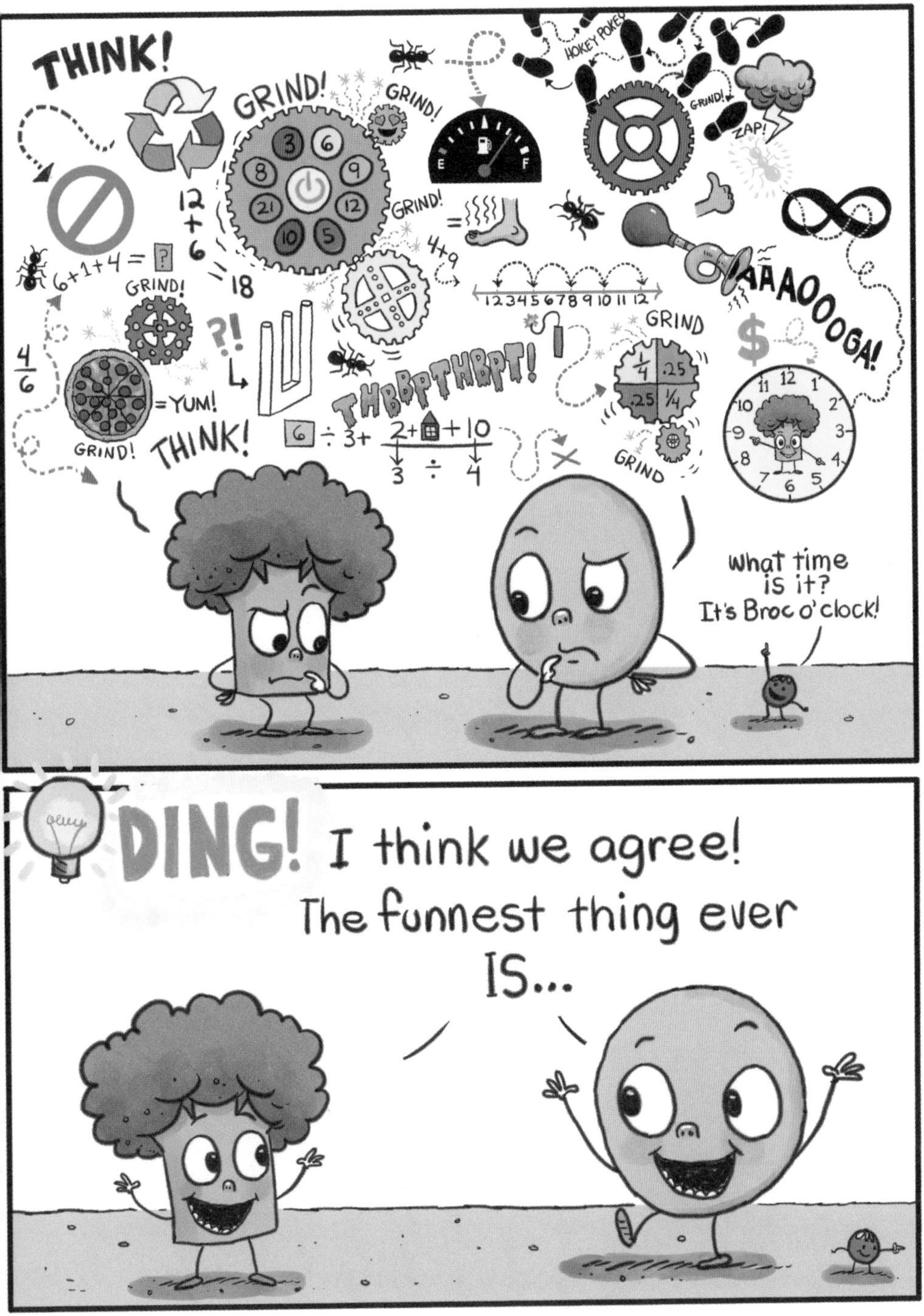
THINK!
GRIND!
GRIND!
HOKEY POKEY
GRIND!
ZAP!
E F
GRIND!
12 + 6 = 18
6+1+4 = ?
GRIND!
4+9
AAAOOOOGA!
1 2 3 4 5 6 7 8 9 10 11 12
GRIND
?!
$
4/6
THBBPTHBPT!
1/4 .25 .25 1/4
=YUM!
GRIND!
THINK!
6 ÷ 3 + 2+ + 10 / 3 ÷ 4
GRIND
What time is it? It's Broc o'clock!
DING!
I think we agree! The funnest thing ever IS...

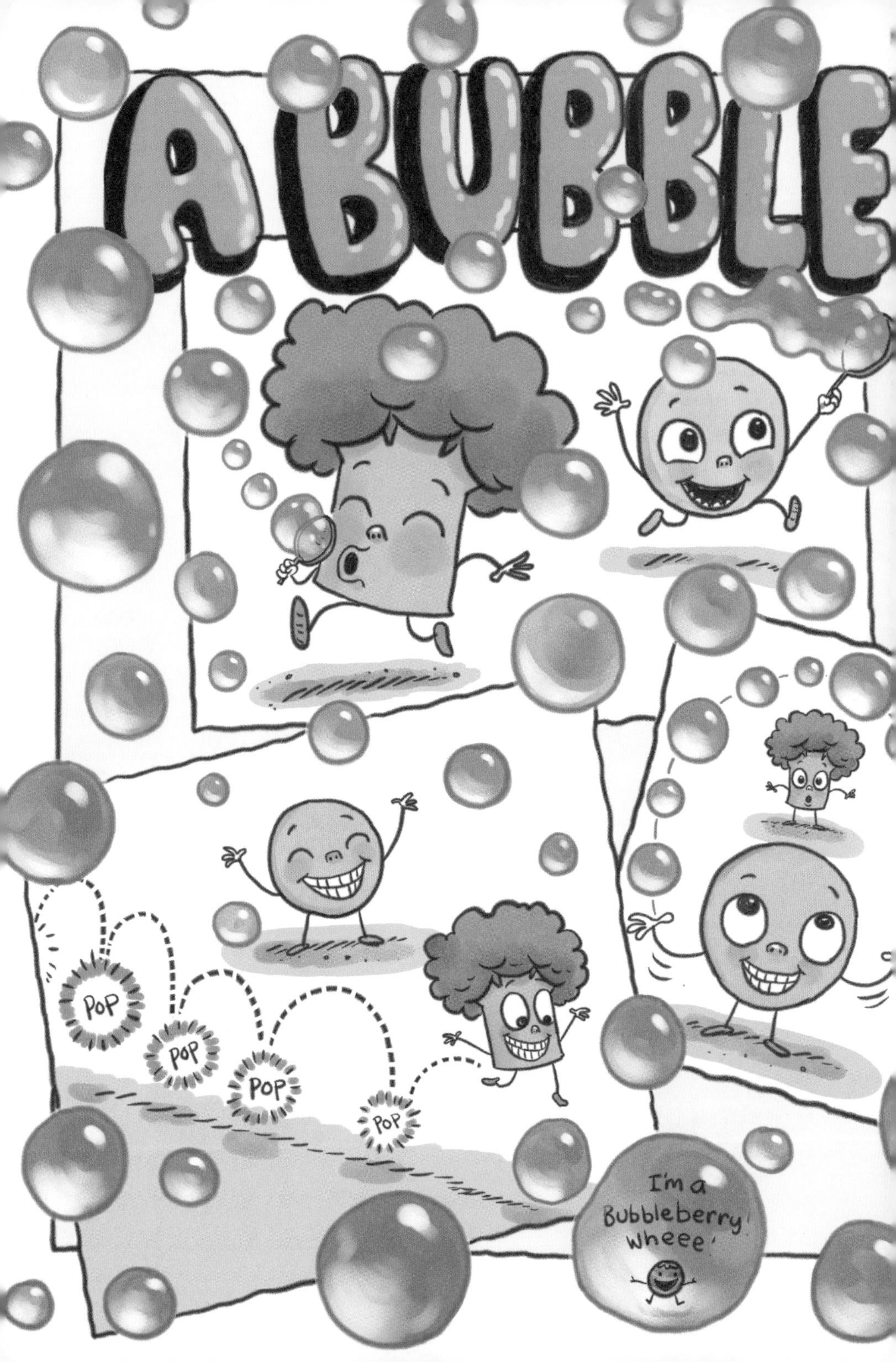
A BUBBLE
POP
POP
POP
POP
I'm a Bubbleberry! Wheee!

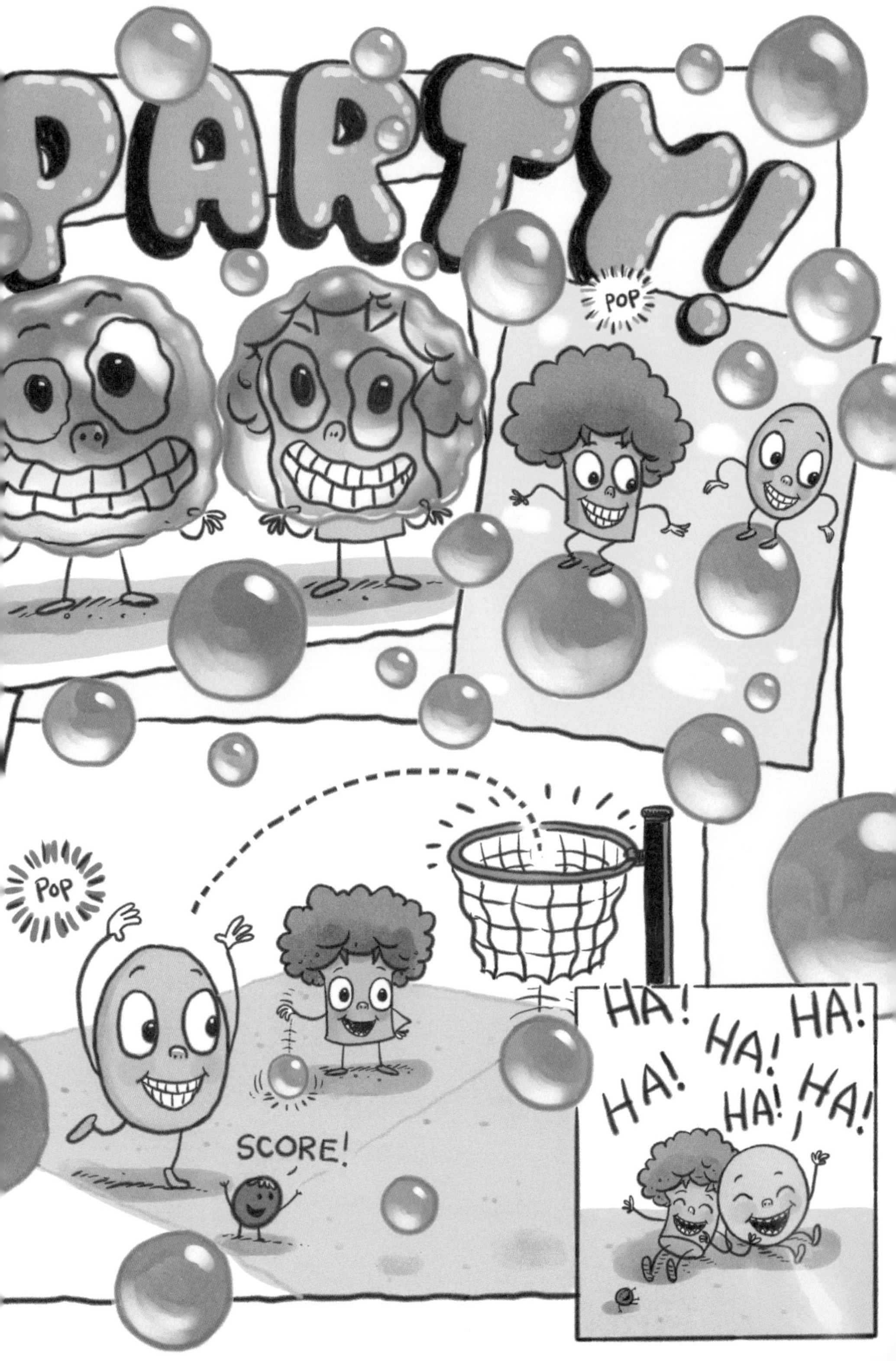
PARTY!
POP
POP
SCORE!
HA! HA! HA!
HA! HA! HA!

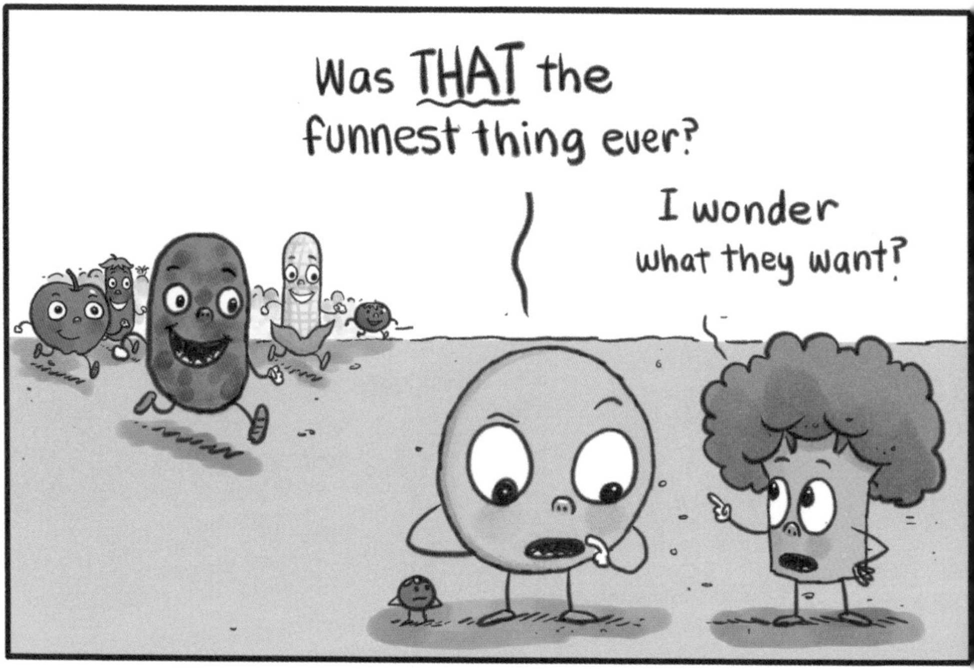
Was THAT the funnest thing ever?
I wonder what they want?

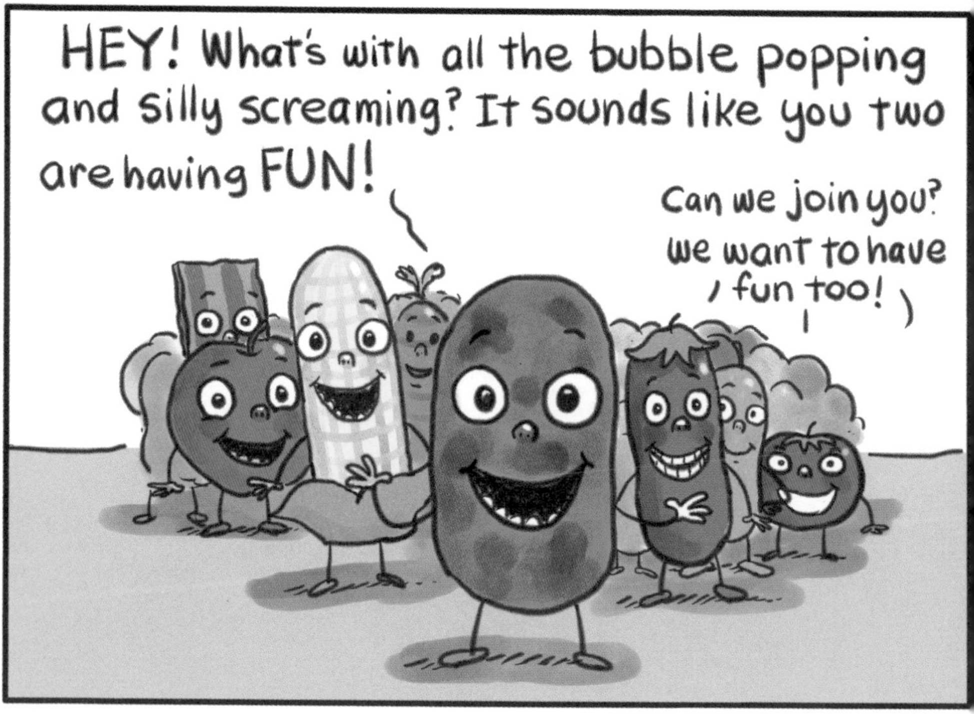
HEY! What's with all the bubble popping and silly screaming? It sounds like you two are having FUN!
Can we join you? We want to have fun too!

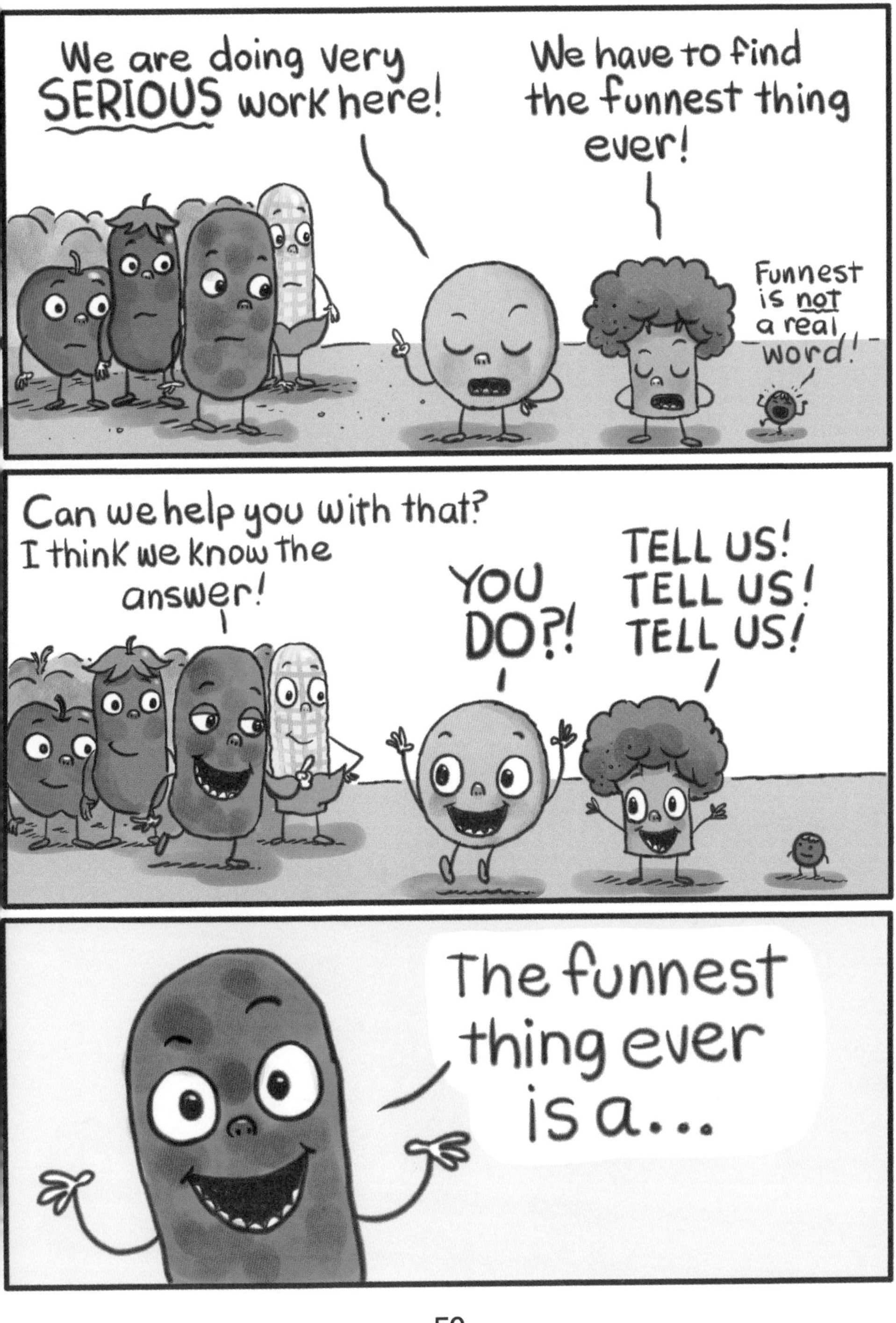
We are doing very SERIOUS work here!
We have to find the funnest thing ever!
Funnest is not a real word!
Can we help you with that? I think we know the answer!
YOU DO?!
TELL US! TELL US! TELL US!
The funnest thing ever is a...

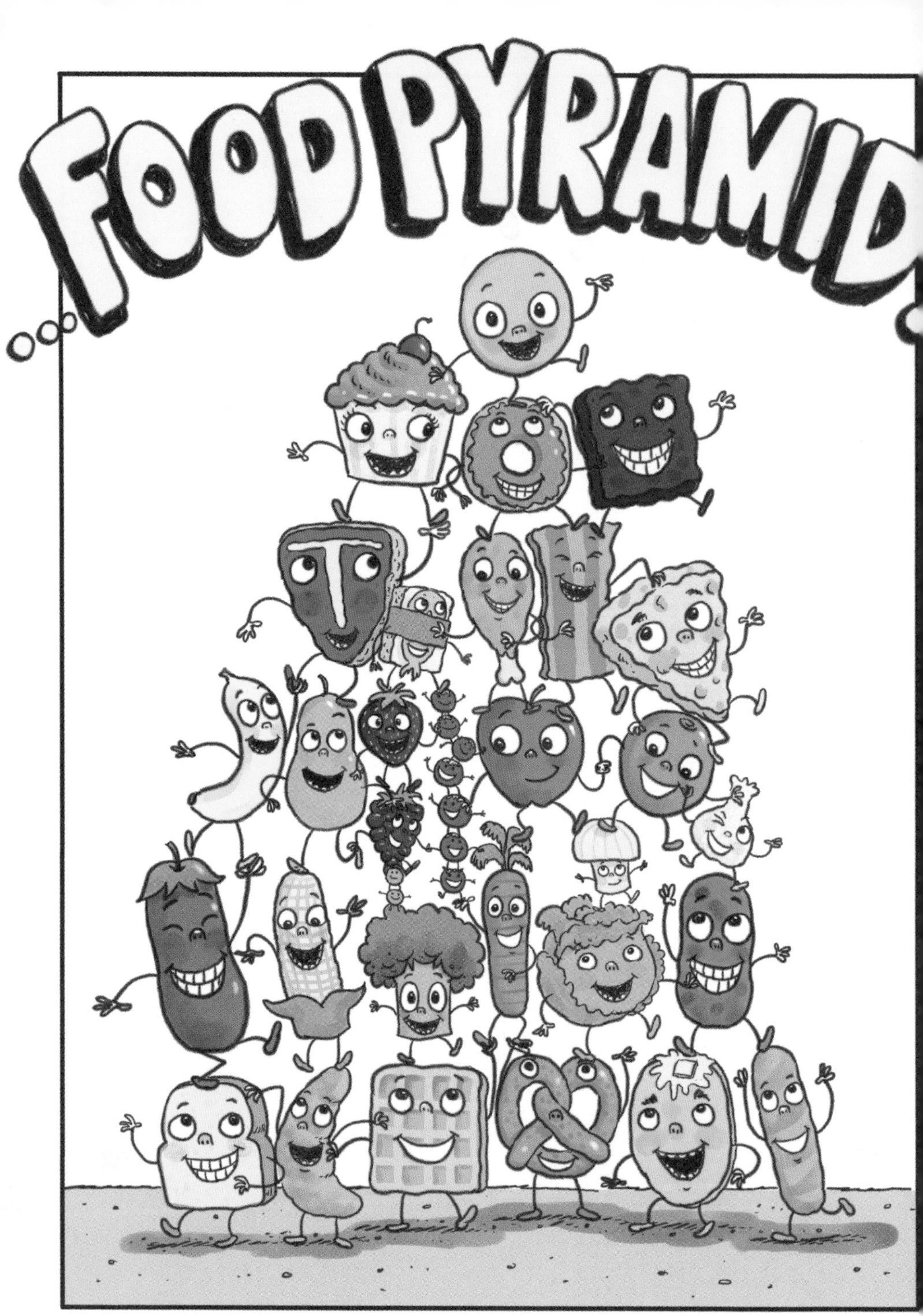
...FOOD PYRAMID

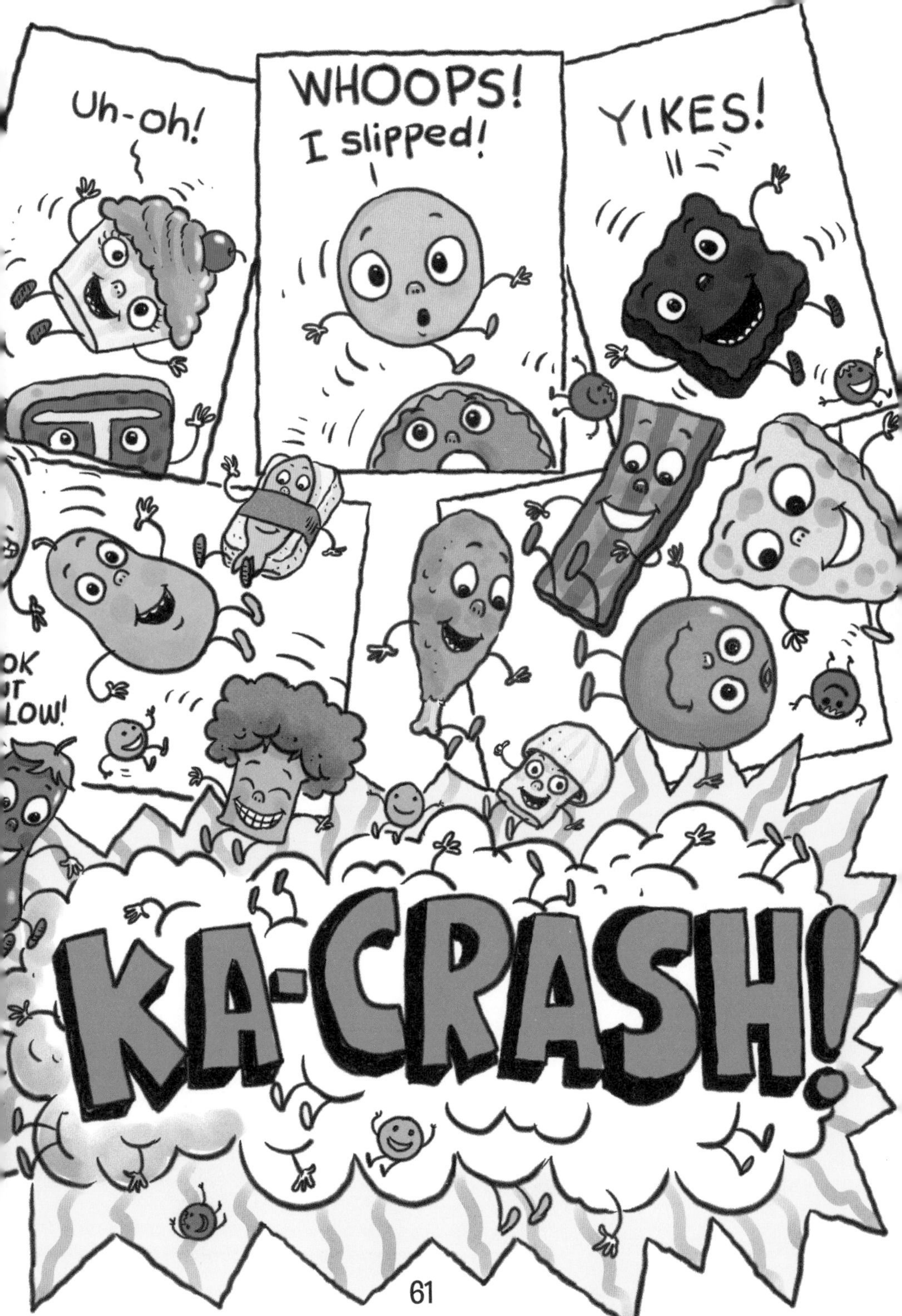
Uh-oh!
WHOOPS! I slipped!
YIKES!
OK
IT
LOW!
KA-CRASH!

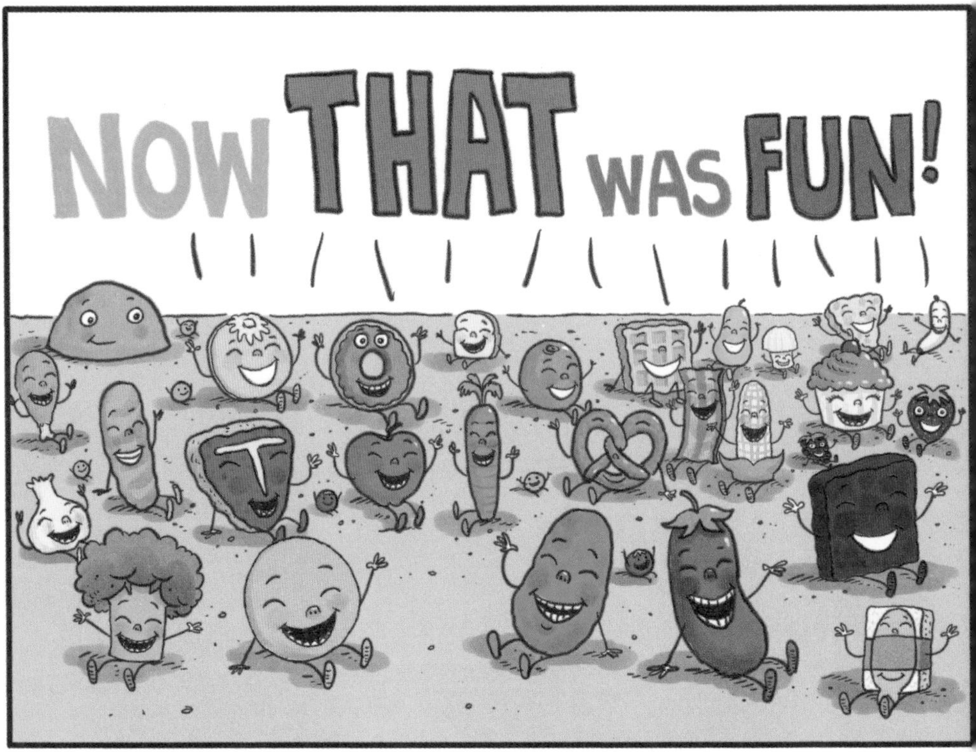
NOW THAT WAS FUN!

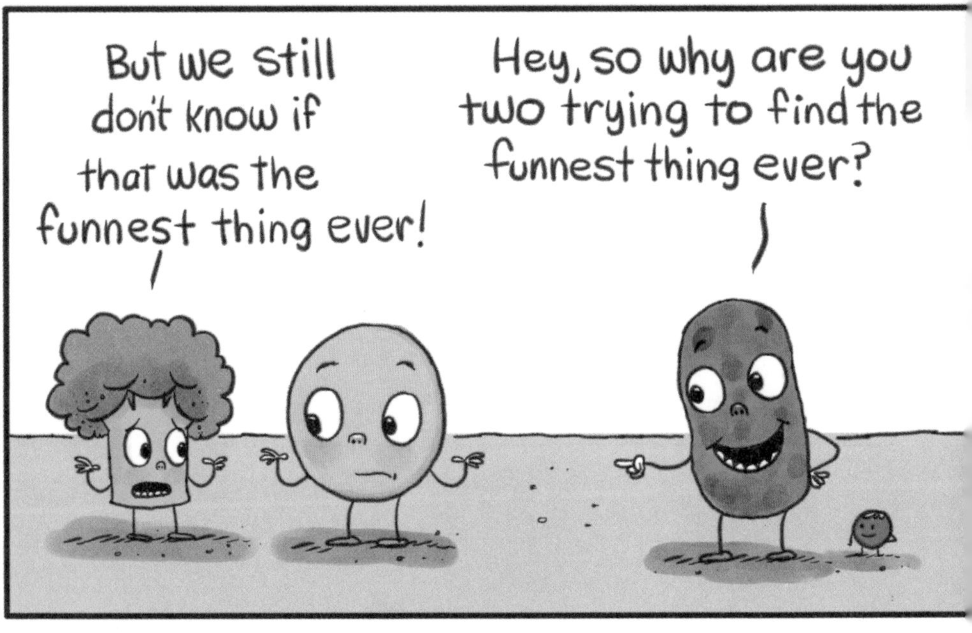
But we still don't know if that was the funnest thing ever!
Hey, so why are you two trying to find the funnest thing ever?

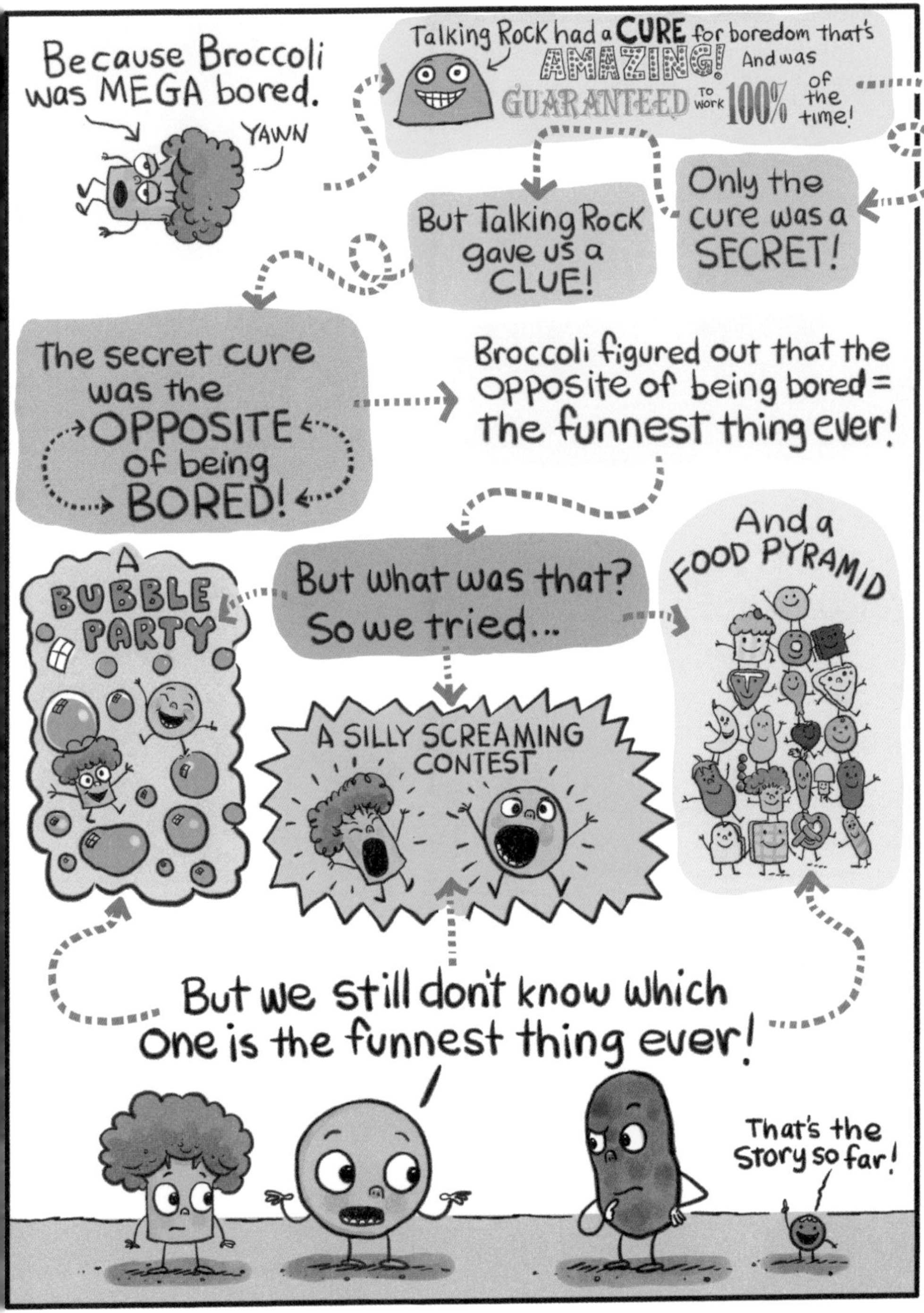
Because Broccoli was MEGA bored.
YAWN
Talking Rock had a CURE for boredom that's AMAZING! And was GUARANTEED TO WORK 100% of the time!
Only the cure was a SECRET!
But Talking Rock gave us a CLUE!
The secret cure was the OPPOSITE of being BORED!
Broccoli figured out that the opposite of being bored = the funnest thing ever!
But what was that? So we tried...
A BUBBLE PARTY
A SILLY SCREAMING CONTEST
And a FOOD PYRAMID
But we still don't know which one is the funnest thing ever!
That's the story so far!

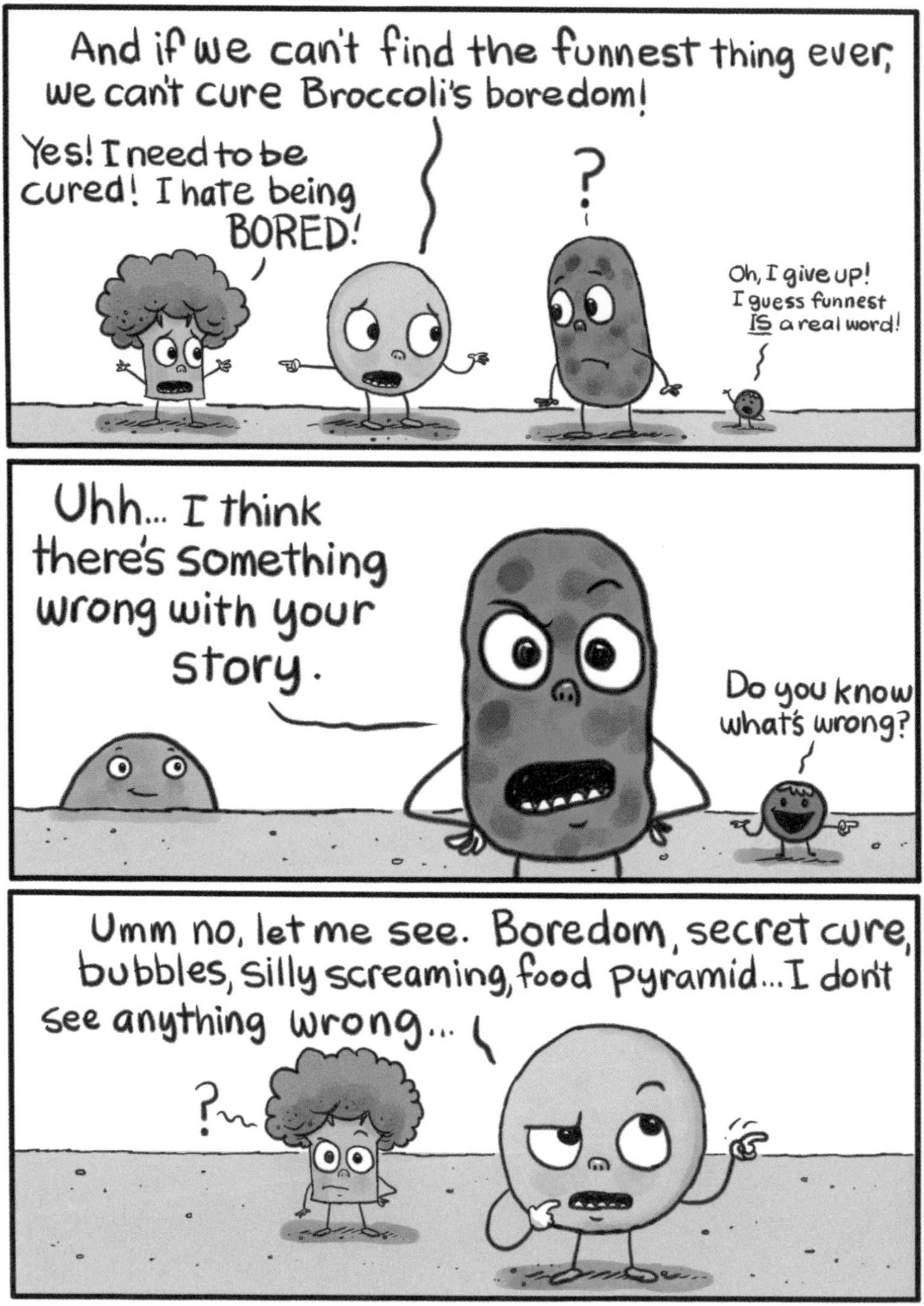
And if we can't find the funnest thing ever, we can't cure Broccoli's boredom!
Yes! I need to be cured! I hate being BORED!
?
Oh, I give up! I guess funnest IS a real word!
Uhh... I think there's something wrong with your story.
Do you know what's wrong?
Umm no, let me see. Boredom, secret cure, bubbles, silly screaming, food pyramid... I don't see anything wrong...
?

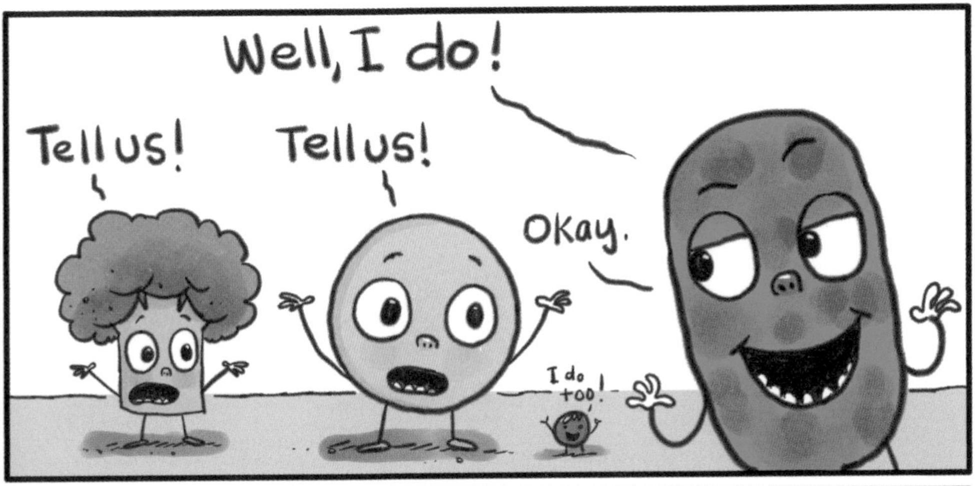
Tell us!
Tell us!
Well, I do!
Okay.
I do too!

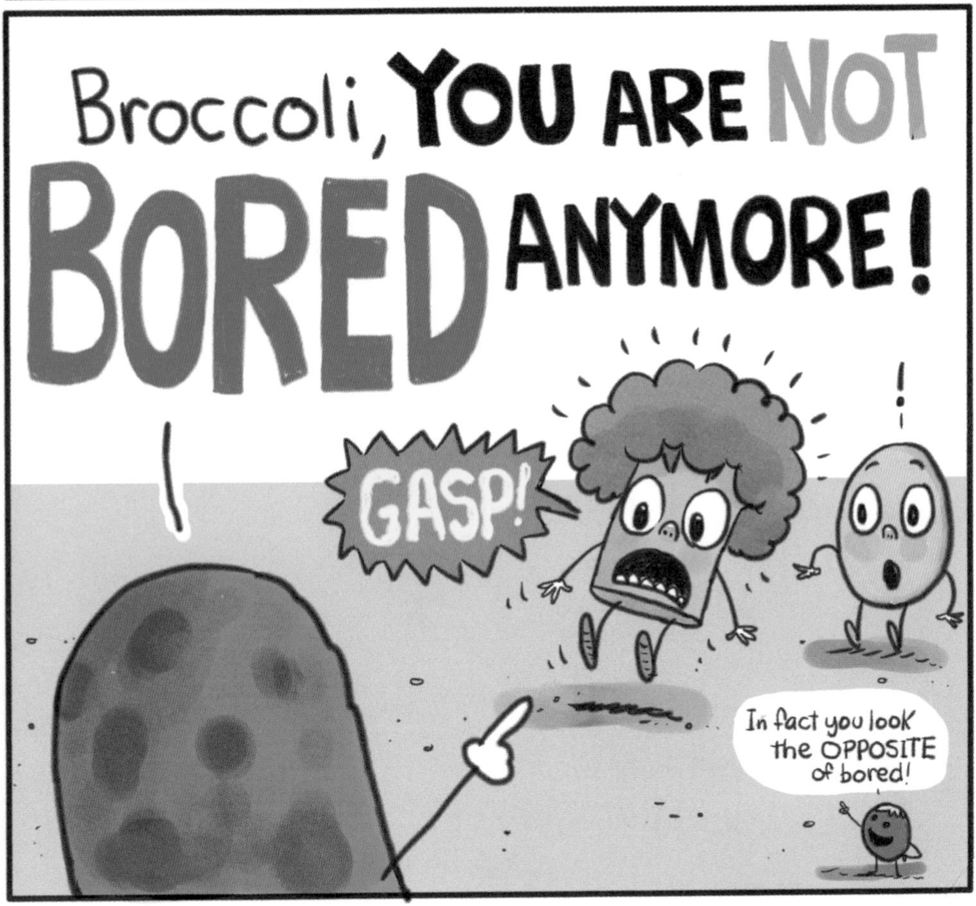
Broccoli, YOU ARE NOT BORED ANYMORE!
GASP!
In fact you look the OPPOSITE of bored!

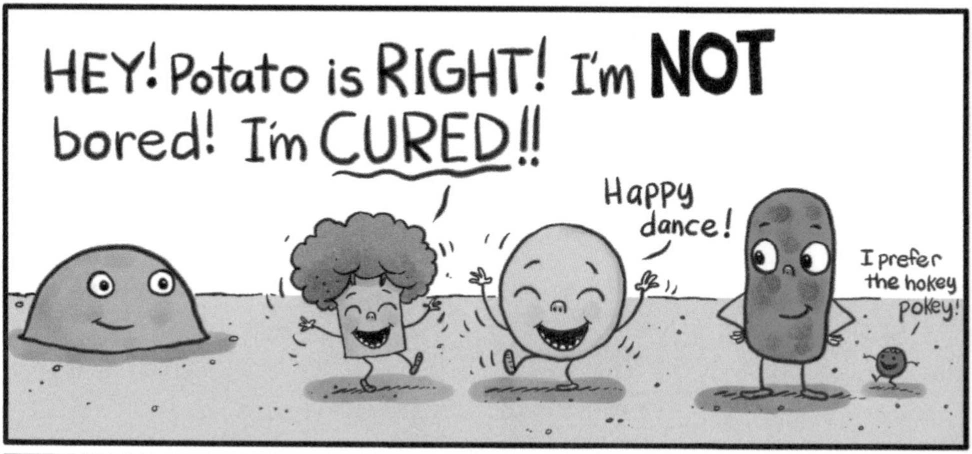
HEY! Potato is RIGHT! I'm NOT bored! I'm CURED!!
Happy dance!
I prefer the hokey pokey!

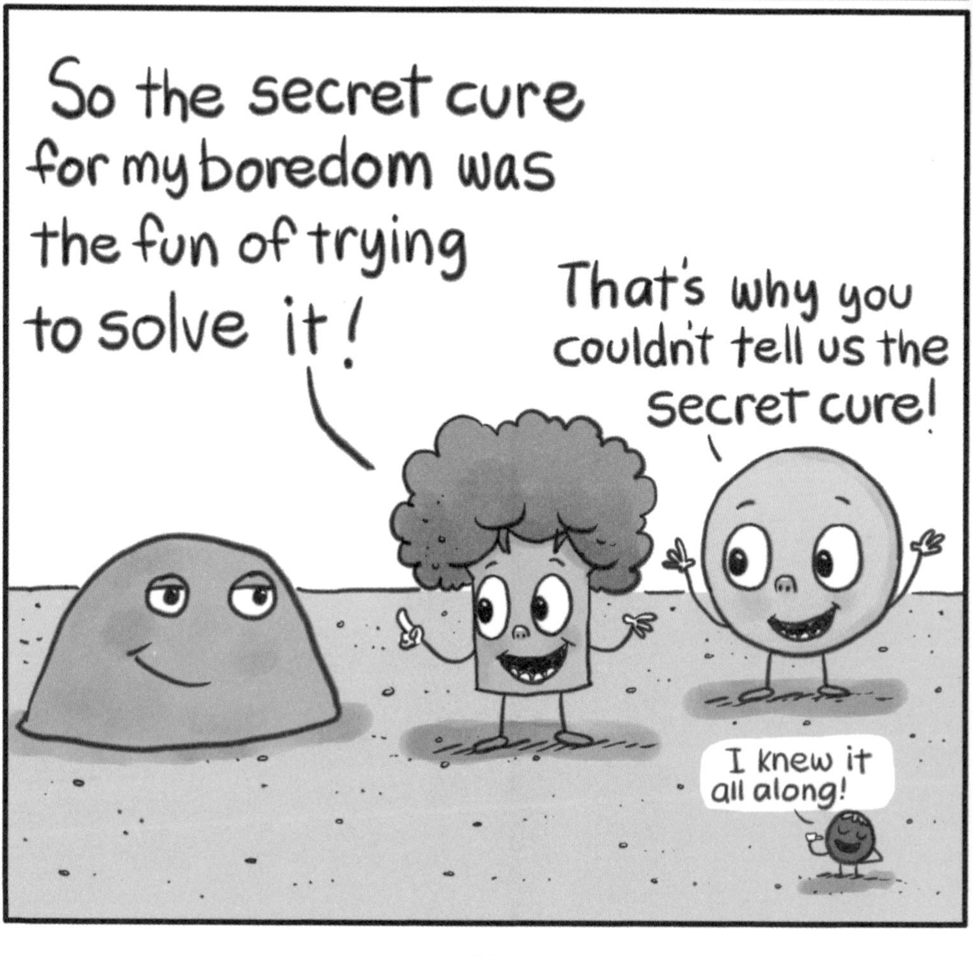
So the secret cure for my boredom was the fun of trying to solve it!
That's why you couldn't tell us the secret cure!
I knew it all along!

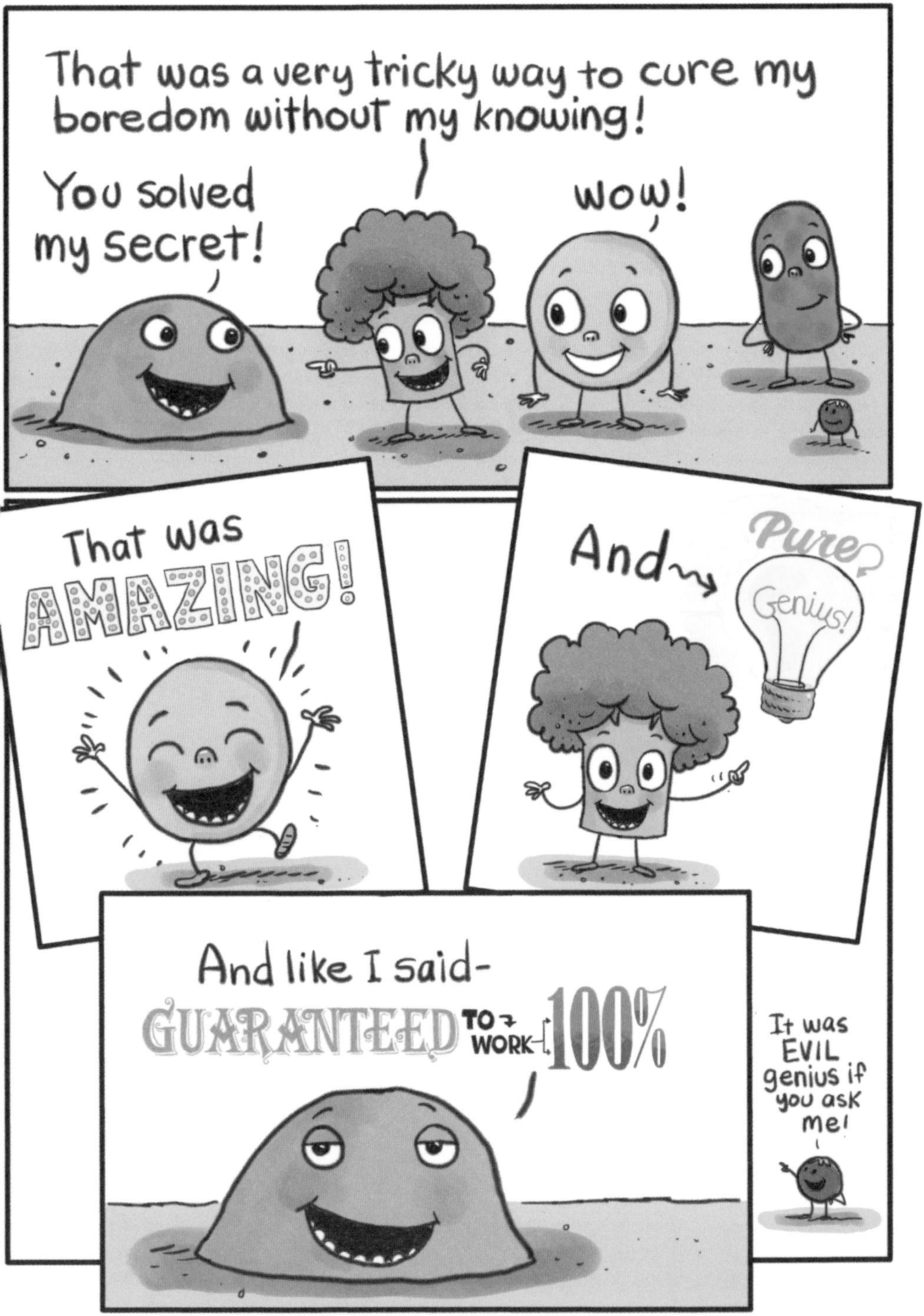
That was a very tricky way to cure my boredom without my knowing!
You solved my secret!
wow!
That was AMAZING!
And
Pure
Genius!
And like I said-
GUARANTEED TO WORK 100%
It was EVIL genius if you ask me!

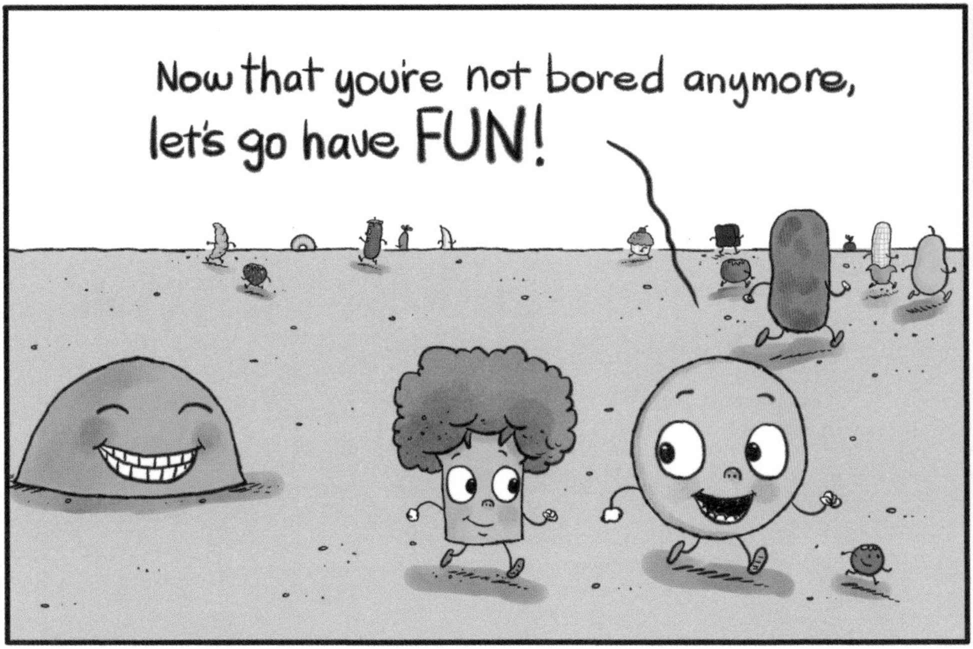
Now that you're not bored anymore, let's go have FUN!

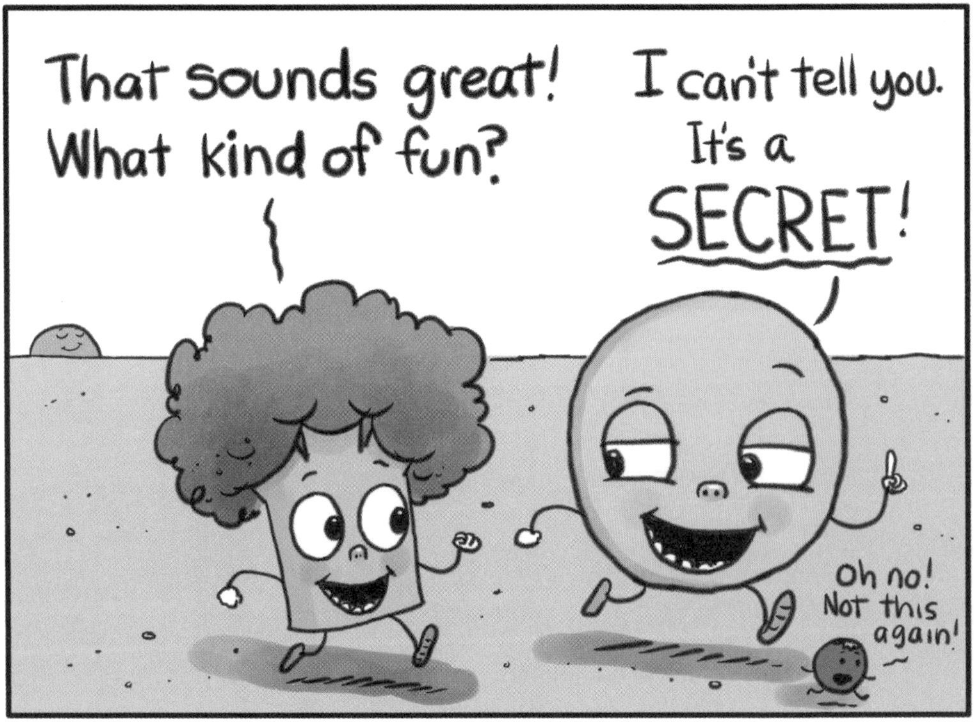
That sounds great! What kind of fun?
I can't tell you. It's a SECRET!
Oh no! Not this again!

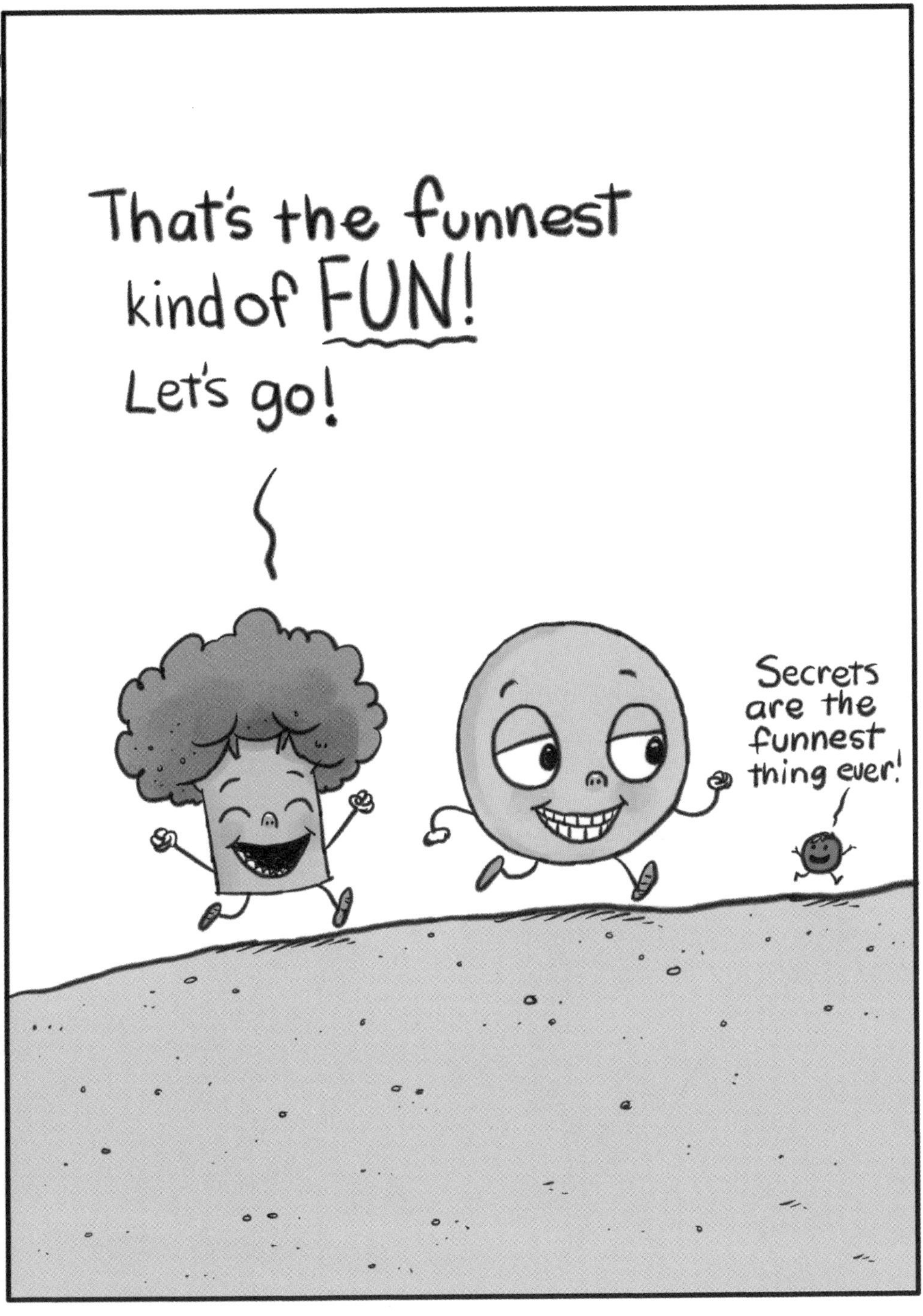
That's the funnest kind of FUN! Let's go!
Secrets are the funnest thing ever!

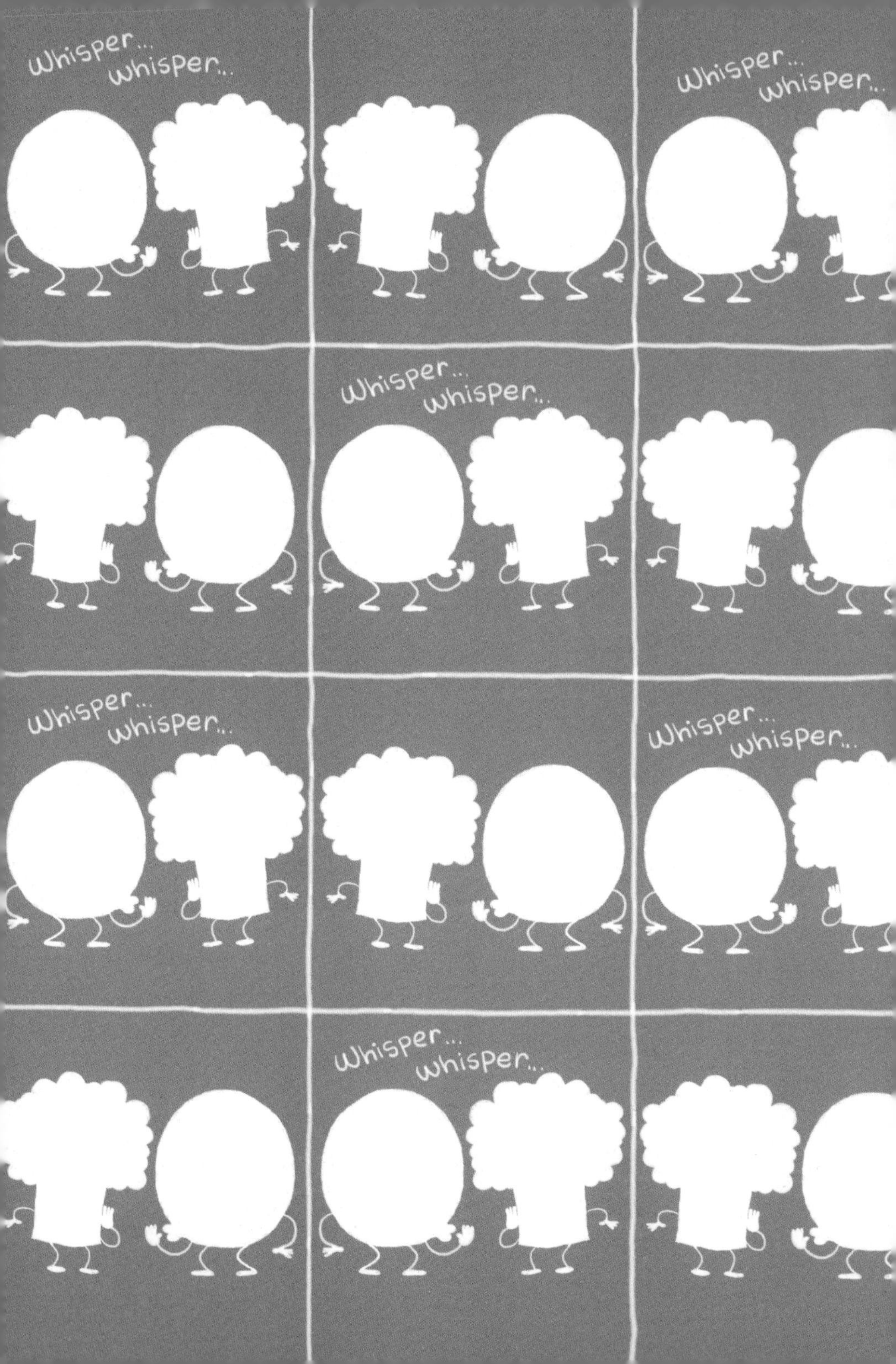
Whisper... whisper...
Whisper... whisper...
Whisper... whisper...
Whisper... whisper...
Whisper... whisper...
Whisper... whisper...

Chapter 3

SECRETS OF THE SCARY FOREST!

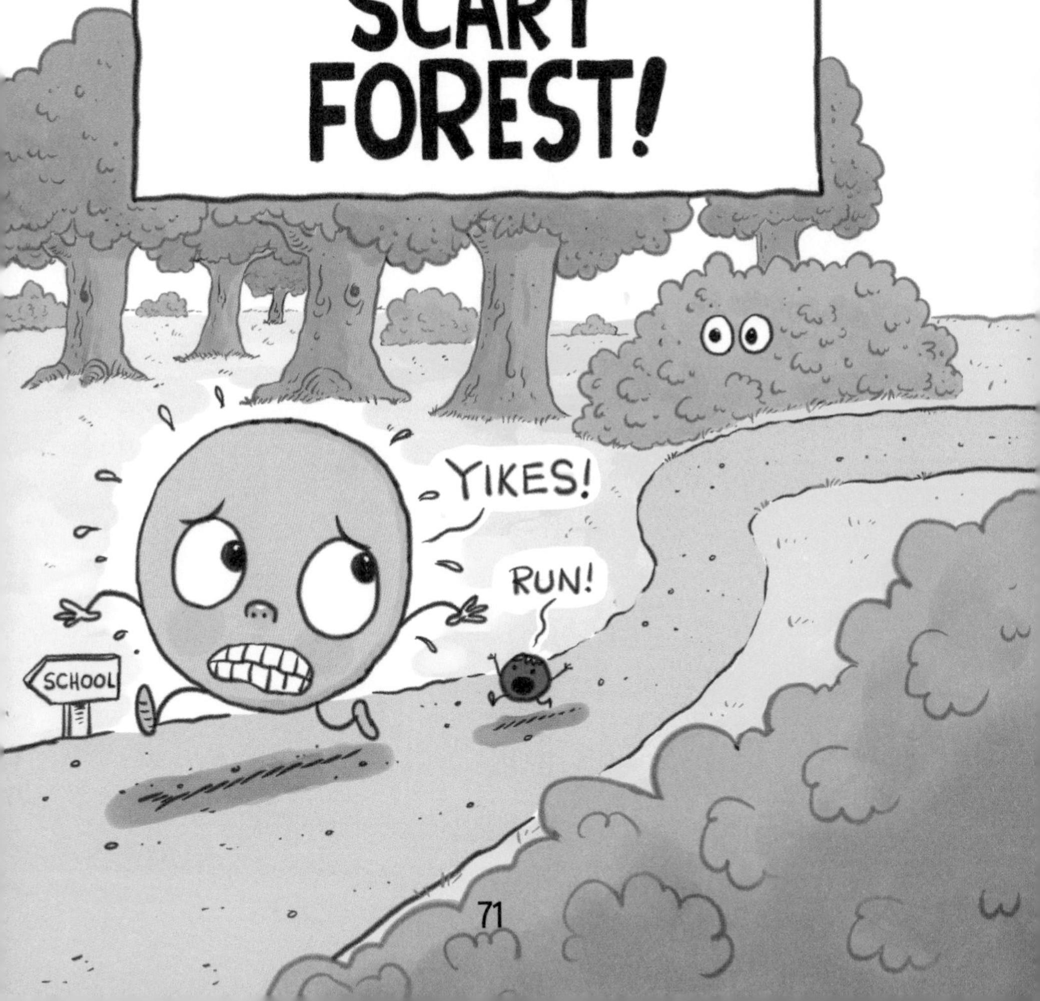
YIKES!
RUN!
SCHOOL

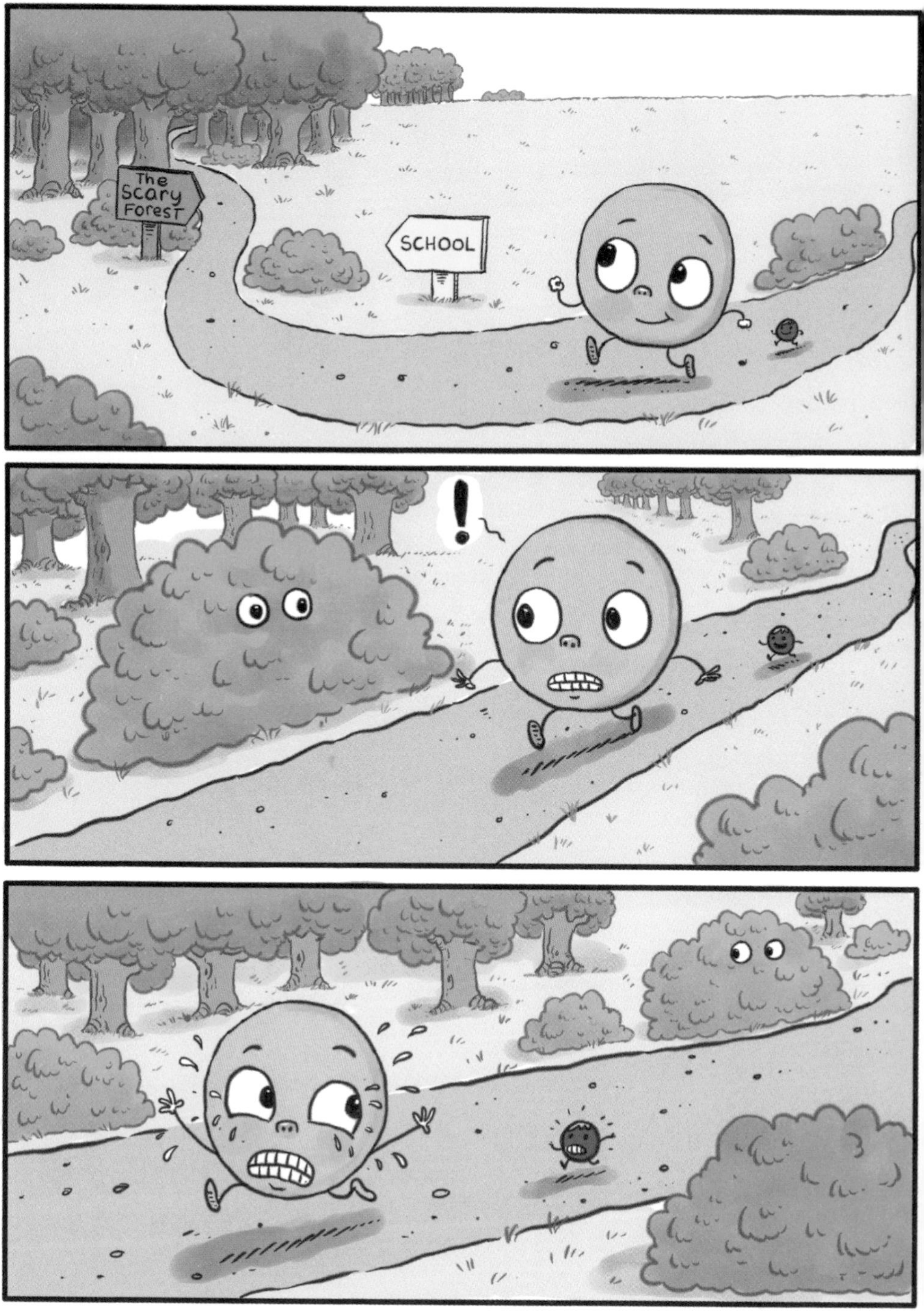
The Scary Forest
SCHOOL
!

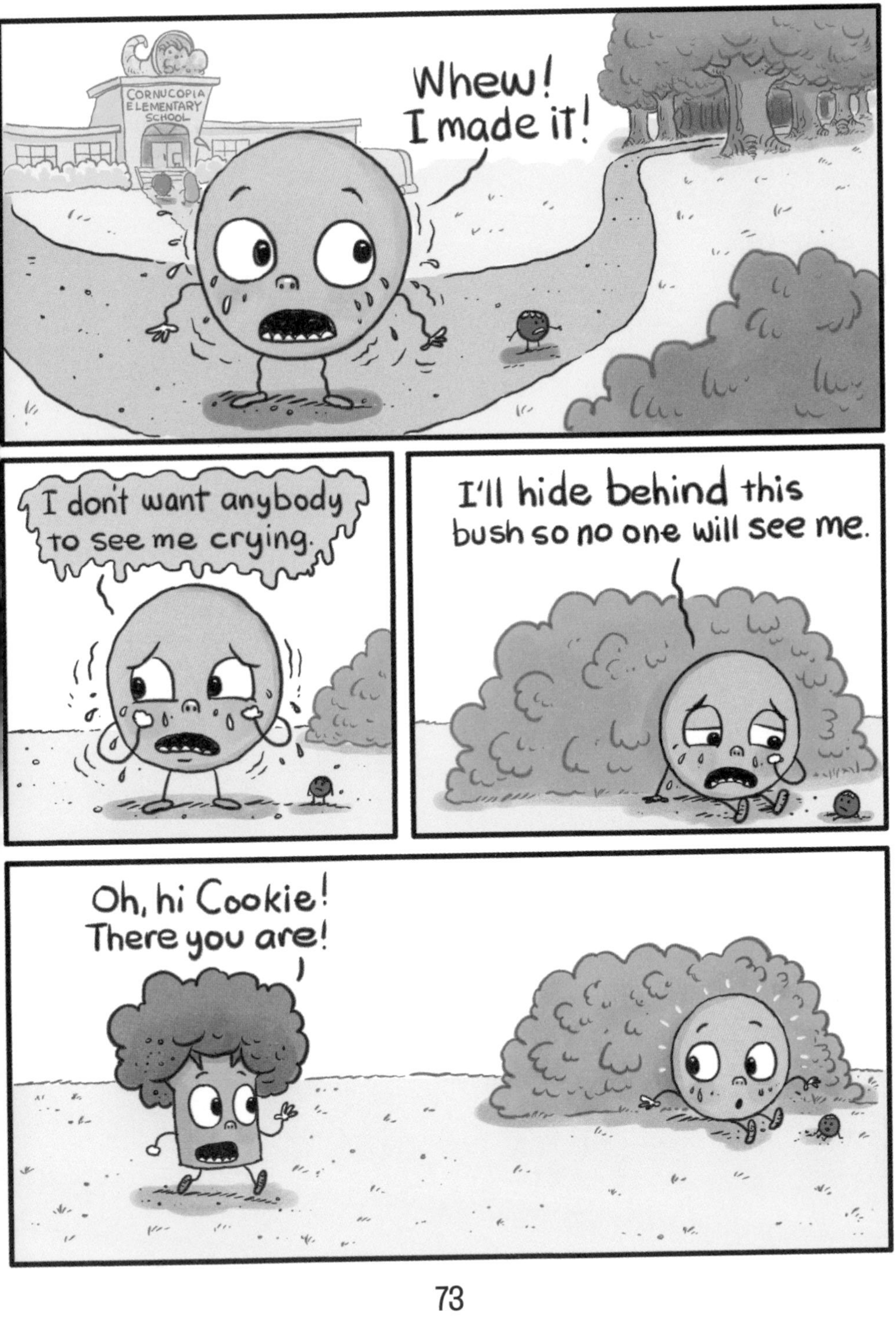
CORNUCOPIA ELEMENTARY SCHOOL
Whew! I made it!
I don't want anybody to see me crying.
I'll hide behind this bush so no one will see me.
Oh, hi Cookie! There you are!

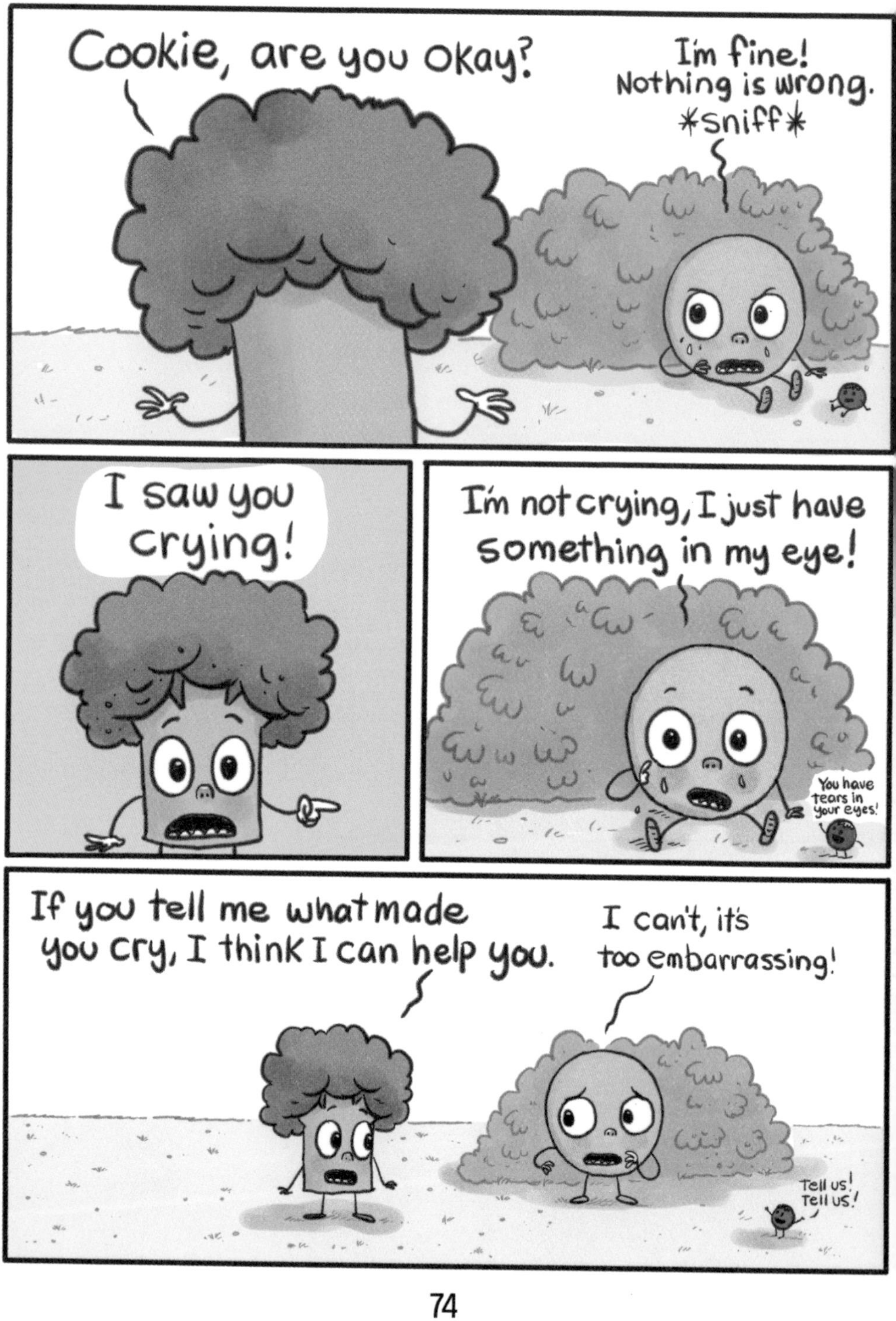
Cookie, are you okay?
I'm fine! Nothing is wrong. *sniff*
I saw you crying!
I'm not crying, I just have something in my eye!
You have tears in your eyes!
If you tell me what made you cry, I think I can help you.
I can't, it's too embarrassing!
Tell us! Tell us!

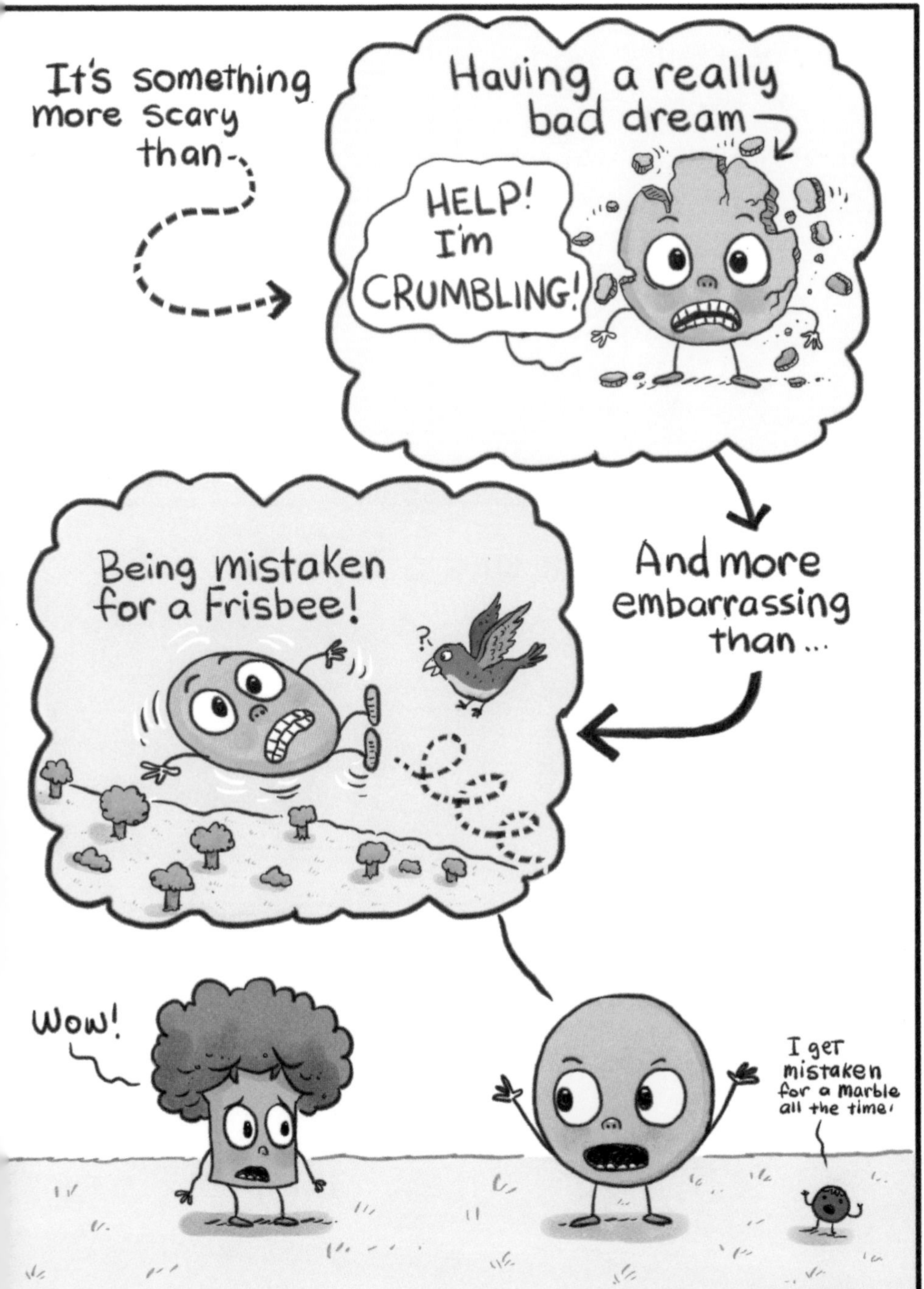
It's something more scary than-
Having a really bad dream
HELP! I'm CRUMBLING!
And more embarrassing than...
Being mistaken for a Frisbee!
?
Wow!
I get mistaken for a marble all the time!

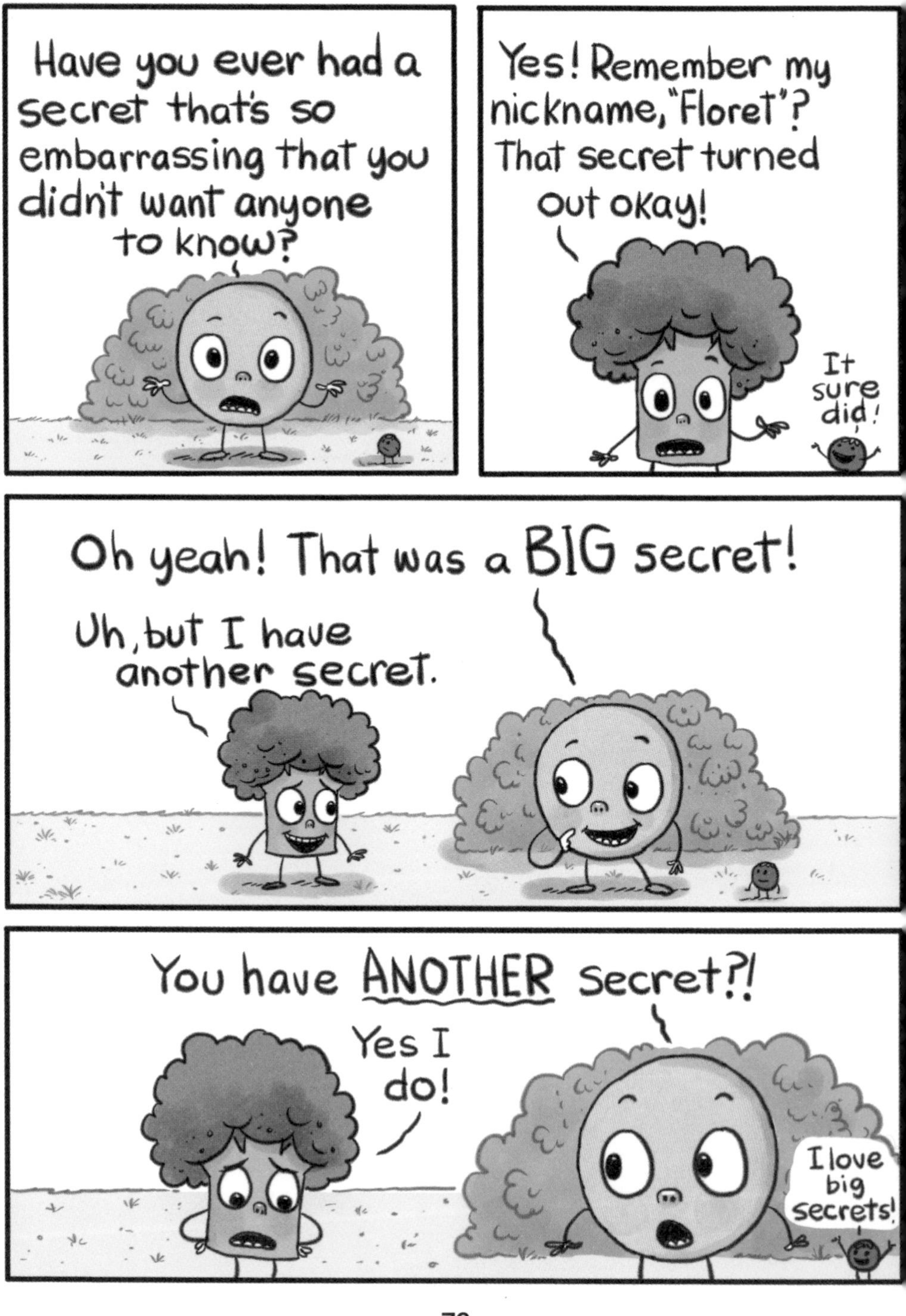
Have you ever had a secret that's so embarrassing that you didn't want anyone to know?
Yes! Remember my nickname, "Floret"? That secret turned out okay!
It sure did!
Oh yeah! That was a BIG secret!
Uh, but I have another secret.
You have ANOTHER secret?!
Yes I do!
I love big secrets!

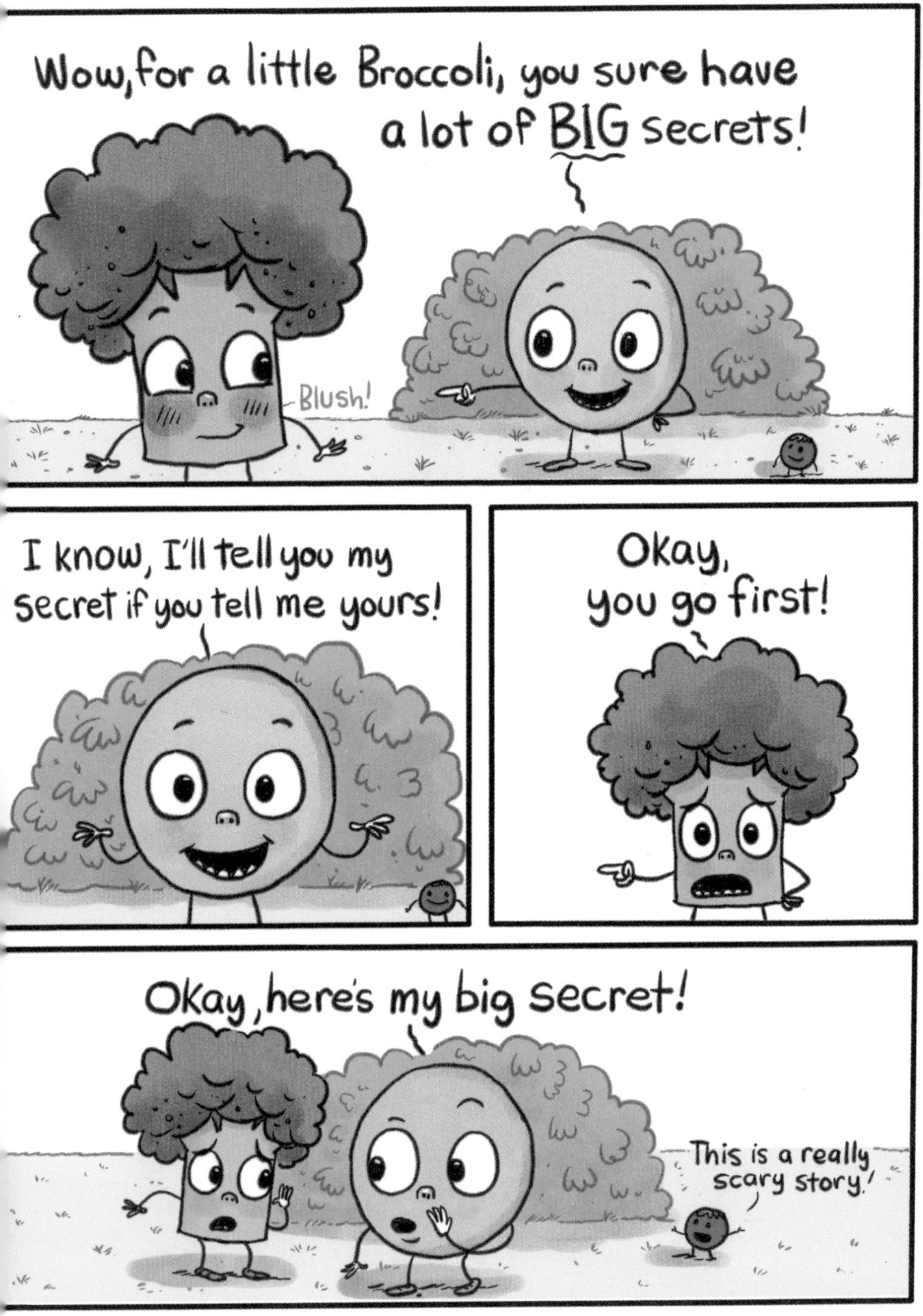

Wow, for a little Broccoli, you sure have a lot of BIG secrets!
Blush!
I know, I'll tell you my secret if you tell me yours!
Okay, you go first!
Okay, here's my big secret!
This is a really scary story!

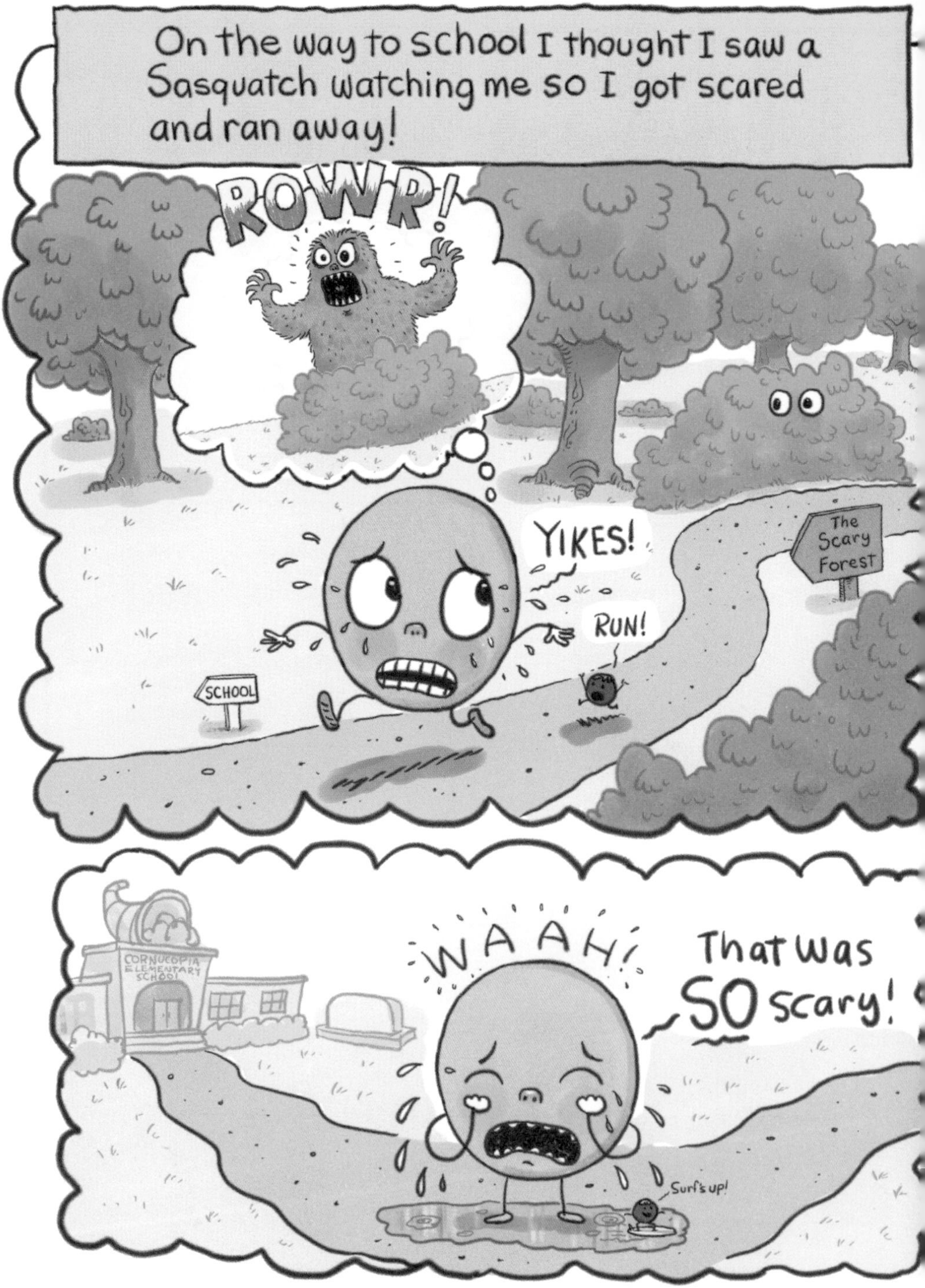

On the way to school I thought I saw a Sasquatch watching me so I got scared and ran away!
ROWR!
YIKES!
RUN!
The Scary Forest
SCHOOL
CORNUCOPIA ELEMENTARY SCHOOL
WAAH!
That was SO scary!
Surf's up!

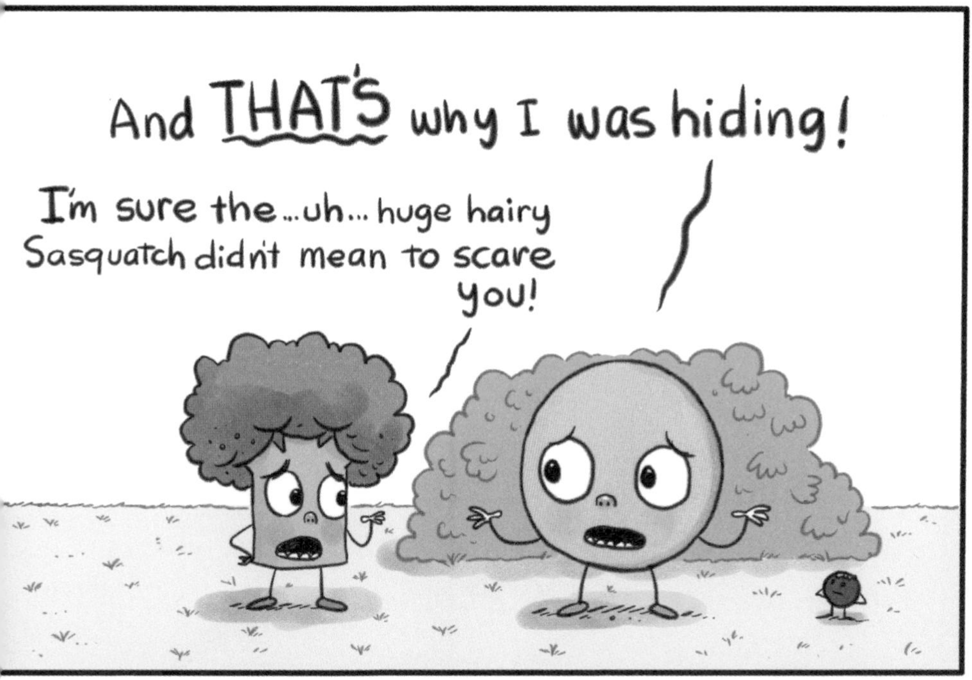
And THAT'S why I was hiding!
I'm sure the...uh... huge hairy Sasquatch didn't mean to scare you!

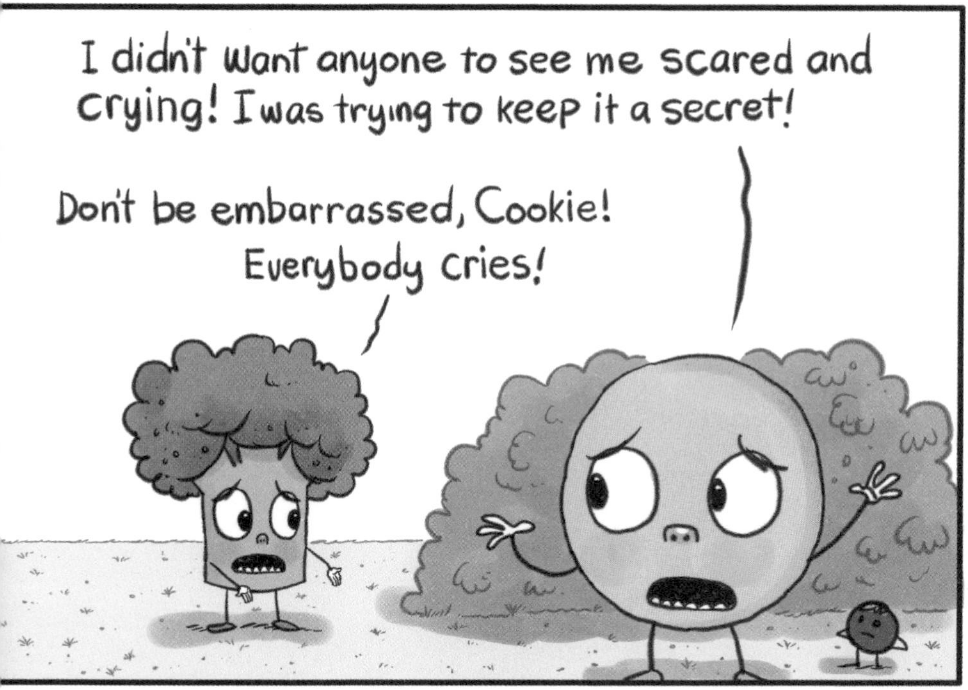
I didn't want anyone to see me scared and crying! I was trying to keep it a secret!
Don't be embarrassed, Cookie! Everybody cries!

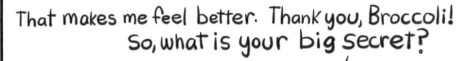

That makes me feel better. Thank you, Broccoli! So, what is your big secret?

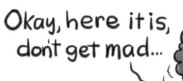

Okay, here it is, don't get mad...

Uh oh!

I thought it would be fun to hide behind the bushes in The Scary Forest and then jump out and ask if I could walk to school with you!

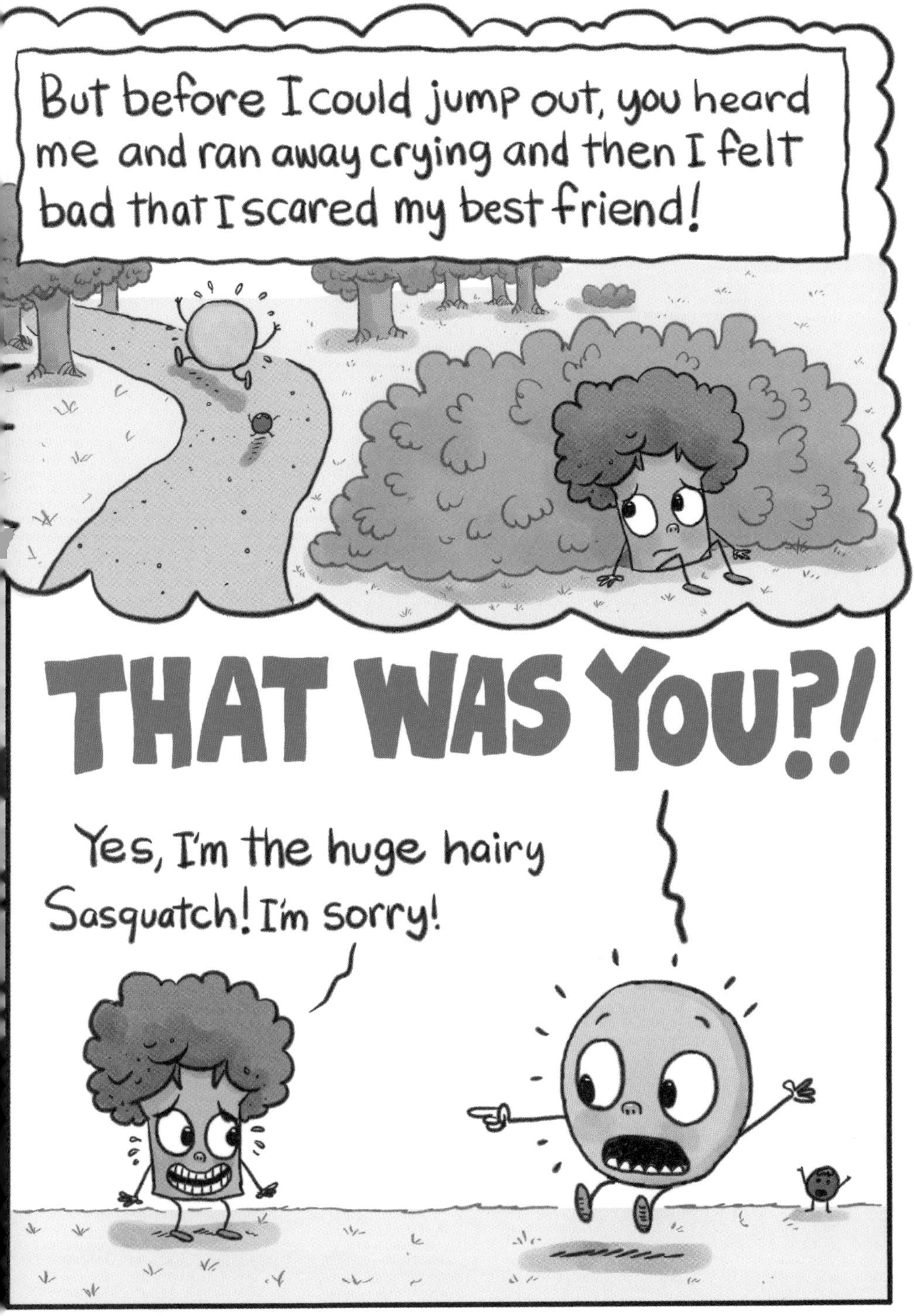
But before I could jump out, you heard me and ran away crying and then I felt bad that I scared my best friend!
THAT WAS YOU?!
Yes, I'm the huge hairy Sasquatch! I'm sorry!

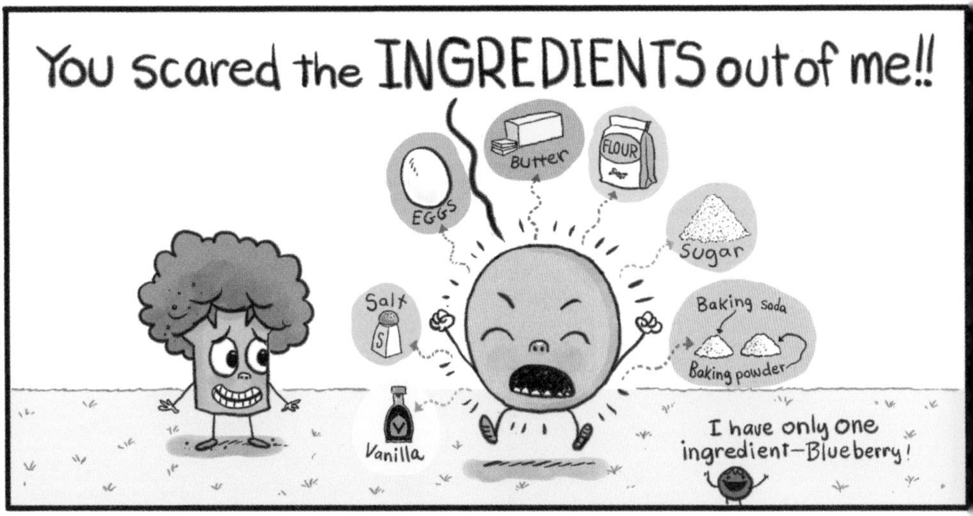
You scared the INGREDIENTS out of me!!
EGGS
Butter
FLOUR
Sugar
Salt
Baking soda
Baking powder
Vanilla
I have only one ingredient—Blueberry!

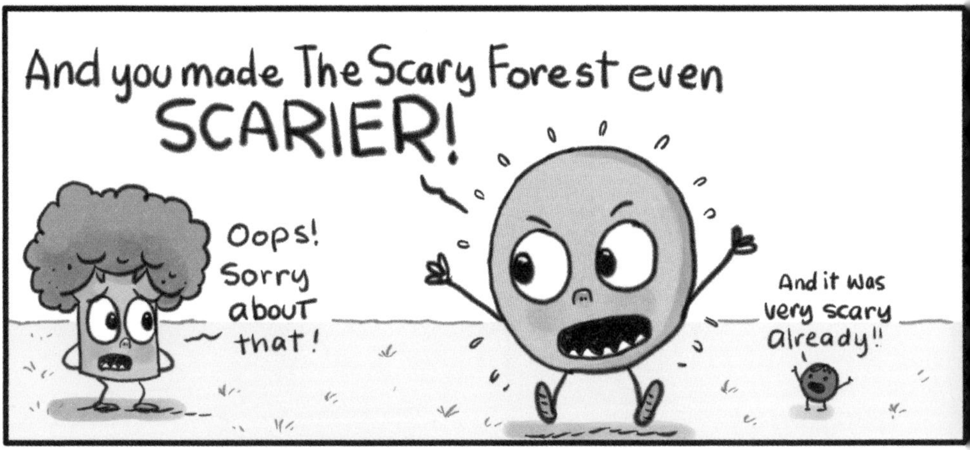
And you made The Scary Forest even SCARIER!
Oops! Sorry about that!
And it was very scary already!!

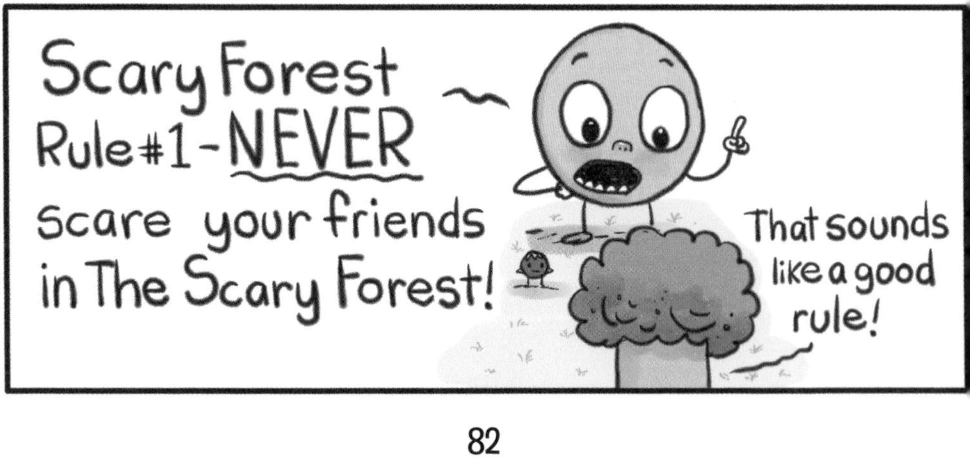
Scary Forest Rule #1 - NEVER scare your friends in The Scary Forest!
That sounds like a good rule!

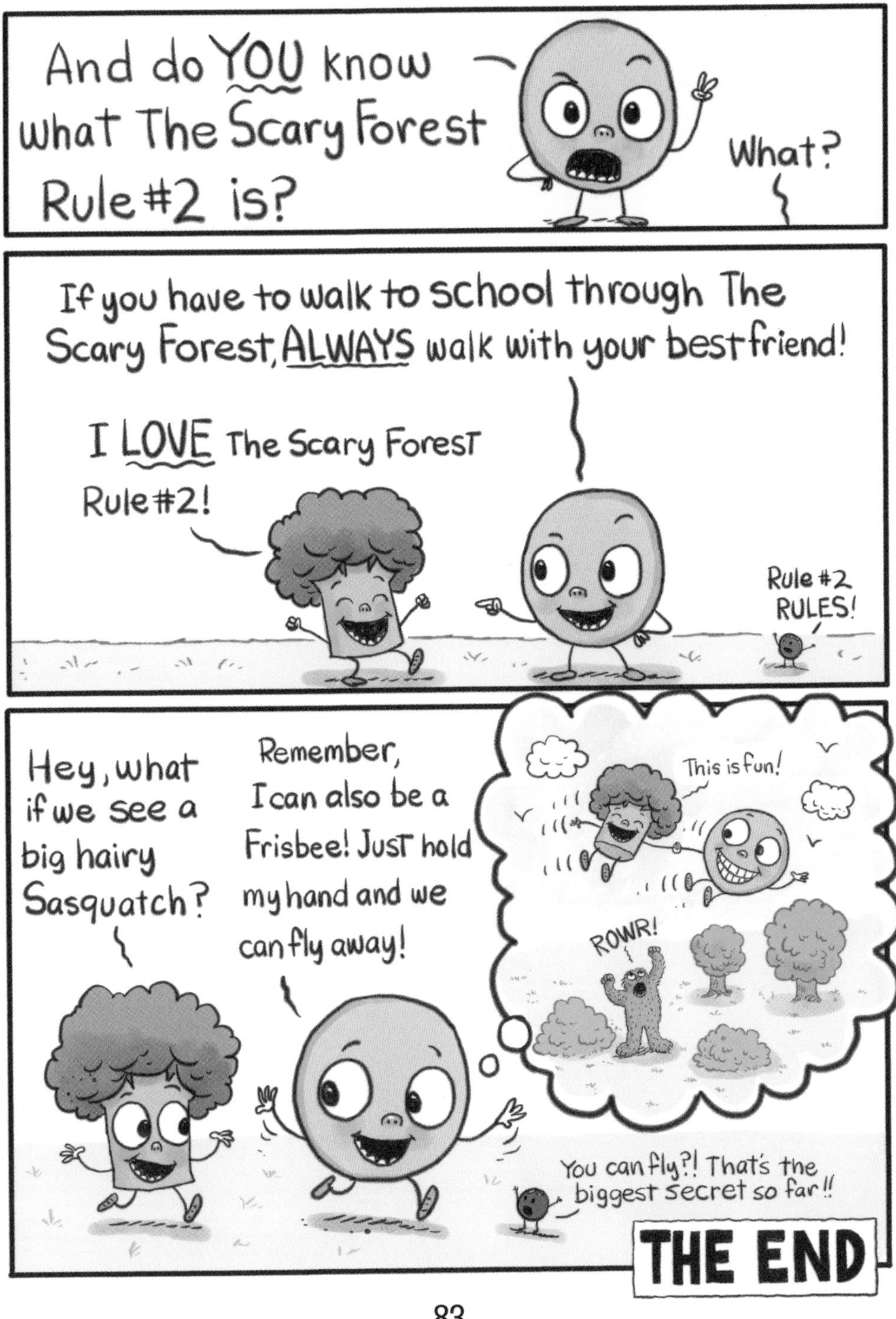
And do YOU know what The Scary Forest Rule #2 is?
What?
If you have to walk to school through The Scary Forest, ALWAYS walk with your best friend!
I LOVE The Scary Forest Rule #2!
Rule #2 RULES!
Hey, what if we see a big hairy Sasquatch?
Remember, I can also be a Frisbee! Just hold my hand and we can fly away!
This is fun!
ROWR!
You can fly?! That's the biggest secret so far!!
THE END

CAN YOU SOLVE THE SECRET MESSAGE

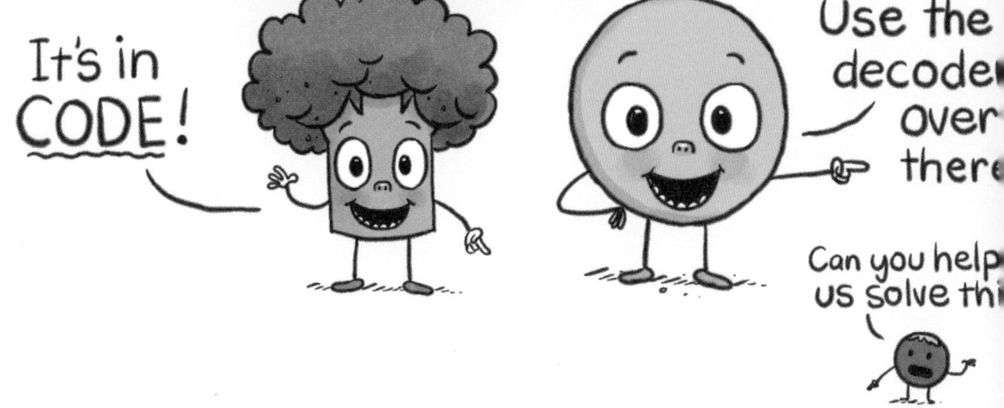
It's in CODE!
Use the decode over there
Can you help us solve thi

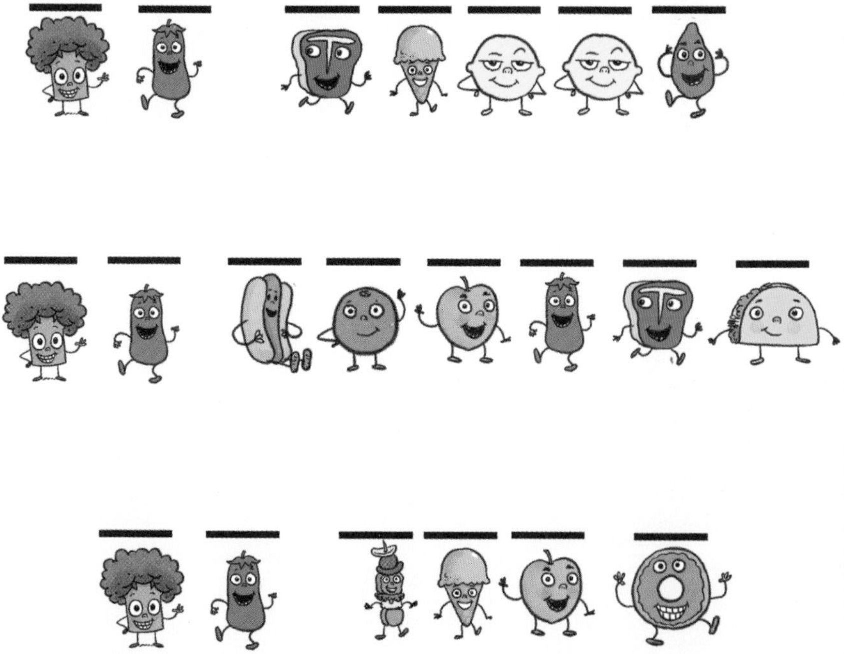

~THE DECODER~

A = Apple
B = Broccoli
C = Cookie
D = Donut
E = Eggplant
F = French fries
G = Garlic
H = Hot dog
I = Ice cream
J = Jalapeño
K = Kabob
L = Lemon
M = Mushroom

N = Nectarine
O = Orange
P = Potato
Q = Quesadilla
R = Radish
S = Steak
T = Taco
U = Unicorn
V = Vanilla
W = Waffle
X = X marks the secret spot
Y = Yam
Z = Zucchini

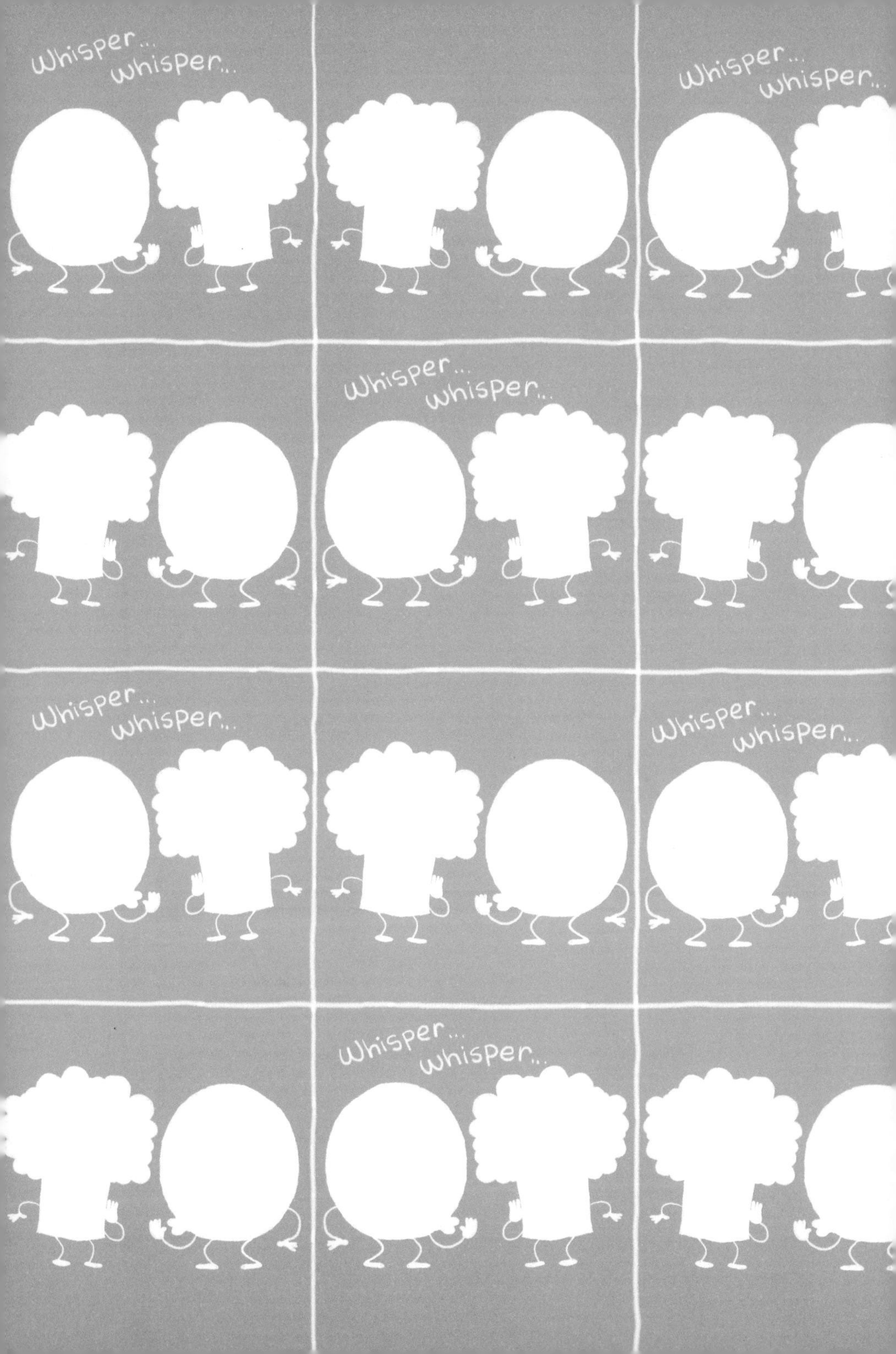
Whisper... whisper...
Whisper... whisper...
Whisper... whisper...
Whisper... whisper...
Whisper... whisper...
Whisper... whisper...

Epilogue

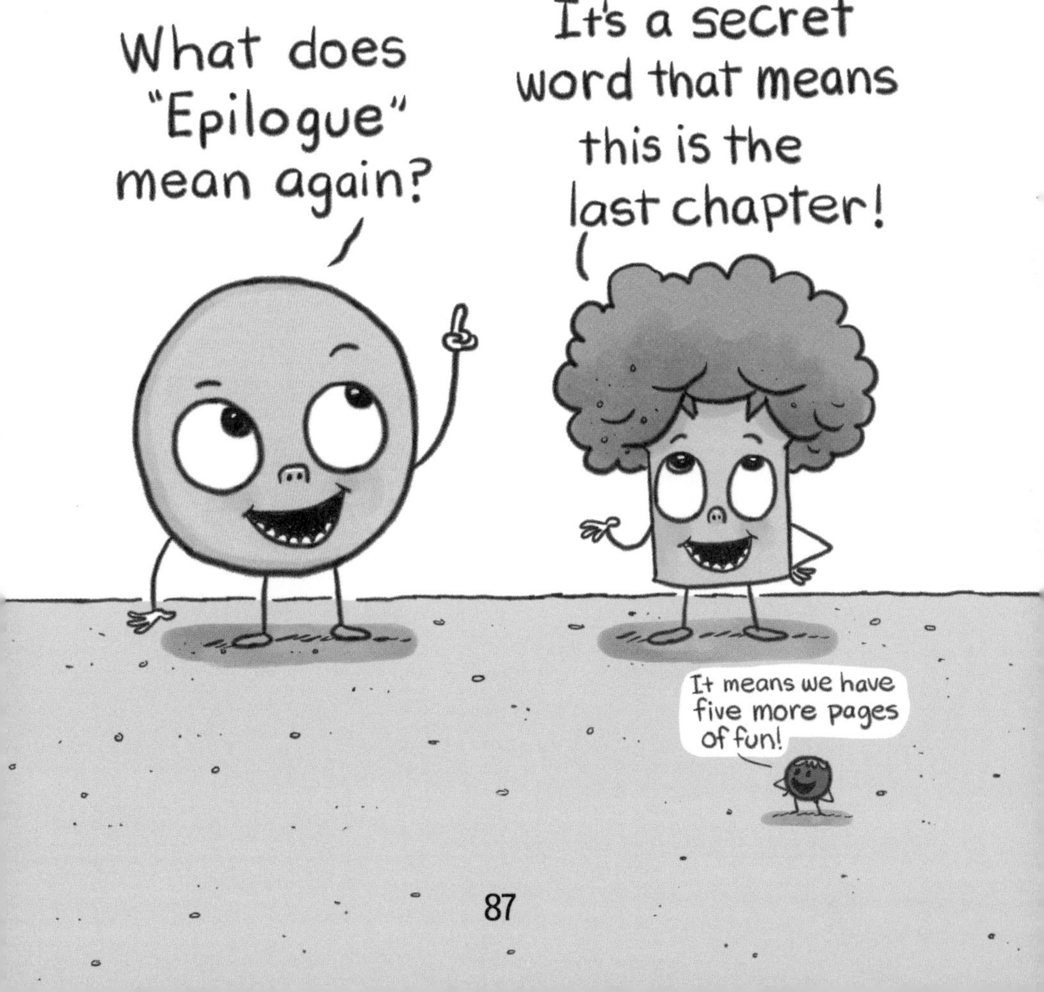
What does "Epilogue" mean again?
It's a secret word that means this is the last chapter!
It means we have five more pages of fun!

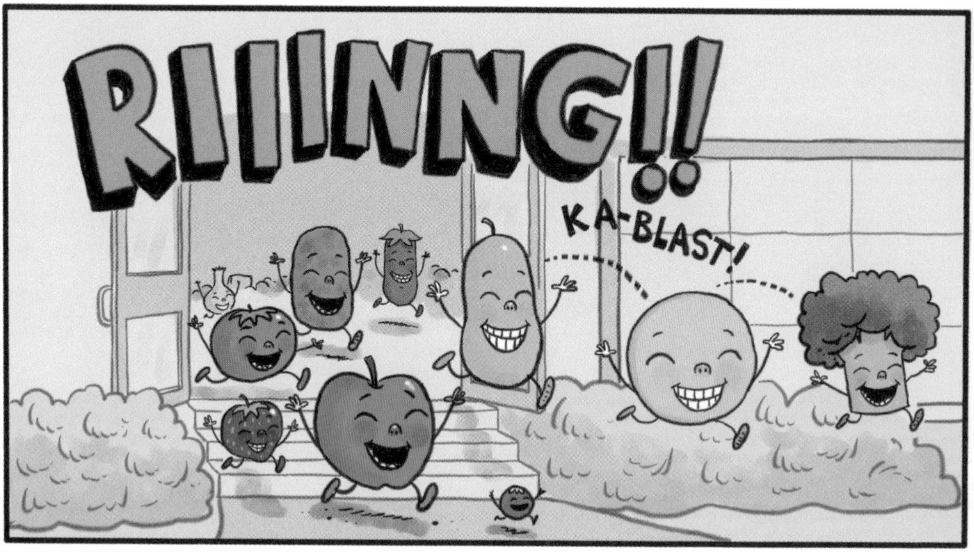
RIIINNG!!
KA-BLAST!

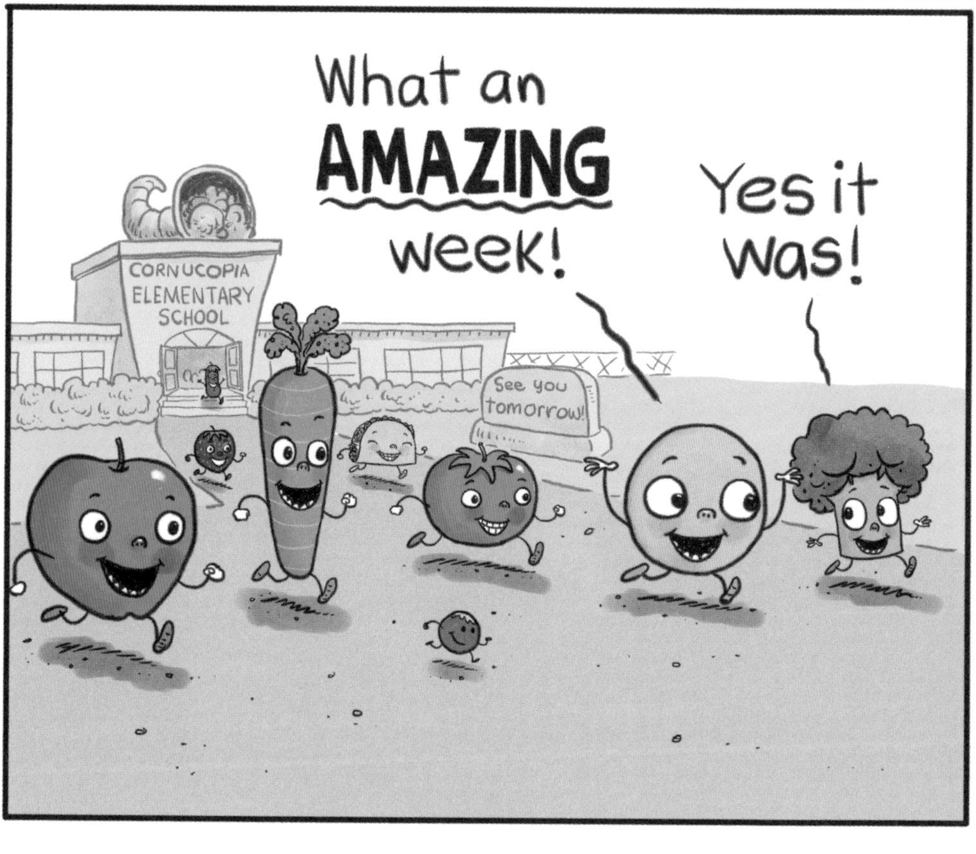
What an AMAZING week!
Yes it was!
CORNUCOPIA ELEMENTARY SCHOOL
See you tomorrow!

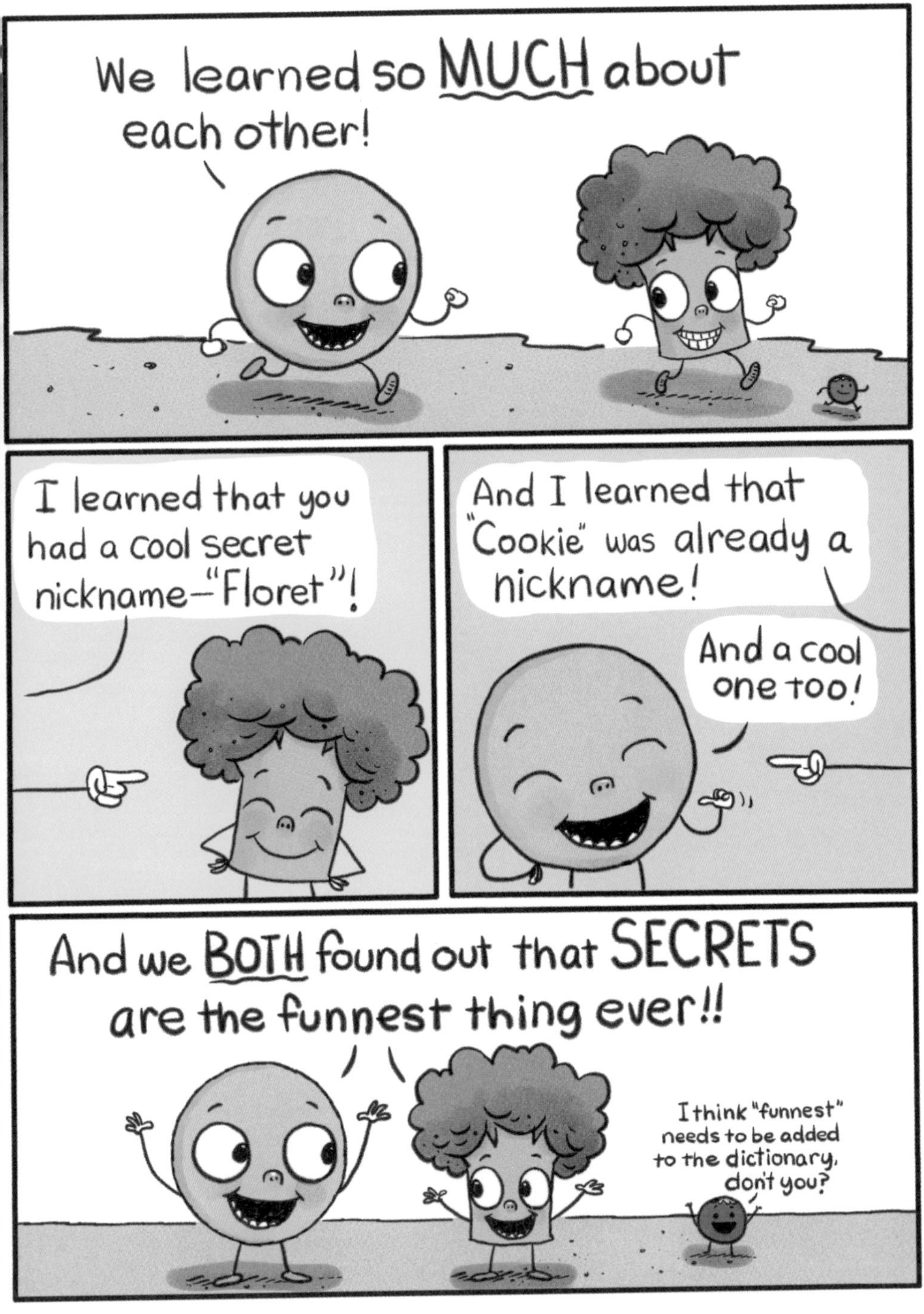
We learned so MUCH about each other!
I learned that you had a cool secret nickname—"Floret"!
And I learned that "Cookie" was already a nickname!
And a cool one too!
And we BOTH found out that SECRETS are the funnest thing ever!!
I think "funnest" needs to be added to the dictionary, don't you?

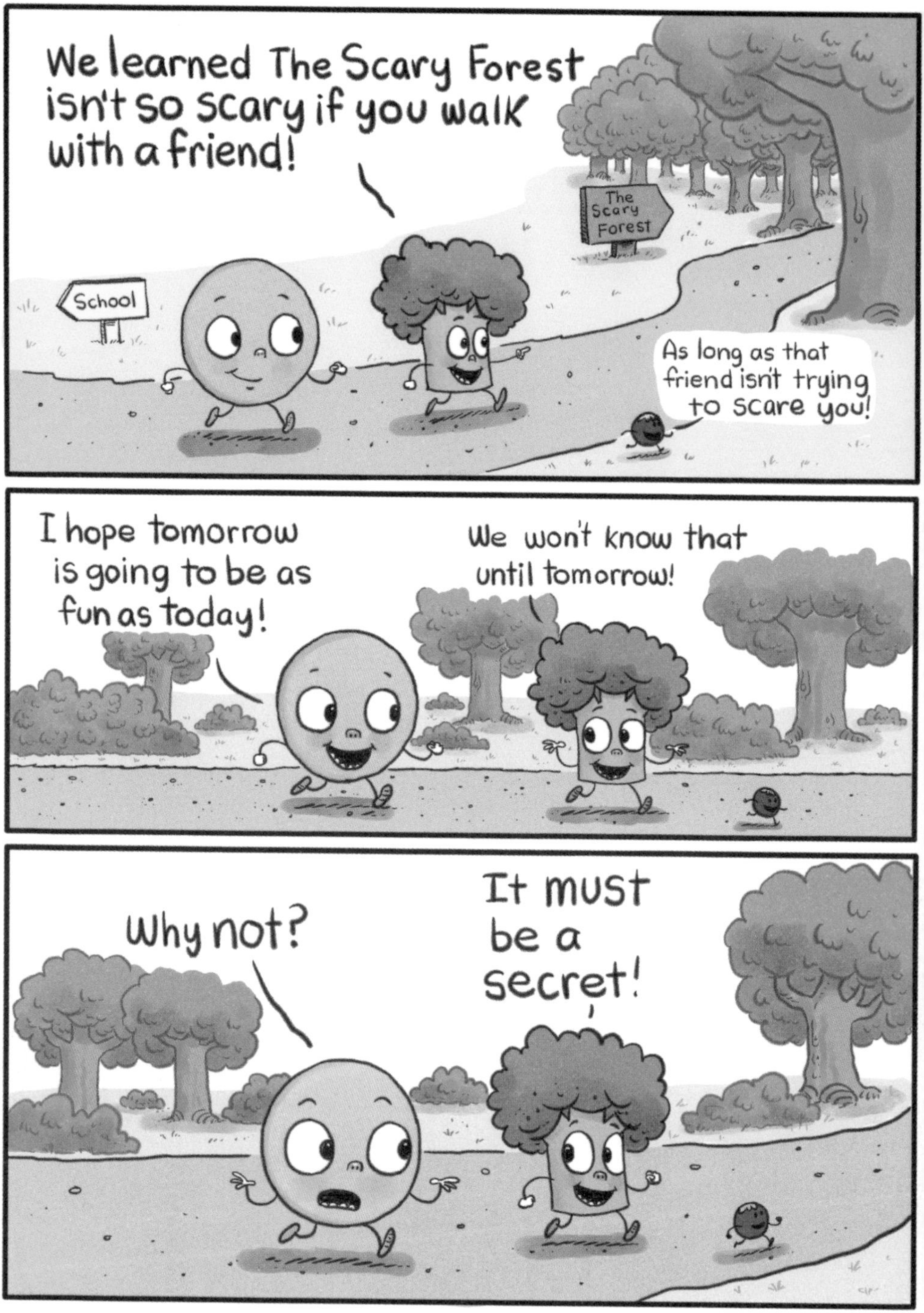
We learned The Scary Forest isn't so scary if you walk with a friend!
School
The Scary Forest
As long as that friend isn't trying to scare you!
I hope tomorrow is going to be as fun as today!
We won't know that until tomorrow!
Why not?
It must be a secret!

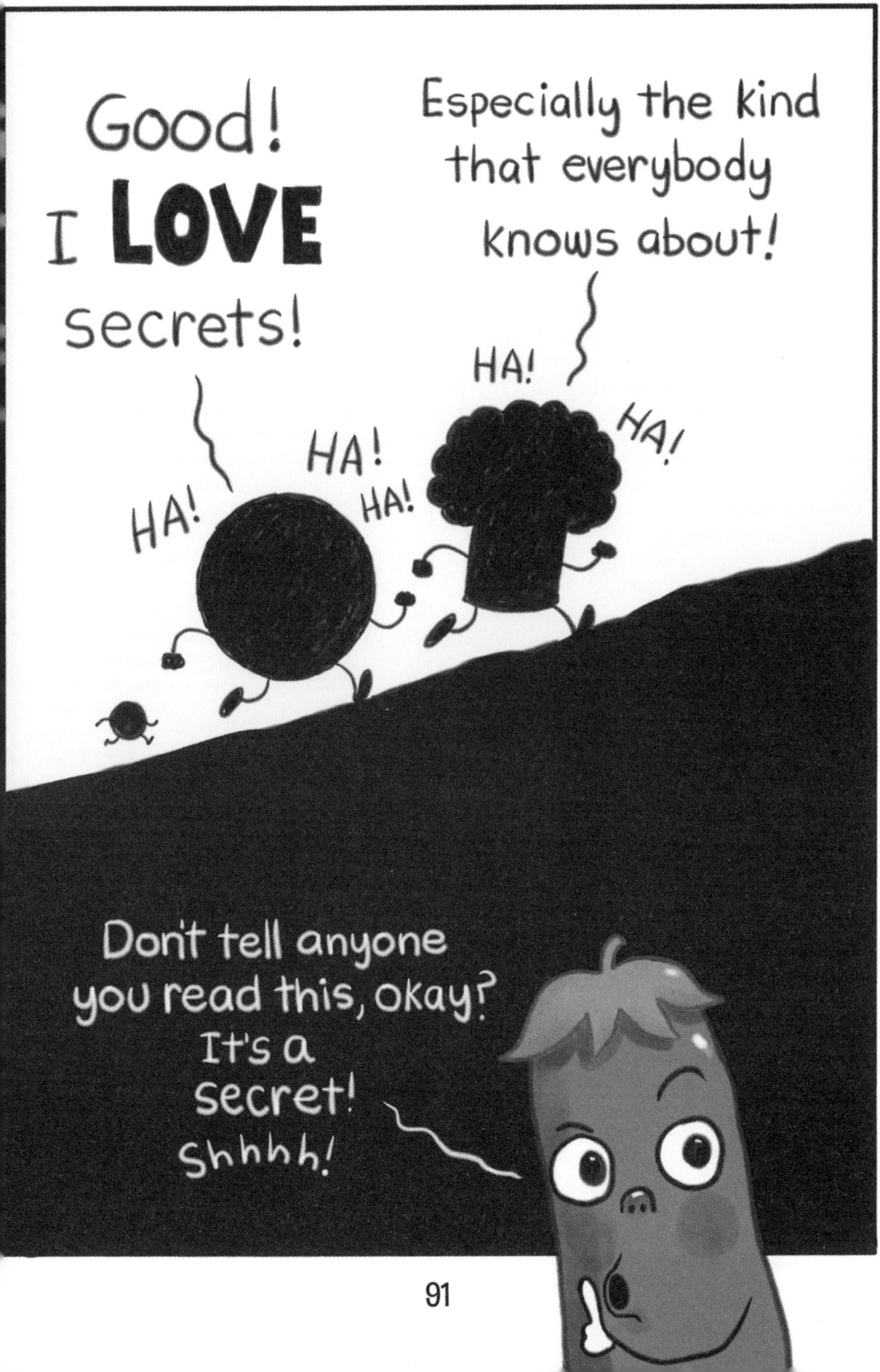
Good! I LOVE secrets!
Especially the kind that everybody knows about!
HA!
HA!
HA!
HA!
HA!
Don't tell anyone you read this, okay? It's a secret! Shhhh!

CHECK OUT COOKIE AND BROCCOLI'S OTHER ADVENTURES!

PRAISE FOR THE FIRST TWO BOOKS IN THE COOKIE & BROCCOLI SERIES:

Texas' Little Maverick Graphic Novel selections!

★ "Readers get a powerful, relatable lesson in the kind of coolness that matters: dismantling unfair systems for everyone's benefit."
—*School Library Journal* starred review for *Cookie & Broccoli: Play it Cool*

"Delightful, owing in no small part to Cookie and Broccoli's odd-couple chemistry. . . . A great start to a conversation between early elementary students and their grown-ups about kind, confident social interaction."
—*School Library Journal* review for *Cookie & Broccoli: Ready for School!*